Bone Deep

For my dad, John 'Jack' Redfern
1924–2018

Bone Deep

Sandra Ireland

Polygon

First published in Great Britain in 2018 by Polygon,
an imprint of Birlinn Ltd.

West Newington House
10 Newington Road
Edinburgh
EH9 1QS

www.polygonbooks.co.uk

1

ISBN 978 1 84697 418 2
eBook ISBN 978 1 78885 023 0

British Library Cataloguing in Publication Data
A catalogue record for this book is available on request
from the British Library.

Typeset by 3btype.com

Printed and bound in Great Britain by Clays Ltd, Elcograf S.p.A.

A note from the author

So many people have helped make this book possible. I can't thank them enough, but I'll try. First, I'd like to mention Mr Peter Ellis, Miller, who first offered me a job at Barry Mill, Angus, in 2014. Little did I know old watermills could be so compelling. I'm very grateful to Creative Scotland, who saw potential in my fledgling project and gave me the generous financial support required to bring it to fruition. Thanks to the National Trust for Scotland, and Ciarán Quigley, for a behind-the-scenes perspective on milling and access to lots of fascinating facts and archive material.

The village of Fettermore, characters and events in this novel are all the work of the imagination, but Barry Mill, which inspired the setting, is very real and one of only a handful of working watermills to survive in Scotland. It is a National Trust for Scotland property, so you are welcome to visit. You may even find Bella's name written on the wall, if you know where to look . . .

Huge thanks to my wonderful, insightful agent, Jenny Brown, for her unstinting support and hard work, and to the whole team at Polygon (it takes a lot of people to make a book), especially to my editor, Alison Rae, and copy-editor, Julie Fergusson, for their expertise, patience and skill.

Thank you to the University of Dundee, always such a support, and in particular the Creative Writing Department: Professor Kirsty Gunn, Eddie Small, Gail Low and many more. A big shout-out to my lovely fellow writers – too many to name but you know who you are. Thanks for your support, and to the super-talented members of Angus Writers' Circle for their constant encouragement. Heartfelt thanks to my writing buddies, the Novellers Dawn, Elizabeth, Kerry and Richard, who have been part of the *Bone Deep* journey from the start, cheering me on with the words we all live by: when the going gets tough, have another latté.

Thanks to the Fobel Shop Four, June, Kenny, Fiona and Parker, for putting up with all my author nonsense and frequent absences, and (last but by no means least) to my family and friends, especially my main cheerleaders, Jamie and Lizzie, Calum and Georgie. Love you all!

A Lyke-Wake Dirge

This ae nighte, this ae nighte,
  Every night and alle;
Fire and sleete, and candle lighte,
  And Christe receive thye saule.

When thou from hence away are paste,
  Every night and alle:
To Whinny-muir thou comest at laste;
  And Christe receive thye saule.

If ever thou gavest meat or drink,
  Every night and alle;
The fire shall never make thee shrinke;
  And Christe receive thye saule.

If meate or drinke thou never gavest nane,
  Every night and alle;
The fire will burn thee to the bare bane;
  And Christe receive thye saule.

*

From Brigg o' Dread when thou mayst passe,
  Every night and alle;
To purgatory fire thou comest at laste;
  And Christ receive thye saule.

This ae nighte, this ae nighte,
  Every night and alle;
Fire and sleete and candle lighte,
  And Christ receive thye saule.

An extract from a North Country burial charm, collected by Sir Walter Scott
in *Minstrelsy of the Scottish Border*, 1802

Mac

January

I'd forgotten about the girl. Her email had suggested a vague time of arrival, but I'd been struggling with a particularly vexing passage and I opened the door wearing my *face*. Arthur named it that: my *face*. I suppose it's a mixture of cross and vacant. Cross because my train of thought has been derailed, and vacant because my mind is still somewhere in the Middle Ages, and not here, on the doorstep, glaring at this scared-looking girl.

'Take your hands out of your pockets. If the dogs see your hands in your pockets they go berserk. They think you're about to dish out doggie treats. Basically you're asking to be mugged.'

At my warning, the girl drops her hands to her sides like an obedient squaddie. What a glum little thing she is, pasty, with dark hair scraped back in a most unbecoming fashion. She seemed larger when I'd interviewed her – more presence, more spark. 'I'm looking for a Girl Friday,' I'd said, and she'd replied, 'Well, I'm a Friday kind of girl.' Quite snappy, I'd thought.

'It's Lucie,' she reminds me.

I try to rearrange my expression into something more welcoming. I do remember. Lucie with an *ie*. Pretentious. Why don't parents give their offspring good earthy names like Arthur? I step out into the chilly air. The rain has stopped but I can still smell it. The girl looks bemused. The dogs wag and sniff her shoes and Floss jumps up. Black trousers, never a good idea.

'Stop that, you silly bitch.'

The girl, Lucie with an *ie*, looks at me with a glint of fire, and I'm relieved that she isn't as defeated as she looks.

'Talking to the dog, dear, not you. Black's not a great colour round here. You'll see every damn dog hair on it.' I lock the front door behind me and pocket the key. 'Now, I'm putting you in the Miller's Cottage. We have spare rooms, of course, but I like my space. No offence.'

'None taken.'

She follows me back down the driveway. For a few moments all I can hear is the irritating grind of her suitcase wheels on the gravel. It's colder than I'd imagined, and I regret not pausing to grab my coat. I belt my old grey cardigan tightly under the bust with my arms. The dogs shoot off towards the road, scattering leaves and birds in every direction. I slow to let Lucie catch up and the suitcase trundle softens a bit.

'Now, usually I rent the Miller's Cottage out to writers and the like, reclusive types, but I can't be arsed with all the cleaning. Do you like cleaning, Lucie?'

She opens her mouth like a goldfish.

I wave a hand. 'No matter. Cleaning may or may not become one of your duties. Did we discuss duties? No? Well, I think we'll just play it by ear. You can take tomorrow off. Get acclimatised.'

We reach the road. I yell at the dogs but the wind's getting up and they pretend not to hear. The wind sends them crazy. They gallop straight across the road. Good job it's quiet. They know where they're going, of course – down the track that leads to the mill. As always, an image of Jim looms large in my mind. I hug my cardigan more tightly.

'This path used to be the main road to the next parish, many moons ago.' I glance across the boundary wall. The view is as familiar to me as my morning newspaper, but still it's stunning; all that sky, purple with rain, and the ploughed field and the sea on the horizon. On sunny days it sparkles like diamonds. Today it's black and sluggish. I breathe in the rich aroma of cow dung.

Seagulls wheel overhead and squeal like cats, or babies. Jim always thought they sounded like babies.

'It's lovely,' Lucie says. I look down at her feet. She's wearing those fashionable canvas trainers. No support, or a single bit of damp-proofing.

'You'll need boots round here,' I say. 'Gets a bit boggy after rain. There's a bundle of old wellies in the cottage. Feel free.'

The track opens up into the mill den. The cottage occupies prime position at the entrance to it, built on a gentle rise. Low and long and white, I have always seen it as a yappy little terrier, a watchdog, while down near the edge of the burn the old mill slumbers, a sleeping dragon. I steel myself not to look at the place. We march past the front of the cottage, the front-door key having been lost a long time ago, until we come to the tradesmen's entrance at the rear. A pergola of trailing ivy forms a shelter over the back door, and there's an old wooden bench against the wall. I rummage through a pile of gravy bones in my cardigan pocket in search of the key. Immediately, all three dogs appear, noses moist with anticipation.

'You can take this key, I have a spare.'

The back door scrapes across the stone floor like a wet sweeping brush. The place smells damp and mushroomy. Sometimes I leave a window open to air the place, but the ivy encourages the sparrows, and they're a bloody nuisance. I'm always afraid they'll find their way in and crap all over the curtains.

'So the phone signal isn't great, I'm told. Can't stand all that technical nonsense. I believe you can get the wi-fi. My son, Arthur, sees to that kind of thing.'

The dogs skitter into the house, fanning out in all directions, while I lead the girl at a steadier pace through narrow, stone-flagged passages, past baskets of logs and kindling and wellies lined up on newspaper. The kitchen is big and bright, although I notice Lucie shiver. She's looking around the place, taking in the oak beams and the shelf with all its old jars and bottles.

'You can do what you want with the place, within reason,' I say. I'm thinking cushions and throws. The young people like their comfort. 'Go easy on the candles, though. I had a woman in here set my curtains on fire.'

Lucie narrows her eyes. They are grey and rather bleak. 'No candlelit evenings for me,' she says. 'You're okay.'

'Fair enough. Now, the heating's on a timer. Don't fiddle with it. But you can try and get to grips with the Aga, if you like, or you can light the fire.' I nod towards the grate. It's one of those old fifties surrounds with the puce tiles and a companion set. She's probably too young to know how to light a fire. 'There are matches and firelighters in that cupboard. You might need to use newspaper to get it going. I generally twist it into croissant shapes and –'

'I know.' She nods. 'We have a coal fire in the parlour at the manse.'

The parlour. I make a face. Very grand. I'm not sure what a minister's daughter is doing here in Fettermore, buried in the country, assisting a cranky old academic. Shouldn't she be at uni, or something? Too old perhaps; she's in her mid-twenties, as I recall. Her application mentioned college. Media studies, or another of those Mickey Mouse courses. She's worked in an ironmongers too, so that might come in handy, if she knows her way round a hammer and nails.

We've come to a natural parting of the ways. I think I've covered everything. Perhaps I should mention the mill. Keep it technical, rather than emotional.

'That's the mill, obviously.' I wave towards the window. 'It's for grinding corn. Oats originally, but now we mill – used to mill – wheat. It was working right up until –' I stumble and she looks at me. I can see she is quite sharp, our Lucie. 'It still operates, but no longer on a commercial basis. Yonder, in the dip behind, is Fettermore Burn. You'll notice it runs past the mill, because the water supply we need to power the waterwheel is taken off at the weir half a mile upstream.' My wave climbs higher. Warming to my theme, I mime channels and ponds. 'The lade brings the water around in a big loop on the high ground, fills up the pond and then drops down to the mill wheel. The fall of the land gives it power. Never underestimate the power of water.' She looks rather anxious, and I quickly adjust my tone. 'And of course it's a very picturesque walk to the weir and to the pond.'

Lucie remains thoughtful, like a child with too much to digest. It's on the tip of my tongue to say, *Any problems, just phone, or pop into the house*, but I don't. She looks like a girl who has the sort of problems I could well do without.

Lucie

My mother threw me out on Boxing Day. Not physically. Even in her heels she'd have struggled to make five-two, but her sense of reproach filled every room in the manse, like the shadow of a grizzly bear. I knew my days were numbered.

Reuben had joined us for worship, and my father was on top form as he scanned his flock from the pulpit. At this time of year, he warned, we remember that the rich and the powerful were not willing to give houseroom to the Christ Child. They'd kept him at arm's length. My mother, sitting beside me, nodded so vigorously that the hard pew rocked a little beneath us.

Afterwards, we had cold turkey and salad for lunch, because everyone was complaining of being over-full after all the Christmas day trimmings. Even then, we'd managed to demolish a whole trifle, and Reuben had been up for seconds.

I sat there, remembering the day he'd first been introduced to the family. There had been trifle that day too, and mother had insisted on giving him the portion with the most cream, lashings of chocolate sprinkles and a cherry on top. That must have been about two years ago. There'd been such a fuss about meeting Jane's new boyfriend. The two of them had rolled up arm in arm, a real couple, Jane looking all smug and entitled. Her grin lit up the hallway.

But this Boxing Day, Mum had landed him a dollop of jelly with such force I thought I heard his bowl crack. Her eyes were as cold as pebbles.

The confrontation came later, as we were clearing the table. I'd taken some plates through to the kitchen. Dad and Jane and

Reuben had gone off to watch some old movie in the parlour. It was just Mother and me. She closed the kitchen door.

'I've been biting my tongue since . . . since last Sunday.'

'Painful.' I turned my back on her and began to run hot water into the sink. My heart was thumping oddly.

'Don't get smart, Lucie. I wanted to get Christmas over. Christmas is such a *family* time.' There was a catch in her voice, but I couldn't look round. I squirted Fairy Liquid into the washing-up bowl and watched the bubbles mount.

'You have *broken* this family, Lucie.'

'That's not fair!' I swung round at that, but she'd turned her back on me, so our eyes couldn't meet.

'Stop it!' She pulled out a chair and sat down heavily at the table. 'It's always someone else's fault with you. You're always in denial, Lucie! Well, I can't unsee what I saw. I *will not* deny what I saw.'

'Jesus, you sound like one of Dad's sermons.' I twisted off the tap and reached for a towel. 'This is real life. Shit happens.'

'You watch your mouth, young lady!' She got up, and we faced each other. Her chest was heaving under her pine-green cardigan – she couldn't unbend enough to wear a novelty Christmas sweater like the rest of us. 'I *will not* be spoken to like this in my own kitchen.'

'Where do you want to go then?' I could feel the heat rising in me, staining my cheeks. 'Where's the best place to go for a really good row, Mother? Oh, I forgot, we don't do that in this house, do we? We just drown in disapproval.'

'If you don't like the way we do things in this house, then feel free to leave.'

I'd been twisting the dishtowel in my hands. Now I flung it across the back of a chair. 'I've already apologised for what . . . for what you thought you saw.'

'I *know* what I saw. Don't insult me, Lucie. Actions have consequences.'

'Oh, stop it with the sermonising! I've had enough!' I stalked back to the sink, glaring at the white foam because I couldn't bear to witness her disappointment.

'Things have to change.' Her voice had dropped. In the sink the bubbles popped under their breath. 'I want you gone, Lucie. Get a job. Get your own place. Get out.'

The Miller's Cottage is an alien landscape where the slates lift in the wind and the windowpanes rattle like loose teeth. With Mac and the dogs gone, I am alone in the kitchen, rooted to the spot, as if I've come a long distance and cannot walk another step. The cold of the stone floor soaks through my trainers like water. Outside, I can see a tiny bird clinging to the telephone wire.

The pine table is draped in an old-fashioned oilcloth, illustrated with cherries so succulent and glossy they look good enough to eat. A sharp twist deep inside makes me groan. I press a hand to my ribcage, grip the edge of the table as fragments of memory crowd my mind.

Me putting cherries on the trifle. Mother checking the clock for the hundredth time, mouthing the time soundlessly, as she always does, then telling me, *They'll be here any minute. Stick that trifle in the fridge, quick!* I remember my father's disembodied voice from deep inside the parlour: *Look at that squirrel on the bird feeder! You can coat the seeds in chilli powder, you know. It keeps the little buggers away.* In my memory he's standing at the front window, hands behind his back. My mother joins him there, and she's saying, *But what about the birds? Do they like chilli powder?*

Memories are weird like that, deceptive. I never saw any of that in reality. In reality, I was skulking in the kitchen, because I was awkward around new people. I was awkward around my own sister, because she always made me feel too clumsy, too slow, too ignorant.

Dad had passed some comment about Jane's new red Mini, and Mum had clipped into the hall in those neat court shoes she always keeps for Sunday. Had it been a Sunday? I can't remember what day it was. I *should* remember what day it was.

Then they were all in the hall, kissing and hugging. Where was I? I may have been looking through the kitchen door, or standing awkwardly in the hall. I was on the outside, somewhere, gazing in. Jane looked amazing – all that hair, copper at the crown, paler at the tips, as if the ends had been dipped in something luscious. She was just finishing her teacher training then, in Dundee, so we hadn't seen each other for a while. She spotted me and rushed forward. *Lucie!* I hadn't moved. I can feel the same stiffness in me now, the way my mouth refuses to curve, the way my arms fold naturally across my belly. She'd changed her mind about hugging me and I think we were both relieved. *Lucie, you look . . . the same!* A bright little crystal laugh. *Come and meet Reuben!*

Suddenly, Reuben was there, holding my hand. Okay, he was shaking my hand in an entirely appropriate manner, but our eyes locked in a way that probably wasn't. It was over in a split second. He dropped my hand and my skin felt cold. Dad was talking about whisky and my mother had steered Reuben away. They left me standing there in the hallway, all broken loose inside. I couldn't move. Reuben's eyes had asked me a question. *Who are you?* Back then, I didn't have an answer.

I suddenly come back to life, drag the oilcloth from the table. Cherries jump before my vision like the images on a fruit machine. I try and fold it but it's huge, inflexible. It threatens to engulf me. I wrestle it to the floor and stamp on it. Eventually, it lies there in an unwieldy ball. I carry it into the hall and fling it as far as I can out of the back door.

Mac

You can tell a lot about folk by how they interact with animals. The girl hadn't really turned a hair when the hounds rushed at her on the doorstep. She'd put up with them parading around her new abode, and seemed unfazed when Jethro cocked his leg against the basket of logs in the utility room. Jethro likes to leave his mark, and Max will eat anything he can find. Floss is more subtle. She's very needy, falling in love with perfect strangers and casting a spell over them with her melted chocolate eyes. *I'm lost. Take me home,* she seems to beg. I spotted Lucie trying to tease a knot from one of her silky spaniel ears. She went up in my estimation, that's for sure, but it's early days.

Instead of returning home, I take a left and head down to the village. I'm eager to see Arthur and impart what little knowledge I've gleaned about our new addition. It was Arthur who'd first mooted the idea of a Girl Friday. He'd said it would set his mind at rest, knowing I wasn't up at the house all alone.

I'm afraid I'd taken umbrage at first, accused him of sneaking in a carer by the back door. 'I'm only seventy, you know. Hardly decrepit! And anyway, I have the dogs for company, and you're only a phone call away.'

I'd tried to keep my recent ill health a secret, but nothing gets past my son. I gave in reluctantly to the Girl Friday idea, taking pains to point out that she would be more of a PA for my writing and research, although a little light ironing wouldn't go amiss. I began to warm to the idea, visualising a biddable foreign exchange student with excellent editing skills, a cheery smile and a nice signature dish of eggs Benedict.

Lucie Snowe did not fit that description. Arthur had yet to meet her and I could only imagine the conversation when he did.

We reach the village and I call the dogs to heel as a tractor chugs by. The farmer raises a slow hand and I dip the brim of my waxed hat in reply. Floss is missing, but that's not unusual. She can take off for days, on the trail of something only she can see. I march the two collies across the road. The cafe lights are warm and welcoming. Max starts to drool, and Jethro lifts his leg on the pavement sign that reads Muir's Artisan Bakery and Tea Rooms. I've always wondered about the use of the plural, when tea is invariably served in a singular room.

Arthur is behind the counter, polishing a glass. *No dogs*, he mouths, but I ignore him and sit by the window. The collies creep under the table. The cafe is Monday-quiet, just a couple of women from the church gossiping in a very genteel way. They glance in my direction. No doubt I will be their next topic. Anita, the waitress, appears at my side. Anita ticks all the boxes on my fantasy Girl Friday wish list. She is quiet, competent and highly intelligent. Her parents are from somewhere in India, and rather well off, I believe. They take a very dim view of her little job here in the cafe, but Anita goes her own way, enjoying a rather hectic student life up at the university, when she's not brewing coffee. Ah, to be back on campus. I experience a little tug of regret.

'I'll have a latte, dear. And maybe a cake. Just a small one.'

She smiles, her head slightly tilted. Her eyes are dark, lustrous and slightly unnerving. I always feel that Anita sees much more than you'd like her to. 'A pancake? A Bakewell tart?'

'Maybe a little bigger than that.'

She trots off and Arthur comes over. 'Well?'

'Lucie's fine. Got her settled in the cottage. I said she needn't start properly until tomorrow. She seems a bit out of sorts.'

Arthur makes a noise that resembles a snort. 'Great. You'll end up looking after *her*!'

'Not at all. There was something about her at the interview

that I liked. Give her time to come out of her shell, and I'm sure we'll rub along very nicely.'

It will be nice to have someone young about the place. For a man in his early thirties, Arthur can be a bit middle-aged at times. He's cautious, like his father, inclined to think things through. Lucie seems to have an impulsive streak, the way she applied for the job like that, fully prepared to up sticks and take on a new challenge. So like myself at that age.

Anita approaches with my coffee and a meringue the size of a large grapefruit. My mind is already leaping ahead to all the little jobs I can now delegate.

'Thank you, dear.' I smile at Anita.

Yes, I think Lucie and I will rub along quite nicely.

Lucie

I never knew tears could be so hot. All those trashy novels I read as a teenager? Scalding tears in every one. Heroine meets hero; hero dumps heroine. Cue scalding tears. I feel like everything has turned to stone, but still waters boil up inside me and overflow. When I'm in bed, alone, they escape, burning trails down into my ears, matting my hair. And in the morning my eyes are on fire.

I put on a brave face, use make-up to hide the shadows under my eyes, pin back my hair because it's too much effort to wash it. My reflection shows a pale, subdued girl. I look cold, shivery, as if nothing will ever warm me up again.

In the night, a baby's cry wakes me. At least, that's what it sounds like to me – a thin wail, out there in the black night – and I come out of sleep shaking inside, my heart hammering. I lie in the narrow bed, cold but sweating, eyes straining, trying to place myself in the dark. I see the loom of a strange wardrobe. The air smells unfamiliar. I make out a thin strip of yellow light where the curtains don't meet, and recognition comes slowly.

The security light is on. That's it, that yellow sliver of light. I lie still, soaking up the heat under the duvet. The noise has stopped, but I can't settle. I'll have to get up, investigate. Security lights don't just come on by themselves.

The rug is cold beneath my feet. I can feel the hard ridges of the stone tiles beneath. I root around for my slippers and wish I'd taken the time to unpack my fleecy dressing gown. I'd dug out an oversize T-shirt for sleeping in, and I hug that more tightly around my chest. Flicking on the lamp, the room comes into sharp relief. Not familiar, yet, but normal. The furniture has its own new landscape, and the only thing I'm sure of is my suitcase, now gaping open, with my clothes spilling out. I should have unpacked, but I'd been so tired. Maybe I could do it now? Sleep already feels pretty distant. I might make a cup of tea. The baby starts crying again.

It's outside.

Wrenching open my bedroom door, I run down cold passages, skidding to a halt in the kitchen. I can still hear it, a soft sobbing that scrapes at my insides like nails. It's coming from the back door. Carefully I make my way through the maze of wellies and baskets and boxes, searching for light switches, snapping them on. My breathing is beginning to calm. I'm trying to listen to the rational part of my brain. It isn't a baby crying. It isn't a sob. It's a whine. I find the back-door key and poke it into the lock.

'This had better be good,' I mutter, turning the handle. The whining stops. I can hear excited snuffling. 'You'd better have a bloody good excuse.'

I open the door and Floss, Mac's spaniel, bounces in, wagging her tail like it's morning and everyone should be up. I make tea. We go back to bed. Floss leaps onto the duvet before I even take my slippers off. I'm too tired to argue. I turn off the light and squeeze myself into the space that's left. We find a kind of shape; I bend my knees, she spirals into the back of them. Within seconds she starts to snore softly. It's oddly comforting.

Mac

I put down my pen and sag against the back of the chair. I've been sitting here since 6 a.m., and now that the words are finally flowing I can't let them go. Things have been a bit stuck of late, ideas bobbing around like fish, and me grown too slow to catch them. But this morning things feel different, as though Lucie's arrival has brought a gust of fresh air, stirring up the leaves of my imagination.

I'd asked her about her family a couple of times, but her replies had been rather muted. I gather she has a sister, but there'd been no warmth to her description.

I'd nodded knowingly at the time. Sibling rivalry. You get that with sisters. Best not to dwell on it. It had reminded me of something though, this sister thing. What was it now? That evening I'd gone through all the dusty old volumes on my bookshelves, not quite sure what I was looking for.

I stretch my arms out in front of me, flex my fingers and rotate my neck. Something cracks, and my insides shrink accordingly. I'm getting paranoid, waiting for the next little blip, holding my health up to the light like a badly stitched seam. I'm getting frayed.

Somewhere in the house, a key grates in a lock. The front door opens, and a ghastly echo carries along the passages. The hall always has that empty-house ring to it, regardless of how many bits and bobs I pad it out with.

The sound of footsteps carries towards me. That will be Arthur. My heart sinks and immediately I go into guilty mode. I am a bad mother. A can't-be-bothered mother. My eyes drop automatically, going to the photograph on the desk. My own mother, wartime drab but happy in a floral tea dress she'd knocked up from remnants. We have bad mother genes, I suspect. There is a coldness in us. I remember Mother feeding a poorly dog tinned salmon while we kids scoffed bread and dripping. The thing is, I fear I'm heading for the ultimate fail. The leaving-your-child fail.

Footsteps approach my study.

'Come in,' I say, without enthusiasm.

Arthur sticks his head round the door, hair rumpled, flour on his glasses. 'Good morning, Ma. How's it going?'

He always asks and I always reply, 'Crap', or some such. He remains unperturbed.

'How long have you been sitting there? Shall I put the kettle on? I've got some of yesterday's flapjacks.' He holds aloft a brown paper bag.

I shrug, conscious of a new pain in my right arm. Which arm is it for a heart attack? I'd been hoping for a quick in-and-out visit – *Ma, have you got any Kilner jars? Ma, can I borrow some vanilla?* – but Arthur seems bent on a let's-have-a-cuppa-and-a-chat sort of thing. I sigh and close my notebook.

'I don't know why you don't use the computer,' he says. 'It would be much easier.'

I get reluctantly to my feet. It always takes a little time to straighten, so I do it casually, like I'm not really trying.

'I'm going to get the girl, Lucie, to type up my stories.'

'Good idea!' Arthur smiles and my heart unbends a little. Guilt is ever present between us. Nowadays, it's mainly his. He plays the dutiful son, making sure I've locked up at night and that I don't starve to death, when really it's me who should be full of remorse. In my low moments I ask myself if I've been a good enough mother, but I'm never sure of the answer. I've always spread myself too thin, competing with male academics with neat little wives to support them. Jim never complained, though I suppose it took its toll – all those times he had to look after Arthur when I was giving a paper at some conference or other. The meals that never materialised because I was locked in the study, elbow deep in research. I can still remember the tentative knocking at the study door, and my son's timid voice: *Mummy, are you coming to put me to bed?* Maybe Jim shouldn't have put up with so much. He should have reminded me that some things are more precious than books. It might have saved a lot of heartache.

'Has she got over her jet lag yet?'

I let out a reluctant chuckle. 'Bus lag, more like. She did appear a little green about the gills. I'll give her an easy week.'

I follow Arthur out into the cold hallway. I feel bereft, away from my warm cell, my books, my pen. I think I may be wearing my *face*. The dogs get up as soon as he opens the kitchen door and there's a lot of tail- and body-wagging, pink tongues and general doggy happiness. Arthur pretends to do a head count.

'Wait a minute – you've one missing.'

'Floss. Been out all night, the rascal. I suspect she's adopted our newcomer. There's a job for you. Perhaps you could drop by the cottage and bring her back?'

He hesitates, glances at his watch. 'I really need to go back to the cafe. I've scones to bake.'

I make impatient noises. 'It won't take you a minute and I'm sure Anita can pop a tray in the oven. Please? And it will give you a chance to introduce yourself.'

'Okay.'

The word doesn't carry much enthusiasm, but I smile and retrieve the brown bag from the table. 'Take these with you as a welcome offering. Lucie might be partial to a flapjack.'

Arthur slopes out of the door, the way he used to do as a teenager when I asked him to cut the grass or carry out some other boring chore. But perhaps he'll find Lucie more appealing than an overgrown lawn.

Lucie

Mac shuffles off ahead, gesturing with one arm for me to follow. She'd told me to show up around nine thirty, start typing up some of her work. She ushers me into her study, a small, untidy room stuffed full of books and papers.

'So what exactly do you do?' I ask.

'I'm a retired history lecturer. I specialise in folklore and the oral tradition.'

I latch onto the *retired*. 'So what are you doing now?'

'I'm specialising in folklore and the oral tradition.'

Her look suggests that I am a particularly dim student. I suppose experts never stop being experts.

'Sounds interesting. Are you writing a book?'

In reply, she waves a hand towards the bookshelves that line her study. They're mahogany, or some kind of expensive dark wood, crammed with every volume you could imagine, from paperbacks to the sort of crusty leather-bound specimens you see on the *Antiques Roadshow*. An entire shelf is dedicated to the books of Dr Margarita Muir. She told me at my interview never to call her Margarita, it was too girly. Everyone calls her Mac.

I move closer to the books and trail a finger along their spines. *The Scottish Farming Tradition. Bothy Ballads: Volumes 1–3. The Scottish Miller's Tale* . . . It goes on and on.

'This will be my eleventh book,' she says, in case I've missed the point. 'A collection of short stories based on local legends. I thought I should get more creative in my old age, so I did a fiction-writing course last year. Can't abide all that technical nonsense – the PCs and the printers and the what-have-yous. Complete Luddite. Always will be.'

'So you write in longhand.' I turn my attention reluctantly to the writing desk, which looks like it has been turned over by burglars. There are jotters and scraps of paper everywhere; pens and pencils; mugs with cold, sour dregs in the bottom. I spy the corner of a laptop peeking out from beneath the debris. Mac picks up a black notebook and hands it to me.

'Begin at the beginning. There are two completed stories in here, and one I've just started. You'll need to plug in that contraption and set up a whatsit for my manuscript.'

I want to ask who typed up her other books. Perhaps her son, Arthur the Baker? He called round yesterday. It had all been a bit awkward, actually. I'd opened the back door to let Floss out, just as Arthur was about to knock. My first impression of him was of his fist in front of my face. I'd stepped back sharply and he'd spent a long time apologising while Floss squatted on the bundled-up cherry tablecloth and peed like a racehorse.

That was a conversation killer. Neither of us could look away from the steady stream of piss bouncing off the plastic. Arthur cleared his throat.

'Um, did you know your tablecloth is outside?'

'Yes. I put it there. I don't like cherries.'

'Right.' He'd rocked back a little on his heels, stuffed one hand into the front pocket of his jeans. In his other he was clutching a brown paper bag. 'I've come to take the dog back, actually. And to introduce myself. I'm Mac's son, Arthur.'

We fumbled the obligatory handshake and the brown paper bag hit the dirt. Arthur swore beneath his breath as he picked it up and dusted it down.

'Oh – these are for you.' He'd handed me the bag with a smile. 'It's okay. They don't contain cherries.'

He'd taken off with a cheeky wink, the spaniel at his heels.

I unearth Mac's laptop, smiling a little as I recall the wink.

At a guess, I'd say Arthur is in his early thirties, a little older than me. I'd labelled him bland and solid, a bit like one of his own loaves. Carefully measured, like you'd always know what you were getting. That wink had given me a glimpse of a younger, more carefree man.

'What's the title of your book?' I ask Mac, as the computer boots up.

'*Fire, Sleet and Candlelight*,' she'd replied without hesitation.

'Snappy.' I type it in.

'It's from the "Lyke-Wake Dirge", one of the ballads Scott collected in his *Minstrelsy*.' She's lost me already, but, like most clever people, she hasn't even noticed and presses on. 'In the north of England and in Scotland, a charm was uttered around an open coffin before interment. I think the juxtaposition of the natural elements of fire and water with man-made candlelight sums up not only what I want to achieve with this collection, but the essence of the Scottish canon, the human compulsion to find out what is beyond the civilised circle of light.'

'Riiight.' I pick up her notebook. *Beyond the civilised circle of light*. A shiver walks up my spine.

'I'll leave you to get on with it then. You can have elevenses in the kitchen with me.'

'At what time?'

'Eleven.' She gives me a look and ambles off.

There is little left of the castle now, and what remains appears to be growing out of the cliff top, lashed together with ivy and moss. The roof has long since caved in and the stone fireplaces are choked with rubble and old crow nests. This was a home once. If you take the time to listen, you might hear it sigh into the silence. You might imagine the tap, tap of the tapestries against the wall as the draught sings down the passageways; you might hear the creak of the hall door, or the scrape of boots and the sound of horses in the yard. You might catch the breathless laughter of two sisters, feel the swish of their skirts as they rush by. After all, the past is only just out of sight.

I look again at the words I've typed. Not starting at the start, as commanded, is fairly typical of me. Being impulsive has consequences; I'm learning that. I'm the sort of person who reads the last page first, spoiling the ending. I ignore operating instructions and wonder why my life is full of devices I can't work. Even if Reuben had come with a manual and a risk assessment written in red, I'd still have jumped right in.

So, typically, I skim the first couple of stories without paying too much attention. The first is about a blind fiddler who can see into the future. Mac calls it a 'gift', but I'm not so sure. This guy seems pretty bogged down by the present. Quickly, I move on. The second story is about a warrior queen who leaps from a waterfall. This one is better. She's rash, impulsive. She'll do anything to get out of trouble. I'm really getting into this one but it stops on a cliffhanger. Maybe Mac has writer's block? Then there's a little snippet about an abandoned castle. Just a paragraph, nothing more. I close the notebook with an irritable snap.

Various old books are lying open on the desk – other people's collections, ballad sheets, an encyclopaedia of fairy lore. I sift through them, gathering up pieces of A4 and securing all the scribbled-on scraps with a large bulldog clip. Maybe I can persuade Mac to take a look at Pinterest; she'd love it.

There are old photographs on the desk too, and I can't resist picking them up. The frames are tacky with dust, and the masking tape on the back is all dried out and peeling. Close up, they smell of mildew. In the first picture, a smiley woman, ration-book thin, poses with her foot on the bottom spar of a farm gate, and in the other, an unsmiling man is bending over some machinery. Judging by the flour sacks around him, he may have been a miller, but since I don't know much about mills, other than the squat stone building I now see when I open my curtains in the morning, I put the photo down. Mac's world is a bit sepia, like the photos, and it makes me sad. I realise this is the first time today I've actually thought about sadness. I suppose that in itself is a start.

Lucie

February

Mac has dismissed me for the afternoon, promising to call if she needs anything. It's a bit of a relief – I find it hard to concentrate when she's around. She's always muttering something to herself, pulling books from the shelves. I moon about the cottage for a bit, getting in my own way, and thinking of all the things I should be doing. I've been here over a week now, and I still haven't unpacked my suitcase. A pile of dirty laundry is growing steadily in the corner of my bedroom.

I'm in the little utility room at the back, trying to figure out the washing machine, when I hear a car. Probably the postman with his endless supply of junk mail. I turn my attention back to the control panel and manage to activate a red light. I'm so absorbed in what I'm doing, a sudden knock on the back door makes me jump.

I open the door and there he is. Reuben. The last person I expect. The only person I want to see. My heart leaps. It's been – what? Two months? He looks achingly familiar, as if we've been apart just days, not weeks. He's alien too. There are things about him I don't recognise: sleepless hollows, lean planes. He looks on edge; his jaw is set, as if he can't stop gritting his teeth.

We lock eyes on the doorstep, not speaking. We've always been the kind of couple that breathes in sync, and we're doing it now – bodies readjusting, realigning to accommodate each other. I take a step back, bare heels colliding with a wicker basket, not noticing the pain. Reuben is gazing at me from under his wayward fringe, face full of questions. I should tell him to go. *I can't see you any more. This isn't right.*

But I don't.

I say his name, and it feels so good to say it out loud. He smiles and I'm lost.

'Come in,' I hear myself say. 'The place is a mess.'

I'm always in a mess. My bedroom was in a mess the first night I ever slept with him. I'd had to bundle my knickers off the radiators and kick dirty plates under the bed. Reuben hadn't cared. He doesn't care now. He wanders past me, hesitating briefly, just letting me know he's close enough to touch me, to stroke my arm. Something flips over in my chest. I break eye contact, swing out my arm like a hostess at a dinner party. *This way. Just keep walking.*

I follow him into the kitchen, inhaling the Reuben-smell. It's nothing fancy, not designer cologne or anything like that, just over-the-counter deodorant, mixed with something indefinable and good. My insides contract.

'So how did you find me?' I sound out of breath and distant. He comes to a stop beside the table. I'd scrubbed the oilcloth after the Floss incident and reinstated it, but a faint smell of disinfectant lingers, slightly at odds with the luscious cherries. Reuben glances around, taking in the shelves with the mismatched pottery jugs and old glass bottles. He's always loved vintage stuff.

'I asked about you at the little cafe.' He turns to face me again. He looks cold, pinched. That dusty blue sweater he's wearing, that was the one he had on the day we went to the coast. We had lunch in a cosy inn with fish on the menu, and we stayed there all afternoon, chatting over pints of cider. We'd stayed there that night too, in an attic bedroom with a creaky floor and an old brass bed.

'But before that,' I ask, 'how did you know I was in Fettermore?'

My mother wouldn't have told him, that's for sure. I tried to make a clean break. He'd buggered off up north and I'd sent him a text: *Don't try to find me. I can't do this any more.*

He doesn't want to say who told him, muttering something indistinct as he hauls out a chair. I have to ask him to repeat it.

He sits down at the table, clasping his hands in front of him as if he's in church. 'Jane. Jane mentioned it at some point. I *have* tried to stay away, believe me.'

'I can't believe you and Jane are still living in *my* home, when I got kicked out.'

'You didn't really get kicked out. You left –'

'To get a job. Yeah, that's the party line, isn't it? You're still all sticking to the bloody script. That's so like good old Mum. Don't rock the boat. Sweep things under the carpet. Has she ever said anything to you?'

He looks at the floor, shakes his head.

'No.' I make a dramatic little gesture with both hands. 'It's always the woman who gets the blame.'

'There is no blame.' It's Reuben's turn to be angry. I avoid his eyes. 'There *is* no blame. Sometimes people fall in love with the wrong person.'

Love? It's easy to say, isn't it? But it's not enough. Now, more than ever, I need proof. Nausea rises into my throat. I sit opposite him, an acre of cherries between us. The things we want to say are too huge to come out of our mouths, so we just look at each other in silence. There are deep smudges under his eyes and his hair looks dark, unwashed. There's a certain satisfaction in that, an acknowledgement that I haven't been suffering alone. Eventually I manage something mundane: I offer him a coffee.

'No, you're okay. I had a cappuccino at that cafe.'

'You had a cappuccino? You *were* in a hurry to find me.' I scrape at the tablecloth with my nail.

'I couldn't just go in and start asking random questions.'

'You could. It's no different to asking directions, is it?'

25

'The baker guy seems to have a good idea where you live.'

His tone makes me look up. His blue eyes are stormy. They do that, change colour with his mood.

'Of course he does. I work for his mother.'

'He said you might be working. He said you might not be home.'

I check the clock on the wall. It's just after three. 'Technically, I *am* working. I'm awaiting further instruction.'

'That's a great job to have.'

'The baker's mother isn't very organised. Sometimes I think she forgets I'm here.'

'So what do you do, when she remembers?'

'This and that. I walk the dogs, do the laundry. Help her type up her work.'

Reuben's eyebrow perks up. Any mention of something quirky, something unexplained, and that eyebrow twitches like it's on a thread. His eyes gleam with a fierce curiosity. I love that about him; it makes me smile.

'Research?'

'Fiction. She's rewriting some local legends that fall into the category of things that are "beyond the civilised circle of light". Fascinating stuff.'

It's my turn to gleam, and he smiles at me. There is appreciation there, love, and I feel a little bit of me melt. I can't allow that to happen. 'There's a story with a blind fiddler and a woman who hurls herself off a waterfall. I don't know if she survives. It's not finished yet.'

His eyes bore into me. 'No. No, it's not finished yet.'

'We can't do this.' My voice is a bare whisper, and even I can hear the tears, not far away.

He gets up from his seat. *Don't get up. Please.*

'You can't just walk away from this.'

He comes round to my side of the table. I lower my head to my arms. The tablecloth is cool against my cheek. I don't want

26

to look at him, to think about this. His hand finds my hair. His touch is soothing but makes my system jump at the same time. The oilcloth turns damp beneath my cheek. 'Look at me.'

His voice is lower. He's crouching down, his hand on the back of my neck, not moving, just warm, gentle. I don't want to turn my head. I turn my head.

I don't know who kisses who first. It just happens. No logical explanation. I want to stay here forever, close up against him, my lips on his, breathing him in. He breaks away to thumb a tear from the soft spot under my eye. My smile is shaky. We knew this would happen. As soon as I opened the door, we knew this was inevitable, but I suppose I had to turn on the chill, make both of us suffer for a while, because it's too easy. There lies the problem. It's always been too easy.

I get up from the table, and he has to step back. We stand a little apart, gauging each other's reactions. I'm not quick enough to hide mine, and we end up clinging together – so tightly my ribs feel bruised. My heart is bruised. I can't let him go. I loop my arms about his neck and stretch against him, catlike. He's shaking, and the vibration bleeds through us and suddenly this is all that matters, just this. There are things I want to tell him. I want to rage at him: *I can't go home because of you. My mother thinks I'm a whore and my sister is always just one heartbeat from learning the truth.*

But the things I want to say fall out of my head. I don't say anything. I press against him, and whisper in his ear. 'You missed me then?'

He whispers back. 'Let me show you how much.'

I have a lost place deep inside me. I feel it when I lie down and press my palms beneath my ribcage. It seems to go on forever; a deep, oozing loneliness that only I can feel. Reuben, who has touched every part of me, can't feel this. Even if he could, he'd never manage to fill the gap. He's still asleep, breathing deeply and evenly beside me. I love the sound of his breathing. My thigh is warm and slick where it's pressed up against his, but the rest of me is shivery. My hands are splayed across my naked midriff, searching for the lost place, examining it. Loss moves in me and makes me want to cry. I turn my head on the pillow. Reuben is nearest the window and sunshine is spilling through the gap in the curtains, illuminating his nose, his chin – as familiar to me as my own. His lashes are spidery black, fluttering slightly in sleep. I wonder if he's dreaming, and what he's dreaming about. *Who* he's dreaming about.

Mac

I'd found the old book I was looking for: Scott's *Minstrelsy of the Scottish Border*. It was like sitting down with an old friend – the feel of the dusty linen boards beneath my fingers, thick yellow pages. *Historical and Romantic Ballads*, proclaimed the subtitle. A line engraving of a knight emerges from behind a tissue paper flysheet.

I'd skimmed through the index: 'Lady of the Lake', 'Fair Helen of Kirkconnell', 'The Cruel Sister'. Flicking to page 352, I'd begun to read. Scott had collected the tale from a lady who, in turn, had heard it from an old woman. Such is the nature of such ballads – a fragment here, a line or two there, and you have an entire picture stitched together from scraps. I grew up with a homespun version of this narrative, but I hadn't thought about it in years, not until Lucie walked through the door carrying her untold story like a suitcase.

Now, I long to revisit it. Reacquaint myself with those other long-ago sisters who played around the mill. I close the book, invite the pair to run through my imagination once again on bare, sturdy feet.

But there's a blockage somewhere, sticks jammed across the mill lade. The words won't come. There's something stopping them, and I think it's because I know the ending. The truth. It shimmers at the edge of my vision like the dart of the kingfisher on the burn.

Yes, I can picture those two little girls, even though I've never had a daughter myself. I'd thought about having another child; company for Arthur. Jim was keen, but the boy had been a handful. Always on the go, demanding attention when I had none to give.

He always loved to bake, Arthur. School holidays were the worst. He'd get up at first light, and somehow the sound of him tripping down the stairs would filter through my sleep-fogged brain. Immediately I'd be imagining scalding water and electric sockets and matches and all the usual perils we mothers torture ourselves with. I'd haul myself out of bed and stagger through the cold house in my candlewick dressing gown, hearing the sound of a kitchen chair being dragged across the flagstones, and I'd go in and he'd be up balancing on the damned thing with the cupboard doors swinging open, stripping them bare of ingredients. How big everything looked in his small hands: white parcels of sugar, glass jars of sultanas and tubs of cherries. The flour in a vast enamel bin on the dresser. The flour came from the mill.

Arthur loved it when we ran out of flour. He would pester and pester, and I would huff and puff, and say, 'Come on then, as if I've nothing better to do.' And we would walk, hand in hand, down the drive and across the road and along the track, with the dogs going mad about the place and the grass soaking our shoes. My mind would be on my marking, or my latest funding application, or the chapter I was trying to write. Arthur's nose would be turned up to the sky, watching out for buzzards, or listening for woodpeckers. Sometimes a blackbird with white feathers in its wings would appear by the mill door. Arthur was a dreamer back then. I don't know if he much cares for it now.

Halfway down the lane you'd hear it – the deep, throaty rumble of the millstones, the steady dunk and splash of the wheel. The boy would start to run, flying through the open door of the mill, into the dark, dusty interior to find his father. I cannot see the inside of the old place now without seeing Jim, sitting on a sack, sharpening this tool or that, wiping things down with an oily rag. There was a quietness in Jim back then, an acceptance.

He was a countryman, old before his time. Steady. I thought he'd always be like that. I thought in twenty years the mill would still be rumbling and Jim would still be sitting there, on a sack, sharpening this tool or that. I was wrong.

The flour, newly milled, would be all powdery and still smelling of the fields. We'd bring the flour up to the house in a tiny sack kept especially for Arthur. No wonder the boy grew up to be a family baker. A family baker without a family.

That familiar urge drives me from my chair. This is the story's fault. This is why I cannot settle, why my heart struggles to find the right rhythm, and I feel sick to my stomach. The story has a mill in it, and the mill calls to me from the page, calls to me in real life, real time. On mornings like this it pulls me from my chair. My pen rolls to the floor. The notebook flutters shut.

I walk the familiar route, heedless, leaving the front door standing open and the dogs, whining, penned in the kitchen. I try not to visit the mill too often. I don't like the way the door sticks on the stone threshold. You have to turn the huge rusty key in the lock and shove it with your shoulder until it finally gives and scrapes across the floor. The noise tears at my insides. That's why I have a pain in my arm, no doubt. I shouldn't be shouldering old doors at my age, not with the aches and pains I have – arms, chest, jaw – that could well be the symptoms of an imminent heart attack. It's this place getting into my bones. As sure as there's sap in the trees, I can feel something viscous and destructive moving through me.

But here I am, with the big key in my fist. There are cobwebs clinging to the plank door, reminding me I haven't been here in a while. I try to tell myself I'm just here to air the place, to throw open some shutters, maybe disturb the dust with the old besom broom. Arthur used to call it my witch's broom. The village kids all wanted to borrow it at Halloween. But that was before the accident. Nobody wants to come here now.

The interior is as grey and gloomy as the inside of a flour

sack. The floor, the whitewashed walls, the oak beams – all wan and listless, as if nothing has moved here in a hundred years. As if the great wheel has never cranked into life, the millstones never turned. The mice have fled. The cat is dead. The blackbird with the white feathers has long since gone. The building is lifeless, and I'm glad.

I head straight to the back wall, to throw open the shutters on the long window. To my right, the two great sets of millstones sit and slumber. To my left, narrow wooden stairs lead down to the basement. Through the window I can see the old bridge. The grime on the windowpane acts like a filter; the outside looks greener than it is, and it cheers me somewhat. The trees are bare but starting to bud. Spring is on its way. The days will be longer, fresher. I will have survived another winter.

I open the window a crack and the fresh scent of water hits me. I crave it, sucking it in, letting my ribcage swell around it. Breathe. In, out; in, out. Only then, when I am in control, am I brave enough to turn and face the mill.

Lucie

I'm huddled in my bathrobe on the bench outside the back door. It's too early in the morning, and when I light up a cigarette the smoke blooms in the air like frosty breath. Smoking is one of the many things I've always done in secret. My mother hates it. From my perch, I can see nothing but a mess of damp, tumbled greenery. My heart is skipping around painfully, while the rest of me is numb.

Reuben moved into the manse just a year after he and Jane first met. They wanted to save money for their own flat. A wedding, or at least an engagement, was assumed. He had his own room, of course, it being the manse. My bedroom was between his and Jane's, so perhaps it was only me who heard the creaking of the floorboards late at night, closely followed, if I listened really hard, by the creaking of Jane's mattress. I would lie in my own bed and fume. How could our mother not realise what was going on under her sleeping nose? It made me cranky in the mornings.

Sometimes I would meet Reuben on the landing, both of us half-dressed, and my whole body would blush. I'm sure he never noticed, because I would vanish as quickly as possible. The sight of Jane and Reuben ogling each other at mealtimes made me nauseous. I hate the way couples communicate in some weird code: a raise of the eyebrow, a secret smile, a warming of the eye. When the two of them were together, they'd usually be wrapped around each other, and from the shelter of Reuben's muscular arm, Jane would make some spiked sisterly comment. 'You're seriously wearing that to go to the pub?' Or, 'You could try smiling once in a while. No wonder you haven't got a boyfriend!'

Once Reuben broke free and put his arm about *me*. 'Don't be so mean,' he'd said with a laugh. 'I like the Lucie scowl. I like a bit of attitude!' I'd spent days wondering if he'd meant something by that. Was there a hidden message there? Was he having a go at Jane, with all her demureness and her playing by the rules?

The day we were introduced, the way Reuben had looked right into my eyes – I longed for another moment like that. But my natural prickliness bloomed in his presence. I avoided looking at him, my chin dipping miserably and my eyes refusing to flirt. My best selfie pout, the one I practised in the mirror, turned into a lopsided leer in front of Reuben, which was neither sexy nor beguiling. I wanted to be more *Jane*, relaxed and chatty and open. I told myself that my sister's boyfriend liked the bits of me that *weren't* Jane.

Then came a day when everyone was out. Jane had gone on a hen weekend with her best friend and a gang of probationary teachers. Dad was visiting the sick and needy; Mum had gone shopping for the day in Aberdeen. Reuben had been bed busted and was sitting in the parlour with a few beers.

'What's bed busted?' I'd asked, loitering in the doorway like the shy kid at primary school.

'Too many guys on the rig and not enough beds. I've been stood down for a few days, so I'm making the most of it!' He raised his beer bottle and grinned. My insides wobbled. 'Do you want to join me? Or maybe you have other plans?'

Other plans? Me? This was new, this was unfamiliar. An invitation to make a decision. I didn't realise then that it was a life-altering one. I tilted my chin up and smiled.

'Yeah. I will join you.'

'Beer or wine?'

'You have wine too?'

He kicked a Tesco carrier down by his foot. 'White. It's not very chilled.'

'Neither am I.' What was I saying? Was I flirting with him? Did that even make sense?

He nodded to my mother's mahogany display cabinet. 'Grab yourself a glass.'

I'm not very chilled. I cringed next to him on the couch and let him splash wine into my glass.

I sipped politely. 'It is pretty warm.'

'I'll stick it in the fridge.' He made to get up and I said, 'No,' way too quickly. Our gazes collided. 'No, don't get up.' He clicked the rim of my glass with his beer bottle, his gaze never letting go of mine.

I was lost. I don't remember what we talked about. We laughed a lot. My faltering encounters with my sister's boyfriend hadn't prepared me for how warm and funny he was. He didn't criticise Jane outright – we hardly mentioned her, to be fair – but he seemed to understand the way she was with me, the put-downs, the snide comments. He made a joke of it all, and the joke was on Jane. As the wine disappeared down my throat I seemed to find a new me – vocal, confident. A flirt.

The kiss, when it came, was not unexpected. We were angled towards each other, heads leaning comfortably against the back of the couch; me cradling my wine glass, he running a finger round the moist rim of his beer bottle. My gaze lingered on his finger and our knees were touching. The sober me would have jerked away; I'd always thought I hated being touched.

He pushed the hair back from my face. His fingers were damp and smelled of booze. When he kissed me, it was the most natural thing in the world. He tasted of alcohol and burgers, but the taste was just right. There was no shyness, no awkwardness, and I never thought about Jane once.

A blackbird lands heavily in front of me, jerking me away from the very thing I'd sworn not to think about. The birds have been doing a lot of squabbling in the ivy, and I guess this one's been kicked out. He looks scared, too; I can see the feathers rippling over his heart. He shoots me a knowing look, and I tell him to piss off.

Suddenly, some unholy sound starts up, a dull rumbling that comes up through my borrowed wellies, throbbing through the wooden bench. It starts off like a burst of thunder, but continues, finding a rhythm I can feel in the bones of my backside. The rhythm is punctuated by the splash of water, and then I know what it is.

Someone has started the mill.

I grind out the cigarette and get to my feet. The blackbird dodges away to a safer part of the garden, and curiosity leads me to the front of the house. Who on earth has set the thing going at this hour? And why? Some part of me doesn't want to see the mill come to life. It's the noise. That banging, creaking rumble has dislodged something in me, wormed its way into the lost place. It's unsettling, discordant.

Behind me, in the dimness of the cottage, Reuben is still asleep. Suddenly, painfully, I know what I have to do.

Mac

In the gloomy basement, the small square window is covered in bluebottles, drawn to the light, all jockeying for position. I can hear their frantic buzzing over the groan and rumble of the gears. I can hear Arthur calling me too, from the front door. I know I should respond, but down here, down in this basement, my shoes turn to glue. I don't know how long I've been standing here, watching the bluebottles.

This is where the flour ends up, trickling through a wooden chute into a jute sack. This is the end of the process. Dust to dust. There is an array of machinery down here: sieves and fans and things that judder and hop; a rough timber partition, which screens off the business end of the mill; gears and cogs, levers and pulleys and steel shafts as thick as a man's arm; the mechanism that links water to wheel to horsepower.

The unstoppable might of it vibrates the timber partition. I don't have to see it to know what it can do.

That moment, five years ago, is seared on my senses. I can still smell a ghost in the machine. Blood and oil and friction. Something clogging up the works. I can hear an imbalance, a wrongness in the grinding of the gears. If I look at the floor, to the left of the partition, I can see Jim's serviceable, dusty work boot. I am running to pick it up, as if that will make things all right, as if I can cancel out the horror by the neat ordering of things. His foot is still inside.

'Ma? What are you doing?' Legs appear on the steep staircase, a torso. Arthur bends double to peer into the gloom. He won't come down here now. 'Ma, come on up. I'm going to shut off the water.'

He disappears. I want to tell him about the bluebottles, but I can't move. Not until the water stops can I bear to move. I hear him shoving the lever upstairs, and everything goes into slow motion. Life comes back painfully into my legs, my hips. I rub my arms. I have an aching cold spot between my shoulder blades, as if I've been stabbed in the back. The water has been diverted, and outside the wheel will dither to a halt like some abandoned fairground ride. Down here, the mechanism judders to a full stop. All is silent, save for the buzzing of the flies.

Arthur is waiting for me at the top of the stairs. He's angry. He doesn't like me being here, and his mouth turns down when I tell him about the bluebottles.

'Ugh. A dead rat under the floor boards, most likely. I'll get some fly spray.'

He'll buy some fly spray, but he won't go down there with it.

'We'll get Lucie to do it,' I say.

'You can't do that,' he objects. 'You can't ask her to do all your dirty jobs. And anyway, she's got company. Key.' He holds out his large hand and I surrender the key. If Arthur had his way, he'd chuck the key into the pond.

'Since when?' I look at him sharply. 'She never mentioned she was expecting company.'

'Since yesterday.' We emerge into bright, cold sunshine and Arthur struggles with the lock. 'And I don't think he was expected.'

I suck in a sharp lungful of fresh air. Dust is clogging up my nostrils and my eyes are stinging. 'What? She never mentioned a boyfriend to me. She'd better not be burning bloody scented candles.'

Arthur's mouth twists. He walks off with the key and I pointedly hold out a hand for it. Now I see it: a strange blue car, parked a little way off to the side. Behind the car, the ground drops steeply away from the cottage, and the slope has been turned into a rockery – by some long-forgotten miller, no doubt, using the biggest sea boulders he could find on the beach. In summer, it's very pretty, all sea pinks and lavender and pale, crystalline lumps of stone. Today it is adrift with snowdrops. The blue car looks like it's lurking. I make a disapproving sound in my nose, dislodging flour and dust.

'He came into the cafe looking for her. Ordered a cappuccino.'

'A cappuccino? Father, brother?'

Arthur shakes his head. 'Definitely a boyfriend.'

As we walk past the cottage, heading for the track, I catch a glimpse of Lucie at the far corner of the building. She's a distance away, but appears to be wearing a dressing gown and wellies. Another figure emerges from inside. A man, fully dressed. There is some tense exchange between them and Arthur grabs my elbow and hurries me along, as if we've stumbled on some ruffians in a dimly lit part of town.

'It's her business, Ma. Don't interfere.'

I shake off his hand but keep on walking. 'She's a closed book. No good ever came of a closed book.'

Lucie

I'd told Reuben to go. Not to get in touch with me again. He could see the pain in my eyes, and he nodded to it. Just that. A nod; an acknowledgement.

'You know I love you, right?'

'How can you say that? How can you love me and be with her?'

'You want me to choose you and rip your family apart? Is that what you want, Lucie?'

'No! No.' I'd turned away then, holding my face in my hands. My skin was burning up. 'I don't know any more. I'm tired. I'm tired of this. Nothing is ever going to change, so just go.'

'Fine. I'm going.'

I'd gone back inside, listening to the sounds of his anger from a safe distance: the slam of his car door, the gunning of the engine.

I stood for a long time, clutching the edge of the table. The oilcloth sweated beneath my palms; the cherries began to run together as the tears formed. I refused to let them fall, but they welled up anyway. I felt like my insides had collapsed, and Reuben had driven his car straight through me for good measure. The sound of his car engine, as he'd roared away down the lane, had stayed with me for a long time.

I have to get out of the house. The hurt inside cannot be contained and I need to move, to walk it off. The millpond seems the obvious destination, even though I have an uneasy relationship with water. I've always fought it. My old swimming instructor pops into mind: an Agatha Trunchbull in a tracksuit. She's assuring me I'll be able to float. *Everyone can float!* Really?

The water is pressing into my chest, squeezing the breath out of me, and the chlorine stings my eyes, the back of my throat. As I lunge towards the rail, the water closes over my head. Not everyone can float.

I will never be able to swim. Back then, I resorted to feigning illness. I'd tell my mother I had a verruca, or my period. I don't think she ever clicked that I had the world's most stubborn verruca, and the longest period. I never learned to swim. And now I am drowning.

I follow the lade-side path to the millpond. Mac has explained to me the logistics of the water, and I think, if humans are so smart that they can design all this, that they can use the natural fall of the land to service their technical needs, why are we constantly struggling upstream?

I find a cold timber bench overlooking the pond and sink down onto it. All the action is behind me, a thin strip of shrubs screening my back from where the burn flows down in the hollow by the mill. I tune in to the soft white noise of its endless rushing. In front of me, the pond is too calm to reflect my mood. The water level has dropped, leaving a tidemark of reddish mud all around it. I can see the sluice at the far end, where the pond feeds the mill lade. In my mind's eye, I follow the lade as it trickles beside the path, all the way down to the now-silent mill.

The trees on the far bank trail their broken limbs in the water. They look like old women's arms, grey and sinewy, up to their elbows in dirty dishwater. Their reflections are motionless in the thin morning light. Everything is stagnant, suspended, and I feel the same way myself, now that the first raw pain has passed.

Other water-based memories come flooding in, like Jane's horrible pool party. She'd have been twelve, and me a year older. Like you *really* want to be seen in public in a swimsuit at the age of thirteen. Of course, mother had insisted I go to the party. 'Don't spoil it for her.' That had always been the mantra in our house. *Don't spoil it*. Again, I'd pleaded illness, and spent the entire time slouched in the viewing balcony, dressed in black, eating crisps, as Jane and her mates squealed and cavorted in the pool below me. I didn't spoil anything, because no one bothered with me, and it became a bit of a pattern, me watching life from the viewing balcony. Until Reuben noticed me, that is.

If I close my eyes I can still be in that first moment of meeting; I can still feel that jolt as we saw each other for the first time. It's sweet and painful. I can see the curve of Reuben's smile, his curiosity. Memories pop in my head like sparks. I open my eyes reluctantly and I'm back by the millpond, shivering in my thin jacket, on my cold bench.

Hugging my jacket around me, I get to my feet. My hips are cold and numb. I know I must go back, face the empty house that isn't my home, begin a new day. Tears spill from me like spring rain. There's something cleansing about allowing them to fall, un-wiped. They drip onto the ground for me to step on. There are no pitiful sobs, no snuffling. Just a steady stream of hopelessness as I follow the lade all the way back to the cottage. I can imagine this rawness flowing from me unceasingly, like the mill burn down in the hollow, racing on and on.

There's a carrier bag hanging on my door handle, and Arthur is just leaving.

'Hey,' he says. 'I didn't think you were in.'

'I'm not.'

His smile wavers. Arthur has a cool, Scandinavian look about him: skin, hair and glasses melding together in shades of gold, his eyes a piercing blue. Sand and sky colours. I wonder if he yearns to work outdoors, rather than being stuck in a hot, sweaty kitchen.

'I was just leaving you some cake. It's yesterday's, but I hate waste.'

'Look, I really don't eat cake.'

'You should. Cake makes people happy.'

'What are you saying? That I'm not happy? I'm delirious,

can't you tell?' I push past him, snatch the carrier from the door handle and let myself in. I glance at him briefly, watch the shadow pass over his face.

'Do you want me to take them away then?'

I feel like a complete shit. My hands are balled up, nails digging into palms. I know I should apologise, but nothing nice will come out.

'Whatever.' I hunch my shoulders, stick out a palm. I can see the little red circles my claws have made. 'Leave them. I'll eat one tonight.' There are two cakes in the bag – fudge doughnuts. Maybe he's hoping to share them over a cuppa? No chance.

I close the door with a muttered thanks, stand with my back against it for a full minute. I imagine his round, good-humoured face, marred by the irritation I'd created. This isn't me, this bitchy person, doling out cheek to well-intentioned bakers. I feel ashamed of myself. Sucking in a shaky breath, I open the door to apologise. Profusely. But there is only empty space. He has gone, taking his poor opinion of me with him.

Mac

Imagine them. Bella is dragging her sister along by the hand. She is taller than is good for a girl, with long limbs and sharp elbows poking out of too-short sleeves. She's dark, with a sallow complexion, quite unlike Elspeth, a year younger, all rosy and blonde and, according to their father, growing into a heart-stealer. Cook has always said butter wouldn't melt in little Elspeth's mouth, but there's been evidence of stolen jam around it more than once. Only Bella knows that Elspeth is the instigator of all the mischief. She is the first to take her stockings off to paddle in the burn and last into bed every night because her fidget-brain will never cease. She is full of gossip, spies at keyholes and is always where she shouldn't be.

I spent the morning writing, and as the sun warmed the chilly air I decided to venture out into the garden. This is where Arthur finds me, back again for some reason or other, his second such trip of the day. I suspect he is inventing reasons to pop in and check on me.

'I should have been there when you interviewed her.' He scrapes one hand through his hair, and I catch a glimpse of grey at his temples. You tend to forget that it's not just you who's ageing.

'You could take her to the beach,' I say lightly, and he just gives me that odd little snort, like his father used to do.

'Are you crazy? She's thoroughly unpleasant. I took her some cakes this morning and she might as well have chucked them back at me.'

I'm grooming the dogs in what I optimistically call my kitchen garden, though I haven't planted anything here for years. Today, it's a rather barren wasteland, the earth set hard in unloved furrows.

'She might benefit from a break from routine.'

'What routine?' Arthur looks at me in that exaggerated way of his, eyebrows peaking above the rim of his glasses like gothic arches. 'Where is she now? And what is she actually doing?'

Floss whines under my hands. Clumps of dog hair waft upwards, transported like thistledown on cold air currents, parachuting down seconds later to snag on weeds or be trampled underfoot. There's nothing worse than clumps of damp dog fur freewheeling round the place, but better out here than in the house. I'm not able to wield the hoover like I used to, with all the pain I'm in.

I concentrate on a knot in Floss's ears. 'Of course we have a routine. Lucie is in the study, on that infernal contraption – downloading or offloading or whatever. I told her to knock off after that. She seemed quite upset. What?' I parry his look.

'You're getting soft in your old age!' Arthur shakes his head in that irritating way offspring do.

'But not soft in the head, thankfully. What do you want, anyway?'

Arthur blows out a breath. He's thoroughly irritated and his nose is red with the cold. He's been spending far too much time cooped up next to a hot oven. A turn on the beach would do him the power of good.

'Don't suppose you have any paper handtowels squirreled away? And sultanas?'

We go into the kitchen, and I shut the back door to keep the dogs out a while longer.

'Check the pantry. I definitely have sultanas. Did I hear sirens a while ago? I was filling up the bird feeders and I'm sure I heard an ambulance flying down the lane.'

Arthur is already rooting about in my old walk-in larder. It's one of those very cool, green-painted closets that always smells of cheese. They would have hung a ham there back in the day, or let the cream settle in big shallow pans. His voice comes out like an echo.

'Looks like a car came off the road at that bad bend. Couple of cops there when I passed. It must have gone through the fence into the field.'

'Dear, dear. Old man Clark's cow pasture? He won't be too happy.'

'He's never happy.' Arthur emerges with his arms full. 'I've taken some sugar as well, and that strong wholemeal flour I bought you a while back. You never used it.'

His face is tight, the way it always is when he mentions flour. We shouldn't have to buy flour, with a mill sitting idle across the road, but death has cheated him of his floury inheritance. Of course we never speak of it.

'Just help yourself,' I say drily.

'I'd better get back. Now, don't go giving Lucie an easy ride. She's here to work.'

'As I've told you, she's doing my typing for me, but . . . I'm struggling with the words at the moment. And anyway . . .' The dogs' metal comb is still in my hand. Absently, I tease tufts of hair from it and feed them to the pedal bin. 'She seems so sad.'

Arthur is loading his plunder into a carrier bag. 'Not your problem! She didn't even tell you about the boyfriend, did she? I think that's a bit sly.'

'She isn't *sly*.' I shake my head, feel my forehead setting in furrows, like the neglected garden. 'I think he was a blast from the past that she wasn't expecting.'

'She seems to have made him welcome, since he was there all night. Maybe there's more than one? We don't know enough about her, and I certainly don't like the idea of strange men hanging around the place. I hope you're remembering to lock your doors at night.'

I work the kinks out of my lower back with my hands. 'I'm

sure she's not the type to . . . She's so quiet. Probably just an old flame. There's absolutely no point in raking over old coals, and I shall tell her that. The beach would do her good.'

Arthur dashes the notion with the palm of his hand and turns away. 'Still waters run deep, and stop poking your nose in, Ma. Anyway, I have a business to run.'

Arthur glares at me and I know the conversation is over. For now.

Lucie

*They sit on the grassy bank and launch seed pods, which bob
downstream like little galleys. Bella has been thinking a lot about
men, about marriage. She asks her sister if she would like to be wed,
and Elspeth says aye, in time. But when will it be the right time?
How do you know? And Elspeth says, 'Well, I'll know, because you
must wed first. The eldest always does.' Bella thinks about that. But
what if Elspeth, the youngest, meets someone first? What then?
Bella has lots of questions but no answers. 'Do you think we're of an
age now, to be wed?' Elspeth shrugs, as if she doesn't much care, and
continues tearing the petals from a gowan. She thinks about it some
more, and then she says, 'But it's not for us to decide, is it?'*

I sit back from the computer, knead the tension from my
neck. I would like to be a writer. I used to keep a diary, when
I was a teenager. Every Christmas my mother would give me
some slim pink or purple volume, way too prim to hold thoughts
like mine. Being virginal and boyfriend-less didn't stop me
having the sort of imagination that would have turned my
mother's hair silver. What I wrote in my diaries therefore was
heavily censored, as if somehow my parents were looking over
my shoulder. The pages bore bland references to whatever boy
had taken my fancy at school – it changed every week – or to
some unattainable movie star or rock god. If anyone had sneaked
a peek, they might have sniggered, or shaken their heads. What
was really going on in my head remained unedited, unashamed.

When I lost my virginity to Robert Guthrie at the age of
fourteen, my verdict never found its way into print. *Was that it?
Was that what all the fuss was about, this dry, painful fumbling*

business? It put me off for a long time. There were one or two other experiments. If I had to write a review, they'd probably all be three star. Until Reuben.

After that first boozy afternoon on the couch, that first kiss, I never did think about Jane. It was strange. The whole thing with Reuben – it was such a perfect fit, I never paused to consider how Jane fitted in with *us*. There was a new *us* in town, and that was real life. Jane was my fantasy sister, relegated to the dark recesses of my conscience; I never brought her out to the light. Maybe that was my coping mechanism. Maybe I'm just a bad person.

Anyway, the day after that kiss, I had to go to work as usual in the DIY shop. Mrs Black looked at me curiously, probably because I couldn't stop smiling. I behaved like an absolute loon. I smiled at the grumpy old man who returned a battery-operated alarm clock. 'It doesn't work,' he growled. 'I was late for my bowling match.'

'Did you put a battery in it?' I asked sweetly.

He stared at me. 'Aren't batteries supplied?'

I pointed to the small print on the box. 'I'm afraid not, but I can sell you a battery.'

There was some swearing. The man demanded a refund and huffed away. I laughed, and squirreled the encounter away to share with Reuben. We would have a giggle about it later. But as the day wore on, a coldness settled around me. What if that was it? A drunken kiss that meant nothing. I didn't have Reuben's number; I knew nothing about his plans. Maybe he was already on the helicopter bound for the rig? We never even got to say goodbye. Tears came down like a black cloud and I struggled to hide them. Mrs Black kept staring at me and I retreated to the loo for a long time. Eventually, blowing my nose, I returned to the counter and there he was. There was Reuben, examining some rawl plugs.

'Gentleman to see you,' Mrs Black said pointedly. My face broke into a wide grin. Reuben's eyes kindled with the special heat he would keep especially for me. Mrs Black retreated stiffly to her office, and Reuben pulled out his phone.

'I just realised you don't have my number,' he said, punching his keypad. He looked up and stole my breath away. 'We really need to keep in touch.'

My thoughts drift back into the room, and I realise I've picked up a pencil, worrying it between my fingers. It's a curiously flat pencil, rustic, and looks like it may have been sharpened with a knife. My father had a pencil like that. He called it a carpenter's pencil. Gingerly, I tuck it behind my ear. It doesn't feel natural or workmanlike. I begin to wonder whose ear it belonged to. Mac's dead husband, perhaps. I imagine him methodically going about his chores, knocking up bookshelves, fixing machinery. Emerging from the mill, white with flour, to sit for a moment in the setting sun.

To have that sort of comforting presence ripped from your life . . . I can't imagine how Mac must have felt. How she feels. Perhaps that's why she writes, to fill the gap. When Reuben first came to stay, and I realised my feelings for him ran way deeper than they should, I started to write in earnest. I wrote about how I felt when I saw him, the crippling shyness, the awkwardness. The way he looked, the things he said. Like a lawyer, I recorded every scrap, every thread of conversation. The words he used, and the way they related to me. Sometimes I would take a notion that I'd got it all wrong, that the phrases I'd thought so meaningful were actually just misinterpretations on my part. Of course he hadn't meant it that way. I was reading things into it, slanting everything so that it was about me, when really it was encoded for Jane.

I thought I could get it all out on paper, purge myself, and no one need ever know. Reuben was my sister's boyfriend. He was a secret crush. A fantasy. In this way I talked myself out of Reuben for a long time. I told myself his interest in me was a figment of my imagination. If his eyes smouldered a little bit darker when he looked at me . . . forget it. Don't listen to your intuition. Ignore your gut feeling. Why would he ever be interested in me, the mousy older sister?

Sometimes it is necessary to spill your feelings onto a white page, to try to put them in order. It's a safety valve, I guess. A way of releasing the pressure, if you can call it that, this deep-seated ache. I find an old scrap of paper and scribble furiously for five minutes with the fat stub of a pencil. Words. Some meaningless, some so heartfelt I cannot read them. A goodbye to Reuben.

Just as I place a final full stop, my phone begins to vibrate in the back pocket of my jeans. I fumble for it, peer at the screen. My sister's name flashes at me: *Jane, Jane, Jane!* As always, guilt nibbles away at my gut. My thumb hovers as my brain completes a quick scan. Not in bed: check. Dressed and decent: check. No Reuben on the scene: check.

'Hello?'

'Lucie, it's me.' *Sniff.* Is she crying? Why is Jane crying?

'What's wrong?' My innards drop. There's something wrong. I can feel it. Dread begins to crawl down the back of my thighs.

'It's Reuben. He's been in a car crash.'

My legs give way. I sink into Mac's leather chair. I can't speak.

'Lucie? Are you still there? Did you hear me?'

'Yes, yes.' My voice is a croak. 'How . . . bad? Is he . . . ?'

'They've taken him to Ninewells Hospital. I . . . I don't know yet. I don't even know what he was doing in Dundee. I thought he was in Aberdeen. He's unconscious. I'm on my way down now, Dad's driving. Lucie, can I stay? Can I stay with you? I need to be near him.'

My breath stops. I can hear my heartbeat in my ears. 'Of course,' I hear myself say. 'Of course you need to be near him. Where exactly did it happen, the crash?'

I can hear her weeping now, openly. She can't speak any more, she says, but she'll call me as soon as she gets news. She hangs up. I'm glad. I can't trust myself to speak.

Mac

'Yes, of course you must go. Arthur will take you to the hospital, won't you, Arthur?'

Arthur's mouth drops open, but he doesn't object. Gives perhaps the merest shake of his head. He takes off those flimsy specs of his and wipes them on the hem of his T-shirt. He does that when he's nervous; I've noticed that before. The girl is shaking, and I feel a certain tenderness steal over me. Last year, Jethro got clipped by a car in the middle of the village (my own fault, should have had him on a leash) and had to be taken to the vet. He looked so sorrowful that I became almost maudlin over him. I can't abide all that mawkishness we're subjected to now. Every time you turn the TV on someone is weeping, or lighting a candle. Weeping and candle-lighting are the scourges of modern society. But the point is, I felt a certain *motherliness* towards the dog, and I feel it now. This young girl is away from her parents and home, and now this. It strikes me that she must be very close to her sister after all, to react so violently.

She's still standing beside my desk, as if she doesn't know which way to turn. Behind her I can see a copy of one of my stories open on the computer screen. I hope it won't get lost in the ether.

'Yes, yes.' I pat her shoulder. 'Chin up, my dear. Arthur will take you to the hospital. But first, do save that whatchamacallit, won't you? Should hate to lose any words.'

She does something with the keyboard and my story shrinks from view. Arthur is there, sweeping her jacket from the back of the chair and holding it out by the shoulders in a very gentlemanly fashion. Lucie doesn't slip her arms in, of course. She wrests it from him almost defiantly, and shrugs into it under her own steam.

I stand for several minutes after they've gone, listening to the old Westminster chimes ring out loudly from the clock on the window ledge. There's the chill of disturbed air about the study. It's odd having someone in your space, going through your things, even if you're paying them to do it. I suppose I've become used to my own company. After Jim . . . Well, I did think, for a while, that I should make an effort to look for someone else. I had a fantasy once, of a kind older gentleman in a bottle-green sweater and moleskin trousers. He'd have binoculars permanently attached to his neck, and like hiking and dogs. He never materialised. Mother always said that humans weren't designed to be alone, although trying to be with someone else is sometimes pretty darn difficult. I linger by the desk, standing in the same spot so recently vacated by Lucie. The laptop screen is black; Jim eyes me from his photograph.

Lucie isn't any neater than I am. My desk is still chaotic – open notebooks, a pack of chewing gum (I screw up my face and chuck it in the waste-paper basket), tissues, crumpled paper, pens and pencils. I pick up a short, stubby one. Jim's carpenter's pencil. My heart wobbles. Where did she get that? He always wore it behind his ear, even in the days when we went out to dinner parties and the like.

I sift through the torn bits of paper. I see Lucie's writing; furious scribbles in pencil. A poem, is it? Does she write? Another thing she never mentioned. I peer intently at the note. Yes, there is a rough poem-shape to it, an early draft of something, perhaps. Irritation prickles. Why is she writing poetry when she's supposed to be transcribing my notes?

It's still love, isn't it?
Even when it's a big fat dirty secret.
I can still feel my hand in yours

even though no one has ever seen us walking
hand in hand.
Your favourite cologne lingers on me,
Even though I have never asked the brand,
or bought it for you.
I'll never be able to wrap it lovingly and plant it
under our Christmas tree.
We will never have a Christmas tree together, you and I.
On my birthday, you wish me all the best,
and I act restrained,
as if I couldn't care less,
but inside
I am waiting for another chance to be alone
with you, to memorise you all over again.
That's still love, isn't it?

Good heavens. What on earth can that mean?

Lucie

I'm kind of half-slouching against the window, as if I can make the car go faster just by glaring at the landscape. The road is winding, narrow, and Arthur is a cautious driver. There are bulging ditches on each side and, coming up on the left, I see unmistakeable tyre tracks forged into the bank. *Oh God*. Nausea grips me, and the car slows down. I don't know if Arthur is responding to my sudden lurch, my fingers gripping the door, or whether he has known all along that this evidence is here.

His voice is gentle. 'Isn't that your visitor's car, the blue Citroën?'

I see a flash of blue down in the field and turn my face away. Before answering, I pick over the words in my head. But Arthur has already guessed my secret. We have stopped, the engine is idling, and he's slightly turned towards me, his hand resting on the gearstick. I don't want to look at him. I stare at the glovebox. It's closed, giving nothing away.

Arthur tries again, still gentle. 'So is he your sister's boyfriend then, rather than yours?'

Blunt. Sometimes I like that in people, but not now, not today. I round on him, see him flinch at the bitterness in my voice.

'What are you, the boyfriend police?'

'I'm not judging, I'm just –'

'Saying. Well, don't. Drive on.'

There's a pause. Arthur checks his mirrors and shoves into first gear. We move off, faster now. Fields flash by; detached bungalows. A Shetland pony in a paddock. I'm still angled towards the window. My breath catches on the glass.

'No one knows,' I whisper. 'No one.'

'You think that, but in a small place . . .'

'No one will know unless you tell them.'

But it's not true, is it? That no one knows? My mother knows. And she is the first person I see when I get to the ward where Reuben is. She is waiting in the corridor, her shoulder bag gripped so tightly under her arm that her chest is all squished out of shape. She's wearing a buff-coloured top that blends in with the hospital paint and she's gripping that bag as if it's the only thing that's stopping her dropping through to the basement. Above the usual clinical smell, I catch the whiff of her floral perfume, and it takes me back to childhood. Without warning, I burst into tears. It's noisy, slightly hysterical, and my mother looks mortified. She doesn't try to comfort me, just hitches the bag up tighter.

'Lucie, do you want a tissue?' Fiddling with the zip gives her something to do, somewhere else to look. It's Arthur who offers me a crumpled bit of kitchen roll. I dab my eyes. The paper smells of suet.

'How is he?' I manage to whisper.

My mother looks at me then, her eyes frosty. 'Jane and Laura are in with him just now. They're speaking to the nurse.'

Laura is Reuben's sister. Their parents are dead, so they're very close, and because she's Reuben's sister I've soaked up all the details of her life. Her husband works offshore, like Reuben. She has three kids, another on the way and a nursing career she's put on hold. I feel I know her intimately, but in reality I've only met her twice and I'd be hard pressed to recognise her.

Mum is looking at Arthur, and awkwardly I make the introductions. I'd thought he would just drop me off, I'm sure he has more important things to do, but he accompanied me all the way in; guided me into a lift when I got lost, pointing out the signs. He'd kept up a conversation of sorts: 'I know this place well. My mother is always having tests. My father, he was never in hospital a day in his life. They brought him here, after the accident, but he was already . . .'

I hadn't known what to say, couldn't really get my head round any of that, with Reuben lying in the building somewhere, stretched out under cold sheets. I've always had a fear of hospital beds: they look so hard, so unfamiliar. Had Arthur's father been in a car crash too? I'd let the notion drift away, kept my head down, plodded on.

Arthur is making some small talk about the cost of the car park. Father has gone down to get coffee, Mum says – it could be a long night. I realise we are here for the duration, a family, a show of strength. I must be a sister, a dutiful daughter. I cannot weep at Reuben's bedside. I must distance myself, as I have always done. I recall the scrap of poetry I'd scribbled in Mac's study. *It's still love, isn't it?* Had I picked it up? Chucked it in the bin? *I can still feel my hand in yours.* I hope I've thrown it away. What if Mac reads it? *We will never have a Christmas tree together, you and I.*

I don't want people knowing this; judging me. Arthur has guessed. My mother knows. Did she ever tell my father? Oh God. *I am waiting for another chance to be alone with you.* Oh God, oh God. *I act restrained, as if I couldn't care less.*

Oh God oh God oh God . . .

Perhaps the one person who doesn't know me at all is my sister.

Cold overhead light burns the white sheet. I can't quite believe the bump beneath the sheet is Reuben. He should be more restless, to be Reuben; take up more space. This is a line drawing of a man, plugged into machines I don't recognise. There's some kind of cage keeping the linen from his legs.

I remember that other light, so recently: sunshine spilling through a gap in the curtains, illuminating his nose, his chin;

spidery black lashes, and the steady rise and fall of his sleeping chest. I'd wondered what he was dreaming about. Now his mind has been emptied by drugs; I can hear the drip of them, somewhere, in a tangle of pipelines. I don't want to look at all that stuff, but it saves me having to make eye contact with Jane. Laura has excused herself to go to the bathroom. I was shocked by the size of her bump. How awful it must have been to receive this news, to find childcare, transport. To be at her brother's side in that condition. I realise with a shock that I have more empathy for this stranger than for my own sister. What am I turning into?

Jane is wearing a yellow cardigan; it was the first thing I'd noticed when the nurse said I could go in, and I thought it was too optimistic for a situation like this. And then I remembered – Jane doesn't even like yellow. I gave her a big fluffy yellow cushion one Christmas and she took it back and swapped it for a pale pink one. Jane has an irritating habit of cuddling cushions when she's watching the telly, or on the phone to Reuben.

Maybe the yellow cardigan was all she could find in that moment of panic, when Laura called. She would have gone numb, breathless. She tries to function, looking for her shoes, her jacket. She grabs a cardigan, any cardigan. She can't do up the buttons because her fingers are shaking.

Feeling sick, I reach for my sister's hand. My palms are sweating. Her hands are stone cold.

'He's strong. He'll pull through.'

She glances at me. Her eyes are dry, and I've made sure mine are too. I'm trying so hard to keep a lid on it. She doesn't speak, and my heart winces. Does she know? How can she know?

'Can I get you anything?'

Jane licks her lips. It's hot in here. The air is dry and chemical. 'It's okay, Dad's gone to get coffee. Lucie . . .' She squeezes my hand. 'Thanks for being here.'

Then I begin to cry again.

The cakes are fresh and appealing. Too luscious for a hospital cafe. I think they should be past their sell-by date and taste of dust, in line with the emotional tenor of the place. Arthur is tucking into a croissant. Why is he still here?

'Why are you still here?'

I'm staring at him across the Formica table. Steam rises from the cappuccino between my elbows. Arthur stops chewing, as if he hadn't realised he was under scrutiny and is now embarrassed. His cheeks colour up and he wipes crumbs from the corners of his mouth.

'I'm just checking out the baking.' His eyes, behind the smeary spectacles, hold a glint of humour. 'They do a nice line in almond croissants. Good, but not as good as the one I had in Budapest in 2006.'

'You remember where you were when you ate good cake?'

'Doesn't everyone?'

'No. I remember where I've had good sex.'

I want to shock him. That's the anger coming out, now that the initial shock has passed. I'm fucking angry. Why did Reuben crash? Why have I now got to go through this charade, when all I want to do is throw myself on the bed beside him? Poor, quiet Arthur is fair game for my rage.

'Oh, you do?' He isn't so easily shocked. 'Where was your best place?'

It's my turn to blush. I glance down at my cup, bathe in the steam. 'An old pub on the coast. A sea view and a brass bed.'

'With Reuben?'

I nod slowly. I can feel his gaze on my forehead. 'Do you know what? I just want to go home.'

'I'll take you home. You'd better say your goodbyes.'

Straightening up, I glance at the overhead signs. There are crowds of people all milling around, buying sweets, fags, magazines. Some are in their pyjamas and robes, drips still attached as if this, *this*, is reality, and we're all incomers. I don't want to get used to this reality.

'Which ward is it again?'

'Orthopaedic trauma. Do you want me to come up with you?'

I don't reply, but he scrapes his chair back anyway, and ushers me out.

Mac

There is mischief afoot. My mouth is dry and I'm getting the smell of horses – no, saddlery. The old heart is pattering along like a train and I'm trying to call out to Elspeth. I can see her in the distance, dangerously close to the water's edge. Where is Bella? Bella should be watching out for her, but try as I might, I cannot catch a glimpse of that dark hair, that pale face. The trees are in the way. Then I hear gunshots: one, two. Close range. Elspeth! Come away! I think I'm screaming . . .

I gasp into wakefulness, finding myself slumped in my comfy armchair. My head is wedged at an awkward angle against the wing of it, nose pressed into green leather. No wonder I'm smelling saddles. I shift cautiously, face all scrunched up in anticipation of pain. This is how we get bloody wrinkles, anticipating the crap life throws at us. The telly is still on, some awful cop show, Yanks shooting each other all over New York City. Close range. One, two. The dream recedes. I remember I've been reading 'The Cruel Sister', and the book has fallen to the floor. Elspeth, and Bella, wherever she is, draw back into my imagination.

Oh Lord . . . I wipe a hand across my face. It feels clammy and my neck hurts. Worse, my heart is still skidding around like a hyperactive spaniel. Pressing both palms against it, I feel hard bone beneath the soft padding of my breasts. Am I losing weight? A glance at the carriage clock on the mantelpiece – just after ten. I must have dropped off during *The One Show*. Groaning, I lurch to my feet. The dogs will have peed all over the damn kitchen.

Those two sisters running through my dreams: Bella and Elspeth. Up to no good, slinking around the mill, picking quarrels. The events of the day have unsettled me, and I can't get Lucie's reaction out of my head. She seemed so distraught, and yet I hadn't got the impression she was close to her sister.

Shuffling down the hall, I wonder if Arthur is back. Did he just drop Lucie off at the hospital? Why didn't he come in to tell me the news? If there is any news. They're very cagey, these days, doctors. It's the same every time I go for tests. You could fill up Loch Ness with the amount of blood they've taken out of me, and still no one will offer a proper diagnosis. Arrhythmia, is the closest they've come. An irregular heartbeat. But why? Why is my heart out of sync with the rest of me? Nobody will hazard a guess, because if they guess, and guess wrong . . . well, they're all afraid of the big lawsuits these days.

The dogs go wild, but at least nobody has peed, and I let them out the back door. The night is crisp and very dark. No moon, even though I look for it. It's one of life's pleasures, a starry sky and a moon of some description. It doesn't have to be full, a nice neat sickle will do. It just makes you feel less alone in the universe, to look at that moon and think that the one you love is somewhere beneath it too. Connectivity, that's what it's all about.

Of course, none of that applies to me now. Back in the day, when Jim was here, I could let myself think like that. I was always the one who was absent. There was always some conference or other claiming my attention, or a teaching assignment, or a book festival. It was always me in a strange hotel room, flinging open the window, looking for the moon. Jim never strayed far, and I always felt sorry for him, somehow.

The dogs are out there in the dark, nosing around. One of them lets out a short, sharp bark. I can hear a fox yipping a reply in the distance and the pungent scent of rosemary invades my nostrils. My heart is still uneasy, and slowly the reason is slipping back to me. There was someone else in my dream, someone I haven't thought of for such a long time.

The bang of a door echoing through the silent house makes me jump. Max, the ringleader, starts to bark in earnest. Is that him? Is that Arthur now, at this time? A logjam of furry bodies in the back doorway prevents me reaching the kitchen first. I think I can hear two voices.

'Ma?'

I meet up with Arthur in the kitchen. Lucie is just behind him, skulking in the hallway.

'Come in then. I'll put the kettle on.' My voice comes out quite harsh. Arthur is rubbing the dogs' ears. He looks exhausted. I make shushing motions at the girl, as if I'm herding geese, and she emerges into the sharp kitchen light. Her face is pinched and white. I hold the kettle under the gushing tap.

'You can have a hot chocolate,' I call out, competing with the noise of the water. 'Sugar for shock.'

Yes, she's in shock. I can see that now. She's shaking and Arthur is guiding her to a chair at the breakfast table.

'I just feel a bit sick,' she says, burying her head in her hands. Her dark hair cascades onto the pine surface and I long to stroke it, to comfort her, as I would Floss or any of the others. Maybe if I'd had a daughter I'd be softer, less afraid of contact. I busy myself with the mugs.

'Come along now, chin up. What news from the hospital?'

Arthur speaks for her. 'Reuben – her sister's boyfriend – is stable, but unconscious. He's got internal injuries, a busted leg and a fractured skull.'

'So quite bad then?'

Arthur makes a stern cutting gesture with his hand and I shrug apologetically, placing a steaming mug of chocolate in front of the dark hair, which is all I can see of Lucie. The hair shivers a bit and draws back.

'I'm sorry.' Her voice is squeaky. 'I haven't eaten anything. I feel a bit . . .'

'Sick? Is she going to be sick?' I'm looking at Arthur; I don't know why. I'm already seeing in my mind's eye the old bucket under the sink, the scrubbing brush, the disinfectant. The dogs are always barfing on the carpet. 'Maybe a Rich Tea biscuit? Arthur, get the biscuit tin. Have a Rich Tea biscuit, it will settle your stomach. Or a tablespoon of brandy. My grandmother always swore by a tablespoon of brandy.'

The hair groans. The biscuit tin is produced and the dogs gather round, brown eyes reproachful, already anticipating a refusal.

Lucie looks up suddenly, as if she's forgotten something important.

'Mac,' she says. 'I have a favour to ask.'

'Mmm?'

'Is it okay if my sister, Jane, stays with me for a few days? It won't be any hassle, I –' She rushes the words out, as if I'm about to say no. I shake my head.

'It's fine. Of course she may. She'll want to be near the hospital and there's things to be taken care of. Has she spoken to the police? Where did it happen, the accident?'

Lucie looks at Arthur. Arthur looks at me and opens his mouth. 'Um . . . not far from here, as it happens. He was . . .'

'Working in the area,' Lucie finishes.

I look from one to the other. There is a puzzle here, and some of the pieces don't quite fit. 'Right. And what about your parents? I have rooms here if –'

'No!' The girl shoots up straighter, as if the very notion of having all her family here together is too terrifying. 'It's very kind of you, but they've booked into a Travelodge tonight, and then they're going home on the train and leaving Jane the car. She's taking time off work. We don't know how long . . . She's staying at the hospital tonight, of course.'

'Yes, of course.'

So that will add a new dynamic – two sisters together, in the Miller's Cottage. How strange. How fitting. Fragments of my dream return. Two sisters. My fingers itch to start scribbling down the details, before they float away. I turn around to retrieve my own mug from the worktop, absently fiddling in the pocket of my cardigan. The dogs surge forward eagerly, and Jethro sits on my foot. My fingers make contact with a folded piece of paper – Lucie's love poem to person unknown.

Interesting.

Lucie

March

Jane has hands like a child, and like a child's hands they are constantly in motion. No longer smeared with poster paint and glue, they are now elegant, fully qualified hands; pointed nails, a delicate gold watch draped over narrow wrist bones. I check out my own nails, with their chipped navy polish. Mac said it looks like I have frostbite. 'No wonder, this study is like a fridge,' I'd snapped. She'd suggested I work from the cottage, to keep Jane company, but the idea fills me with dread. My awful secret has been given a dreadful shaking. I'm terrified it will break loose and destroy us. I tell Mac that I'm fine. Work is a good distraction.

That first evening, I light the fire in the sitting room of the Miller's Cottage. It seems like the right thing to do, under the circumstances. Fires are comforting. I'm sitting cross-legged on the floor, feeding the grate with bits of damp wood that stink of rot and are threatening to extinguish what little flame we've got. I bought a chilled bottle of Pinot Grigio from the village shop and now it sits next to me, open, in the hearth – not the best place for it, but, thanks to my efforts, there is zero heat coming from the grate and plenty of smoke. Jane is sitting on the couch, legs curled under her, the gold bracelet of her watch shimmering in the firelight as she describes an anecdote with one hand, the other cupped around her wine glass. The watch had been a Christmas gift from Reuben, because Jane hates to be late. I received nothing. A gift may have been taken as evidence, he'd

66

reasoned, and used against him. Jane's wine is diluted with soda, in case 'circumstances change' and she is called to the hospital.

'So we went to view this gorgeous little cottage. You remember the one at the junction where the Inveraray road forks to the left?' A half-moon motion of her hand. 'Mum used to take us to the woods there, to see the tadpoles in the pond. You were always scared of the water, scared of the little slimy things.'

'*We* have a pond,' I mutter.

She ignores me and presses on with her tale. I realise I've invented a new 'we' – Mac and Arthur and me, even though I don't particularly want to be part of a 'we' that doesn't include Reuben. Jane's 'we' has been to view a house. Jane's 'we' is talking about getting engaged. She fingers the watch band, imagining a smaller gold circle, no doubt. There is such sadness in her eyes, I immediately feel guilty.

'Have some more wine.' I rouse myself to reach for the bottle, but her hand immediately caps the top of her glass.

'No, I'd better not. I need to be able to drive, in case . . . in case the hospital calls.'

We both glance at her silent mobile, sitting on the arm of the couch. She picks it up, checks the signal, the battery. A loud rapping at the back door makes us both jump. I glance at the clock on the wall. It's just after nine.

'Could be Arthur with more cakes.'

There are two cops standing there when I open the back door. I taste the wine on my breath and feel guilty for no reason. They take off their helmets when I invite them in. The male cop has to duck under the lintel. The female cop is shorter than me, but there's a knowing glint in her eye that says *don't underestimate me*. I won't. I lead them into the sitting room. Jane has put down her wine; she's clutching a cushion, not knowing whether to get up or stay seated. The cops perch on chairs, and the male one fishes a notebook from his breast pocket. They have come to inform us – Jane – about the details of the accident.

Jane has had to go through all of the shitty stuff you get left with in a situation like this. She's had to be there for Reuben's sister, Laura, who is struggling to cope alone with all those kids until her husband can get back from some distant oilfield. She's had to deal with the insurance company, and the garage people; the car is a write-off. Writing something off seems to take a huge amount of time and energy and all I've been able to do is hang around and make tea and offer the right words in the right places.

The cop informs us that the accident happened on the B333, near Fettermore. Jane peers at me for some kind of clarification, but my mouth has gone so dry my tongue won't work.

'Just down the road from here,' the female cop fills in helpfully. Her gaze is swinging round the room. She's already observed the damp wood and my ripped-knee jeans. She doesn't rate me much as a hostess, or a sister.

'Was he going to Dundee then?' Jane scrunches up her nose, managing to look like a distressed Reese Witherspoon, rather than Miss Piggy, as I would.

'Erm, possibly, although . . .' The female cop looks at the male. 'It's slightly off the main road. Perhaps he had to detour into the village for something.'

'And the crash site . . . it is slightly out of the village,' says the male cop, 'and the car was facing due east which means he . . .'

I break in with a cheery, 'Anyone like some tea? Cake?'

I have a whole plastic tub of blueberry muffins, courtesy of Arthur. The male cop pats his super-fit stomach and declines with a smile. They eventually get up to go, promising to keep in touch. I hurry them through the back door and lean against it when they're gone, struggling to breathe.

When I get back to Jane, I can tell she's been thinking this through. She's sitting bolt upright, stroking the arm of the couch in a most unfriendly manner.

'So . . . where was he going? Had he popped in to see you?'

'Um . . . Did he even know I was here? I've been working a

lot, up at the house, so I may have missed him if he did drop by.' My heart is rattling in my ribcage. I have an urgent need to pee.

Jane picks up the cushion again and hugs it to her chest. 'I did mention to him where you were, but . . .'

'Oh, well that's it, then. Maybe he decided to drop by in passing. You know, if he was working in Dundee.'

'He never said he was working in Dundee.'

She's picking away at some loose threads on the cushion. I want to grab hold of her hand, arrest her. Never pick at loose threads.

'They do lots of maintenance work in Dundee, on the rigs. They tow them into the harbour.' I'm gabbling now. 'You should see them at night – Mac says they're all lit up like Christmas trees.'

'Maybe that's it.' Jane doesn't sound convinced. 'It's just . . . Och, never mind.' She subsides, cuddling the cushion closer.

'What?'

There's something she's not saying. I can feel it.

'It's just that Reuben has been acting a bit strange. Oh, look – I don't want to talk about it now, when he's so ill . . .' Her voice breaks up a bit. My voice is stuck. *What?* I scream it on the inside. *What?*

She's shaking her head, shaking away some groundless notion. 'He's just been really distant, not always answering my texts. Oh, it's *nothing*, but . . .'

'But?' I sink down beside the hearth again, reach for my glass and take a big gulp of wine.

She looks up at a space above the fire, to the right of the clock. Her eyes are too sparkly. 'If I didn't know Reuben better . . . I'd say he's been seeing someone else.'

Mac

Their father is a giant of a man. He sleeps late into the day and goes out at night, coming home splattered with mud and smelling of horse sweat and other men's cattle. Sometimes, when they cannot sleep, the sisters creep down to the hall and crouch in the shadows and listen to their father carousing with his men. The men drink wine the colour of blood, and whisky, and there is an air of triumph about them. Sometimes, their father spies his daughters and summons them over to sit on his knee, or on the arms of his chair, and calls upon his war band to drink a toast to them, and the dogs growl mightily if any man lurches too close. Once, Elspeth wrinkled her nose and told her father that he smelled of a perfume that wasn't her mother's and that had provoked laughter in him as loud as thunder.

My pencil pauses. I become aware of two things: I've been staring at the page for ages, and someone is staring at me.

Anita comes over to see if I need another coffee. I hadn't been sure about decamping to the cafe to write, but the house seems suddenly very empty, with Lucie spending time up at the hospital with Jane. I've got used to her grumpy presence, the way she swears at the dogs, the murderous glint in her eye when I ask her to do the ironing. I suppose the sad fact is that she is a *presence*. Sometimes, you only know you're lonely when you find yourself with company.

The bonus of working in the cafe means that Anita is on hand to provide me with a constant supply of hot beverages, and it's warm, too. March has come in like the proverbial lion, all teeth and claws, and up at the house, the draughts can't be contained. I've taken to shuffling around with a woolly tartan rug around my shoulders. Arthur says I look like a bag lady without the bags.

'How do you know if someone is cheating on you?' I chew the rubber at the end of the pencil and look up at Anita. 'I've used the old perfume cliché here, but I fear that's just what it is – a cliché.'

Anita frowns. She pretends to think about it, standing there with my dirty coffee mug in her hand, but really I know she's just thinking how bonkers I am. She's never really 'got' me, and yet in many ways she is my staunchest ally. All that time, when Arthur was going through the break-up with Nancy, Anita was my spy in the camp, my eyes and ears. I had thought that perhaps she and Arthur might . . . but rumour has it that Anita is betrothed to a distant cousin back in India. Does she ever wonder what the distant cousin is up to in distant climes? Probably not. When not clearing tables she immerses herself in her coursework – something to do with forensics, I believe. She had her textbooks in here one day – human identification through bones and so on. It all seemed quite macabre for a young girl. I know her tutor, a round, unimaginative chap, who inhabits a very different world to mine. We once had quite a frank discussion about science versus the arts, and he had the nerve to warn me that my foray into fiction writing would put paid to my credibility as an academic. 'You'll be destroyed by your own imagination!' he'd chuckled.

Eventually, Anita speaks in her soft, measured way. 'In a recent Australian study, researchers found that men can recognise women who cheat by merely looking at facial photographs. It would seem that men have evolved to detect the possibility of an unfaithful female in order to make sure any offspring are genetically theirs. My own opinion is that one should never dwell on the possibility of infidelity. It becomes a self-fulfilling prophecy. More coffee? You should eat – it's nearly lunchtime.'

'Yes . . .' I am distracted. A self-fulfilling prophecy? That isn't right, and I want to tell her so. 'I'll have the soup. That's all fine and dandy for the men, but what about the women. How do women know their man is being unfaithful?'

'Soup it is.'

She glides away. From somewhere beyond the bead curtain that divides the shop from the kitchen, I can hear Arthur singing along to the radio. No, that self-fulfilling prophecy idea is preposterous. I never dwelt on the possibility of Jim leading a double life. I was too busy to dwell on anything. Something dark and sleepy stirs in my belly, and when Anita brings the soup – pea and broccoli – I wonder whether I'll be able to digest it.

I'm not sure why these old feelings have suddenly decided to surface now. I seem to be spending an awful lot of time pondering recent events. I heard sirens on the morning of the accident. A surprising collision on a little-used back road. Lucie's unexpected visitor. I must admit I'm a little disconcerted by the way all these pieces are coming together. Arthur's words keep coming back to me. *Still waters run deep.* As deep as the millpond. That other story too is tormenting me, asking to be written, to be recorded. *Things need to come to light.* That phrase over and over in my head. I woke up this morning mumbling those words. The voice I heard was Bella's.

The door bursts open and suddenly Lucie is standing there, all windswept and sulky-mouthed. Her gaze tumbles over me and finds Arthur, who's just emerging from the kitchen, wiping his hands on a tea towel. Anita catches my eye.

'Did you leave cakes on my door again last night?' Lucie demands. She can be terribly blunt. I see Arthur recoil a tad, slap the towel on the counter with more force than is strictly necessary. The two church types in the corner raise their heads.

'I left a box of chocolate and date brownies, to be exact,' he says warily. 'I thought you and your sister might –'

Lucie throws up both hands, despairingly. 'Why didn't you knock?'

'Because I don't generally get a great reception!' Arthur raises his voice, just a little. The old ladies lean in and whisper, and Anita suddenly finds a job for herself behind the counter. I'm unsure about this tension between them. It feels dangerous, out of control.

'Well, the dog's eaten them. There was paper all over the outside this morning. I only stopped in to tell you because –'

I grip the table 'Which dog? Chocolate is poisonous to dogs!'

Lucie flounces around. 'Exactly! That's why I came in! I don't have time for this.' She half turns, and through the window I see her sister's car. The sister is staring at the shop door, fists clenched on the wheel.

'It'll be Floss . . .'

'Probably Floss . . .'

Arthur and I both speak together. Lucie grips the door handle and makes to go. She seems softer, suddenly.

'It probably was Floss. I thought I'd better tell you. I wouldn't like anything to happen to her, and I don't have time to . . . I have to go.'

She opens the door, slowly.

Arthur steps forward. 'Is everything okay?'

She looks at him for moment. Something passes between them. I'm just feet away but it passes over me. I experience a moment of disquiet.

Her voice is little more than a whisper. 'I don't know. The hospital called. Reuben is awake.'

Lucie

Reuben is awake.

I'm standing at the foot of your bed, Reuben. I've deliberately put acres of white sheet between us, because you shouldn't be looking at me. Jane's place is up there beside you, stroking your face, holding your hand. I can't hear that first, precious exchange of words, but it seems intimate, meaningful, and I am bereft.

Jane helps you sip water from a cloudy plastic glass. She wipes your mouth with a fresh tissue.

'Come on, Lucie!' Like a traffic cop, she beckons me over. 'Come and say hi!'

Reluctantly, I tiptoe into your line of vision. Under the stubble I used to find so sexy, there's a sudden edge to your face; your eyes have grown carefully neutral. Nothing wrong with your memory, then. You try out a smile, and when you speak, your voice is low and hoarse with disuse.

'Lucie, this is all your fault.'

I go cold, like someone's drenched me from above with icy water. Is this the way it's to be? Are you going to reveal all here, when you're in no fit state to take any blame? Did you have a light-bulb moment when your lights were out? Beside me, Jane giggles, not quite getting the joke. Her gaze drifts between your face and mine. I'm afraid to speak.

'Remember you asked your mother for those books?' Your eyes look kind of desperate. I have no choice but to play along.

I nod. 'Oh, yes . . . the books.'

'I thought I'd drop them in to you, in passing, seeing as I was going to Dundee. But you were out.'

'Yes, I must have been out.' My jaw tightens. How long have you been lying there, Reuben, dreaming up lies? Thinking up ways to avoid the truth in your white-sheet prison?

The truth. I think we're edging closer to it, aren't we? It's swimming there, just under the surface, like a big fat trout. I could almost touch it, if I wasn't so afraid of the water.

'Do you know what?' I flash them both my brightest smile. 'I'm going to head off now, leave you two lovebirds together.'

'But how will you get home?' Jane says.

'Bus. There are loads of buses. Then you can stay as long as you want.'

I edge out, her half-hearted objections ringing in my ears. You say nothing. You're still holding her hand. I brush past a nurse, turn and run down the corridor. Without Arthur's patient directions, I get lost, but eventually I end up at the cafeteria. I need to sit down, take a few minutes. I order a latte and an almond croissant. They *are* pretty good.

The bus stops at the bottom of the road that leads up to the mill. I'd already noted, as we juddered to a halt, that the cafe is still open, the front window a square of warm fuzzy amber in a dismal day. I pretend to dither, but actually my legs are already taking me across the road. Through the foggy plate glass, I can see the waitress sweeping under the tables. I open the door slowly. Mac is standing at the counter with her back to me. She is in full flow.

'And I said to him, no you are *not* doing my garden again. After last year? Good heavens, the silly man chopped down an apple tree full of fruit and then tried to hide all the apples. Who chops down a fruit tree? I asked him to *prune* the lilac. He doesn't know his arse from his elbow. I said to him, I said . . .'

'The apples weren't wasted, to be fair.' Arthur comes into view from the depths of the kitchen. He looks tired. 'We had apple crumble, apple turnovers, apple jelly, spiced apple chutney – Oh, Lucie . . .'

Mac swings around, and I'm trapped in the full glare of her attention.

'Well? How did it go?'

She makes it sound as if I've been performing in some kind of drama. I've certainly learned to act.

'Let her sit down. Lucie, I'll get you a hot drink.' Arthur grabs a clean mug and busies himself at the coffee machine. The waitress pulls out a chair at the nearest table, and I sit down heavily. Her smile, like her eyes, is watchful. Mac comes to sit opposite me. I can't avoid her questions.

'He's awake. I've left Jane with him. There's no point in the two of us being there.' Arthur rests a steaming latte in front of me. 'It's Jane he wants to see.' My tone is light, humorous, even, but Arthur catches my eye for a split second before he moves away.

'Did she ask him where the crash happened?' Mac insists. 'Did she find out what caused it? Speed, I imagine.'

The waitress speaks quickly, softly. 'That's such a bad bend, even if you know the roads.'

'Anita . . .' From the other side of the counter, Arthur is shaking his head the tiniest bit. Anita bites her bottom lip and hurries away to resume sweeping. When I catch his eye, he just smiles and picks up his tongs to load more cakes onto a white plate. I hope they aren't for me. The hot, steamy atmosphere is making me queasy.

'It's early days, but they're saying that Reuben could be out quite soon.' My tongue lingers secretly, hungrily, on his name. 'He'll have to have intense physio, and probably another operation on his leg.'

'That seems positive then. Your sister will nurse him back to health. It's what you do, isn't it? In sickness and in health, all that stuff. That's what you sign up for.' Mac's voice has a bitter edge that I hadn't been expecting. She turns sharply to the counter. 'Aren't I getting a coffee? Actually, make it tea. If I have coffee at this late stage I'll be up in the night, peeing on the carpet like the bloody dogs.'

Arthur is cleaning the spout of the espresso machine. There's a bit of bad-tempered banging, and I think I hear him swear beneath his breath. 'Ma, you've been here since this morning. We're trying to get finished up.'

Mac widens her eyes at me. 'Did you hear that? I have been *working*. I bet J. K. Rowling never had to put up with this abuse at The Elephant House.' She pushes at her notebook. It's sitting between us, the pen placed neatly on top. I hadn't noticed it, but now a faint flush of anticipation perks me up like a caffeine hit.

'Have you been working on your stories?' I've been pestering her for ages to finish that one about the castle, but she's been procrastinating.

She inclines her head, as if she has a secret and can't voice it. I make a grab for the notebook, but she gets there first and sweeps it into her bag. 'Stories have to play out in their own good time. Now . . .' She gets slowly to her feet. 'Since I have outstayed my welcome, I will take myself off and leave you two to chat.'

She begins muttering about keys, and all the rubbish she carries in her bag – notebooks, pens, cough sweets, a compact umbrella – is hauled out and dumped on the table in front of me. Mac surfaces with the key, a twinkling, elusive fish. 'Got it! My mother used to pin it to my knickers, and no wonder.'

Behind the counter, Arthur groans. Anita seems to have disappeared. The thought of being alone with him is scary, but I don't quite know why.

Mac

A sudden squall of rain blows out of nowhere as I trudge up the road. I should have asked Anita to drop me off. She's always bombing around in that old banger of hers, even though she lives not ten minutes from the village. She'd been talking about going to meet friends, so maybe she was running late. She certainly didn't linger. One minute she was taking her pinny off and the next she was gone.

So Arthur has Lucie to chat to. She's not the easiest of folk, but she seems to unbend a little when he's around. There's a gentle spark between them, and I'm not sure how I feel about that. He's been lonely since Nancy left, but I'm not certain Lucie is the right girl to fill the gap. I zip my anorak up as far as it will go, and bend my head into the squall, letting the rain belt off my waxed hat. It's been a good writing day, productive. Bella and Elspeth have grown today. A young man has come on the scene; courting the father, before he can pay attention to the daughters. Things are hotting up.

I come to the bad bend. After my conversation with Arthur, I'd been looking out for the tyre tracks in Clark's field. I saw them on my way to the cafe; great gouges cartwheeling into the pasture. The car had ploughed through the hedgerow and taken the fence with it. I've been complaining about that fence for months. The stock were always getting out onto the road, and I wonder now if that has some significance. Did the driver swerve to avoid a stray bullock? Or was his mind taken up with other matters?

The car is long gone, towed away by the local garage on the

instructions of the police. Clark has been out fiddling around with fencing wire, but even in the gathering dusk I can see that the field is empty. The two old ladies in the cafe had seen it being towed away. They thought I might know something and they'd asked me in a whisper, as if there was a breath of scandal attached to it all. It was a *strange* car, and a young man driving it. *A stranger.* What would I know, I told them. There are more houses than mine up that road. If there was a stranger in town he most certainly had nothing to do with me or mine. End of story. Arthur hates me gossiping, so I made sure it was all tied up while he was out the back. By the time he returned I was sipping my soup and ignoring the two old bats in the corner.

With a jolt, I realise I'm still standing in the road, staring at the tyre tracks. Such an out-of-the-way place to come to grief. The driver, whoever they were, must have been in quite a hurry. I plod on. Only five minutes more and I'll be home. I can just about see the end of the drive. There's a little whimper from the direction of the hedge, and Floss comes scampering to meet me. I rub her damp ears.

'What are we going to do with you? You should be in the kitchen with your brothers. You'll never settle.'

At least she seems none the worse after her chocolate feast. We walk the last few yards to the gloomy house. In my mind's eye, I am already pottering about the kitchen, plugging in the kettle, reaching for the biscuit tin. There are warm furry bodies against my cold legs, damp snouts in my hand.

My mind drifts back to the strange car in the field, the whispers of the old biddies. I know what village tittle-tattle can be like. Jim and I always kept ourselves to ourselves, but gossips have a habit of trying to second-guess you. Visit the shop red-eyed and they'll make up what they don't know.

I fumble with my key, hurrying to get through the door as if the past has awakened and is lumbering after me like some monstrous beast. The collies start barking as soon as my key hits the lock, the noise distant and echoing in the empty house. I try to calm myself. What's done is done. I'll let them out first, take my tea into the chilly garden and look up at the sky. The hall is cold. I drag off my wet things, flip the hat onto the newel post. I don't bother with the light; the gloom is much less disturbing. You can sink into it, imagine familiar shapes in the margins. In my mind, the echoing house creaks with unseen footsteps. I catch the whisk of Bella's petticoat high up on the stairs, the glimmer of a white calf. Elspeth giggles in the shadows. They are at that lovely age of innocence, before males intrude and spoil everything. All my thoughts of a nice cuppa vanish, and I know I will go to my study; write late into the night. The tale of 'The Cruel Sister' needs to be finished.

Lucie

Arthur offers me a refill, but I shake my head.

'Are you okay?' he asks. 'You don't look too good.'

'Thanks for that.'

'I mean you look pale. You're pure white.'

'I feel a bit . . .' My stomach heaves and I clap my hand over my mouth. Arthur had been leaning against the counter, but as I jerk to my feet he jumps, possibly fearing an *Exorcist* moment, and points to the back.

The toilet smells of overripe lemons, which makes the nausea ten times worse. I lower my brow against the cool mirror, noticing how my skin is bone white under the harsh strip light. To vomit or not to vomit – for a moment it could go either way. Slowly, the queasiness subsides.

Arthur smiles at me when I return. He looks worried. 'By the way, I phoned the vet, about Floss.'

'And?'

'She said Floss would be fine, with the amount of chocolate that was in those brownies. Not enough to do real harm, but it will probably make her . . . sick.' He glances at the toilet door. I scramble into my seat.

'I'm fine. It's the heat in that hospital. They turn it up to the max.' I push away the latte. 'Maybe a cold drink?'

He rushes away to get me a plain lemonade with ice. He's very kind, but I don't even thank him. He asks again about Reuben.

I shrug, as if the pain is nothing. Just shrug it off, nothing to see here.

'So how long will your sister be staying?'

'I've no idea.' I sip the drink through a straw. It's horribly sweet. I realise I don't want anything and push it away. I don't want to talk; I don't want to sit. I don't want to be by myself either. Arthur grabs a chair and joins me at the table. It's oddly intimate.

'Are you . . . are you going to keep seeing him?'

'What?' I scowl at him. All mention of Reuben exists only in my head. I have never spoken about him, not like this. For a moment, my tongue refuses to move. I cup the chilled glass with sweaty palms. 'I – I don't know. I don't have a choice.'

'You don't have a choice?' Arthur's back clicks straighter. I sense the shadow of a knowing smile, just out of sight, and it makes me defensive.

'I love him.' My whisper is fierce, protective. The not-quite-smile disappears, and Arthur looks suddenly older.

'We all have a choice. It's not always easy.'

My thoughts of the previous night come into sharp focus. I take refuge in a sneer. 'Oh, you'd know, would you?'

'I know what it's like when a relationship ends, yes.'

I lift the lemonade, put it down again, unsure what to say. 'What happened?'

'Her name was Nancy. There's not much to tell, really.'

'Still – it's good to talk.'

Silence stretches out between us, and I get the sense that I've stirred things up for him. Maybe he hasn't thought about Nancy in a while. I shouldn't have asked. It's none of my business. Arthur eases the tension with a half-laugh. He slumps back in his chair, angling his body away from me. When he speaks again, he seems to be talking to a random spot on the floor.

'It's old history. Nancy worked here. She was a mate of Anita's. We got . . . close. Always a bad idea when you work with someone. It gives you nowhere to go.'

'Did Nancy go?' I find myself looking at the top of his left ear, fascinated by the colour match between his spectacle frames and his hair. No doubt Nancy found him attractive. He is attractive, in a quiet, unassuming way. I'm not sure where my thoughts are taking me, so I rein them in just in time to hear the end of his very brief story.

'And that was it really. She wanted to travel, and I couldn't. Not with all this.' His gaze flickers around the room.

I think of the mill, and his mother. 'You're trapped,' I say.

'There's always a moment,' he replies carefully, 'when you have to make a choice. In every tricky situation, there's a logical decision to be made. Some people immerse themselves and flounder around. Then they wonder why they're drowning.'

I suddenly realise he's swung the conversation back to me. Nancy is history. She made her intentions known, and Arthur decided to let her go. This is his way of telling me I'm making life difficult for myself.

'But what if you're pushed?' My voice sounds feeble, an apology. 'Good people do bad things because of circumstance.'

Arthur looks at me with some sympathy. 'No one pushed you – you jumped. But there's always a way out. That too is a choice.'

I go to bed early, the way you do when you're exhausted, thinking you'll fall asleep as soon as your head hits the pillow. That almost never happens. You just lie awake, your brain downloading data like a runaway iPhone. I lie in bed with the lamp on, gazing up at the bumpy ceiling. I feel small, crushed, like the whole weight of Reuben is pressing my spine into the mattress. But it's not a good weight, not his heat and his gentle roughness and all the good bits. This is the heaviness of pain, of deception, of despair.

I suppose at the start of the affair there was an element of triumph. I found it incredible that someone like Reuben would fancy someone like me. I was everything my sister was not, dark, quiet, awkward, and Reuben was colourful and careless. I was never quiet and awkward with him, especially in bed. Then triumph slipped into something darker, an unhealthy craving.

My body surprised me, the way it reacted to him, ached for him. My conscience shut down. We took chances, creeping into bed together when the house was empty, trading hot-eyed glances across the dinner table. It was a game, I suppose, and Jane wasn't part of it. I never set out to fall in love with him, and I suppose he thought he could keep me at arm's length – emotionally, anyway. At first, I think Reuben enjoyed flitting between two sisters. Every man's fantasy, isn't it? It would never have occurred to me to give him an ultimatum, to make him choose. Star-crossed lovers are blinded by starlight.

There is no way out of this without heartbreak, and the thought makes me sink deeper, until, like Reuben in that hospital bed, I am a mere outline.

All I can think of is how quickly Reuben tried to save himself. Part of me had been longing for him to have an epiphany under those white sheets. *You're the one I really love, Lucie. It isn't Jane, it's always been you.* Part of me thought that, one day, Reuben would have the courage of his convictions. Part of me thought that 'one day' would be now.

What if Reuben never had any courage? Something inside me wants to weep. The sheer effort of reassessing things, of seeing Reuben in a new and unflattering light, is too much to bear.

I decide to get up. The bed is suddenly a desert, and I can still smell Reuben on my pillow. Dragging on a robe, I stumble into the kitchen, flicking on every switch, flooding the cottage with light, making day out of night. Nights are pretty pointless when you're alone. Soon the kettle is bubbling into life, and I'm singing along to Take That on the radio. I'm not really in a bubbly, singy mood, but I don't want to be alone with the strange turn my thoughts are taking. I have an unblemished, unshakeable connection with Reuben. There is no room for a stain or a wobble.

Mac's notebook is lying on the kitchen table. When she'd been rooting through her bag for keys in the cafe, she'd managed to leave the thing behind, and I'd picked it up, promising Arthur that I'd return it to her. She's been scribbling a lot lately, closing the notebook whenever I enter the room, as if breaking off a secret conversation. I'm curious, but also a bit reluctant to open the book for reasons I don't quite understand. I make a mug of tea and eat two Jaffa Cakes before I eventually sit down to read it.

The sisters know they are of an age to marry when the young Lord Musgrave comes to call. At first it is Father he woos. There are meetings late in the evening: serious words and serious drinking. Once, Elspeth and Bella hid behind the window curtains, but the drapes were thick with dust and Bella couldn't hold back a sneeze. That gave them away, and father bellowed for the maid to take them upstairs. But at least they got a good look at the young lord before being towed away. He was a little rough around the edges, but the quality of his clothing smoothed him out. He wore a fine silk shirt and a cloak of burgundy velvet that smelled of herbs.

The next time he calls, Bella and Elspeth are invited to meet him. Bella breathes him in like a fresh rain shower as she pours red wine into his cup. Elspeth talks too much and giggles too loudly and tosses her lovely hair about. She's wearing a yellow dress, and her hair and the dress glow like buttercups before the fire. Father smiles and nods from his heavy chair.

The next day, the young Musgrave's man delivers a parcel with a letter attached. Father breaks the seal and Bella unwraps it with shaking fingers. Excitement grips her belly like hunger pains as she uncovers a tiny pair of pale kid-leather gloves.

There may have been the sound of a car engine. I might have heard the door slam and the scrabble of the back door latch, but I am engrossed. I read on, the notebook gripped between my fingers.

'Oh, how beautiful!' Bella holds up the gloves for all to see.

Her father wafts the letter at her. He looks relieved and sad all at once. 'They are not for you, daughter. They are for little Elspeth. Our young lord fancies her for his wife. I thought as much!'

Suddenly my sister is here. Her car keys land on the table

beside me with a clatter. Everything about me tightens and I snap shut the notebook.

' . . . going back home in the morning to pick up some fresh clothes,' Jane is saying, patting the kettle to see if it's hot. 'My mouth is so dry. I'm dying for a cuppa – do you want one? Why are you still up? It's after midnight.'

She's still wearing that cardigan.

'You need to ditch the yellow dress,' I say.

'The what?' She pauses to stare at me, a teabag dangling from her fingers.

'You need to get rid of it – the colour, it's kind of inappropriate.'

'What dress?'

'The yellow one.'

'Dress?' She plucks a second teabag from the box, still peering at me like I'm demented. 'What dress? What are you talking about?'

'That – yellow – cardigan!' I say it slowly, like she's the idiot.

'You said DRESS.'

'I did not, I said –'

'You said ditch the yellow dress. I don't even own a yellow dress. Look, Lucie, it's been a long day.'

She's saying some more stuff but the notebook has opened again. Had I opened it? The text dances before my eyes.

Elspeth crows and snatches the gloves from her sister's numb grasp. They are a perfect fit. She flexes her fingers like little cat claws, testing the suppleness of the leather. The seed of jealousy in Bella's breast takes root with a pain so sharp she has to turn away.

'Why are you being like this?' Jane is saying. 'I've been at that hospital for eight hours. I can barely see straight and now you're just ignoring me.'

Closing the book again, I stretch out my fingers like cat claws, testing the air, and when I look at my sister, I *really* look. It's been such a long time since I've made eye contact or connected with her on any level not coloured by furtiveness or point-scoring, I'm not sure how to react. I have a child's image of what she should look like, all shiny pink lips and wide eyes with symmetrical spiky lashes. The mobile hands, the tinkling bracelets. The pretty gold watch Reuben bought her so she'd never be late. Jane is a routine freak. She never stays up beyond ten thirty and before bed she writes her to-do list for the next day, and applies expensive cleansers and toners. Who tones their skin, for fuck's sake? Jane is so together, but now, as I look, I can see she is starting to fall apart, and I am shocked.

This woman is a stranger. Her skin is over-stretched and delicate, her make-up has migrated to the fine lines around her mouth and her nose is shiny. There are deep, dark thumbprints under each eye, and black dots where her mascara has flaked off. I get up clumsily from my chair; the scrape of it sounds brutal in the quiet kitchen. I gather up the teabags.

'Hey, sit down. I'll make tea. Do you want some toast?'

She sits heavily in the chair I've vacated, and I imagine my own residual body heat seeping into her coldness. I want to hug her, but I don't remember the last time we hugged.

She's shaking her head. 'I've had way too many carbs today. I'm living on pastry.'

'Tell me about it!' I splash boiling water into two mugs. 'Arthur the Baker seems to think I'll expire without a daily dose of his cake. I'm starting to put on weight.'

'I noticed that.'

She's staring at my bum, I can feel it. My sudden burst of goodwill evaporates. I slap a mug of tea in front of her and select the old pine chair at the head of the table.

'So . . .' The first sip of tea burns my top lip. 'Are – were – things not too good with you and Reuben, before the accident?'

Her face shutters. She blows gently into her own mug and I think she isn't going to reply. 'Things were the same as always. It's just that . . . I can't help thinking . . .'

'You think he's been cheating?' Let's not beat about the bush.

My heart is jabbing at my breastbone. Inside me, something deeply buried yearns for an explosion. I want to blow things wide apart, and trawl through the debris.

'It's just a feeling I have.' Jane's jaw is set in that stubborn tilt I recall from childhood. This is my sister, the peeved little golden girl. This is the look she perfected when she didn't get her own way. When she was wrongly accused of starting an argument, when she wasn't voted in as class rep, when one of her uni essays was marked down to a C . . . this was the look. Part of me always took a perverse delight in seeing her thwarted.

That night I'd stayed with Reuben in the old fisherman's inn, we'd pretended to be a proper couple, drinking pints at the bar, pressed up close together, with the locals smiling fondly at us. Okay, I'm remembering it like a nostalgic TV drama. Maybe they were just wishing we'd get a room. Jane had phoned Reuben that night. She thought he was on a golfing weekend with his mates. He'd pressed his mobile to his ear, lied to her, his hand all the time squeezing my knee, and I'd kept silent as a little mouse.

I'd experienced a heady rush of something like triumph, but I don't feel triumphant now. Jane can't look at me and her voice is faint and metallic.

'He keeps getting texts that he deletes immediately.'

'You've checked his phone?' I have kept all of Reuben's texts. I cannot bear to delete them.

'Of course. Being jealous turns you into a monster.' She gives a humourless laugh. 'He knows I suspect. He's enjoying the intrigue.'

My heart plummets to a new low. Is that me? Is that what I am – mere intrigue?'

'I'm sure you're mistaken.' I must mean more to him than that.

Jane shrugs. Her fine golden earrings shudder beneath her fine golden hair. 'Now isn't the time to talk about it.' She stretches out her arms and the horrible yellow cardigan rides up to her elbows. 'So I'll go back home in the morning, look out some clean pants and deal with all the domestic crap; all the "life goes on" stuff. Lucie?'

'Yes. Yes, I'm listening. You should take some time out, get some rest. I'll go and see Reuben tomorrow.'

'Thanks. Thanks for being here, Lucie.'

I mirror her smile and avoid her eyes. I can't afford to see my sister as that broken woman again.

The day I do . . . that is the day I'll have to let Reuben go.

Lucie

I am in a place of darkness.

Literally.

I mark the full stop in purple ink and close my notepad. It's cold, and I'm beginning to regret my decision to come here, to the millpond, in the middle of the night. Jane went to bed, but I still wasn't sleepy.

Floss, surely an insomniac, turned up at the back door again and lured me out into the night with her whining and scratching. I was all set to be cross with her, but when I opened the door, the dog looked ready for a midnight ramble. I stepped out into the moonlight, and something came over me. I was entranced. It made me think of that Christmas poem, the one where the moon gives the lustre of midday to objects below. The wildness beyond the cottage was illuminated, a ghostly imitation of daytime. I had the world all to myself. I didn't even pause to grab a torch, buoyed up with a strange sense of something burgeoning. I stuffed my bare feet into cold wellies and set off, pyjama legs flapping and robe tight-belted against the chill.

The pond, blackberry-dark, glints juicily under the full moon. Something prickles in the undergrowth behind me, and bird-like creatures swoop low over the water. I'm pretty sure they're bats. It occurs to me that the nocturnal world is just a mirror of the daylight one, but less complicated, with everything following its natural course. It is complete, and getting by just fine without me. I shiver and pull the neck of my robe tighter, horribly aware that I'm sitting on a bench in the dark in my pyjamas, writing poetry in a notepad I found in the kitchen drawer. Folk have been locked up for less.

I'd set out with a sort of hopefulness – maybe I can get past this, be the sort of sister Jane thought I was. It's okay to be alone. The sky won't fall in. You just need to make sense of it all. Opening the book again, I ready my purple gel pen and look to the sky for inspiration.

I see the pale underside of the moon;
a faint seeding
of stars.

See . . . there's a whole big universe out there. You can't move on until you kick Reuben into touch. You know you have to. You can't keep waiting for – what was it Jane had been waiting for? Circumstances to change? Only you can change them.

The truth has been hooked. From the dark-berry waters of the pond the slippery fish has landed. You have to make a decision.

I look up,
but looking up exposes
the soft parts of yourself.

You started it. You're to blame. You have to end it before the guilt destroys you.

A bird sets up an agitated calling on the far bank, making me jump.

End it . . . end it . . . end it . . .

What sort of bird sings at night? One who can't sleep. Fuck it, I shouldn't be out here. I stuff the pad back into my pocket and get to my feet. Floss appears like magic, and as I bend to pat her head, a heavy splash startles me. The noise reverberates through my system, but when I spin towards it, there is nothing to be seen but the water spreading slowly in neat circles.

What the hell was that? What size of fish would you need to make that kind of noise? Floss whines. I hold my breath and wait, all my senses straining. I'm never at my most comfortable near water, but the added dimension of something unknown lurking beneath the surface makes me want to run screaming for home. There's nothing to see but faint circles in the water, the gentle slop against the bank. I search for a rational explanation. Maybe there are pike in there? You read about people netting monster pike all the time. I have an image in my head of some weird prehistoric-looking fish, lurking in the muddy deep.

The moon slinks behind a cloud and everything is swallowed up. Only sparkles remain – glints and droplets and the paleness of leaves. My eyes are fixed on the spot where the thing disappeared. That splash, such a heavy weight . . . My vision blooms in the dark; my eyes grow wide. Out there, something surfaces. A glimmer of yellow. Something yellow, floating just beneath the surface. Then it sinks slowly out of sight.

Not everyone can float.

I run. I run all the way back to the cottage, skidding on mud, tripping over the thorny snakes of brambles, with Floss galloping at my heels. I have no idea what I've just seen in the pond – that heavy splash, the glimmer of yellow – but all I can think of is Jane and that stupid yellow cardigan. I run straight to her bedroom, crumple outside the door, my breath coming in short gasps and my heart thudding with terror. I know it's not her. Didn't I say goodnight to her just an hour ago? But I'm afraid to open the door. I am so afraid to see an absence of Jane, when for all these months I've been praying for just that. All those times I've wanted my sister to disappear off the scene . . . My head is filled with that yellow cardigan, imagining it saturated with pond water, weighing her down . . .

I burst into the room.

Jane is asleep, as I knew she would be, breathing deeply and evenly.

Relief washes through me until I feel weak from it. I retreat silently and close her door.

Mac

April

Other gifts arrive from the young Lord Musgrave: love tokens, lockets, even a pony, white as new milk. It is unusual for the younger sister to wed first, and Father pretends to be angry, perplexed and put out in equal measure. There are long discussions in secret between the two men, and much ale is consumed. Eventually the deal is struck, and a wedding date set. Elspeth has never been thwarted, after all.

Bella can't bear to be in her mother's bower any more, as the talk turns to flowers and dresses and bairns. They even discuss the wedding night, making Bella turn crimson inside and out. She begins to dread that she will never know such a night, that no man will ever come to her father's castle to seek her hand. Maybe she will die here, unloved, with just the old hound standing guard over her body. The hate seed burrows deep, and germinates.

Love tokens. Doesn't that conjure up something sweet and timeless and real? My fingers are stiff with cold. I put down my pen and tug the blanket more tightly round my shoulders. If I look like a bag lady, so be it. My circulation is shot to hell, all a result of this heart problem they cannot get to the bottom of. *Love tokens.* I press my palms against my ribcage, as if searching for the butterfly ghosts of some lost emotion, but all I can detect is a slight, tight burning sensation, the result of too much banana on my cornflakes.

Jim once carved for me a love spoon out of apple wood. I think I can still remember the tickle of possibility deep inside, the belief in magic.

A memory surfaces. An elderly spinster aunt, living alone here in Fettermore, in the house by the church, my mother packing me off at regular intervals. *Make yourself useful. She has no one else.* The house smells of broth and mushrooms, and the dust on her fine mahogany dining table is dappled with cat-prints. I wipe them off, make tea, volunteer to shop. From the cupboard under the stairs, the old dame drags a tartan shopping trolley, deep and wide. I notice cobwebs in the corners. It is a relic, the type of monstrosity that negates my whole self-image. My mini skirt, my cute beret, my whip-smart understanding of the nuclear arms race and the ethical treatment of animals: my whole being droops like a pair of un-elasticated pants as I drag the relic along the village street. Folk stare at me from cottage windows. I am an incomer, a foreigner with a posh accent and a borrowed shopping trolley. I still remember that walk of shame.

I lived for the times when my old aunt ran out of flour. It meant I could escape to the mill. Jim would be there, a young man just out of school, helping his father. He'd fill my measure with fresh, powdery flour and smile and voice mundane country thoughts that meant nothing to the young, urban me. *Been a good growing season.* His slow, blue-eyed smile. *Looks like we're in for a dreich day.* I started to tell him about my life in Edinburgh. My visits to the mill became more frequent. I'd wait for him in the half-dark under the apple tree, imagining the taste of flour on his lips.

The apple tree was the oldest one in the mill den. It would be even older now, if that ignorant gardener hadn't chopped it down. Back in those days, people knew how to prune trees, and one day, in the month before I left for Cambridge, Jim presented me with a love-spoon, carved especially for me from one of the branches.

It's in the drawer somewhere. It must be. The need to find it is overwhelming. I push my chair back from the desk and get heavily to my feet, completing a 360-degree spin around the room. I feel disoriented, as if the stacks of books are bearing down on me.

I bend double, hugging my laboured breathing close to me. The love token. I must find it. *You kept it. You did.* Every bitter bone in my body laughs off the notion. Memory chimes in with a snigger. *You snapped it over your knee. You fed it into the Aga.*

I stumble back to my chair, wilt beneath the blanket. The breeze of my motion has disturbed the pages in my notebook. The weight of ink anchors the written pages, but the blank ones flutter like wings. I have so few blank pages left.

Fear goads me into motion again. I am a whirlwind, popping open cupboard doors, shuffling the things on my desk. I haul open the top drawer, scan it for clues. There is the carpenter's pencil, the one Lucie used to pen a love note to a man who could never be hers. Anger unfurls in me like a sail, driving me on. I drag out the drawer, dump its contents on the tired carpet: old receipt books, recipes scribbled on envelopes, spent batteries, pencil shavings. There in the back corner lies the thing I hadn't known I was looking for. Another love token. A sapphire pendant on a gold chain. I begin to laugh.

Seizing the blue stone, I cup the cold weight of it in my palm, remembering the story of it. In the light from the desk lamp the blue stone sparkles and my eyes nip as if I've stared too long at the sun on the sea. I recall finding it, maybe twenty years ago. It's a story as old as the hills: misty-eyed heroine discovers the receipt (the cost of it! And from *that* jeweller!), then creeps away, confident of a gorgeous, glittery surprise on Christmas morning. Only the surprise never comes, and you know full well that she's going to be opening a set of non-stick pans while her heart breaks. One of life's oldest clichés.

I let myself sink back to that time. Had I smelled her perfume on him? No. There had been no clues, no indicators, other than that Christmas gift, the one that was never intended for me. There had been nothing leading up to that to soften the blow.

Back to the present and I'm kneeling on the carpet, my insides heaving and the necklace still clutched in my fist. Tears drip between my fingers. When I can bear my own grief no longer I howl and hurl the thing at the wall. The sparkling stone hits the plaster with a hard click, and the too-silent aftermath echoes round the room. My head spins like a broken wheel. Sagging there on the carpet, I don't know if I feel better or worse.

The urge to destroy is monstrous.

I leave my study, my books, my blanket and my warmth. I don't care what time it is. I have the mill key in one hand, the pendant in the other. Smashing it against the wall has damaged the precious stone not one jot. I *have* to get rid of this. Life is so fragile. Every night I torment myself with the thought that I might not wake in the morning. There are loose ends I cannot leave behind.

There's frost in the air. My breath goes before me in the dark. I can hear the soft hoot of an owl, the steady white-noise whoosh of the lade, skimming through man-made channels.

Once inside, the mill settles all around me, chill and clammy. My footsteps echo and my pulse takes on a new, unsettled rhythm. My hand scrabbles pathetically over the electrics, as if the flick of a switch can banish all things malignant, the dark presences that linger here. *Beyond the civilised circle of light.*

I make my way to the water lever. The heft of it in my hands, the smooth, shaped oak, used to give me a kind of comfort. It was timeless, this action of diverting the water, of setting the ancient wheel in motion.

The first time Jim showed me how to operate it, I felt giddy with power, with the notion of all that water under my command. Even now, I feel an elemental thrill as, outside, the water noise changes and the wheel loosens and begins to turn. Inside, the machinery creeps into life.

I stand back, let things get up to speed. The initial grinding gives way to a busy clack as the sieves and chutes find their rhythm. In the far corner the millstones come to life. A gunpowder smell fills the air and sparks fizz in the gloom. The stones are running on empty. I hurry to the hopper. Some grain still remains, but it's sticky and damp. I poke it with a stick and some of it dislodges, trickles into the eye of the stones, and they begin to grind greedily.

I allow myself a little smile and extract the pendant from my pocket, pick off bits of fluff and dog biscuit. I hold it up briefly by the chain and watch it spin. There's an old wives' tale, that if you hold a pendulum such as this over a pregnant woman's belly it can tell you the sex of the child. Jim tried that with me, when Arthur was on the way. He tried it with a bent nail and some miller's twine, but we didn't quite know what to expect and the experiment ended in laughter and a lot of ribbing. 'What will it be, do you think?' I'd whispered excitedly in the dark and Jim had kissed me softly and joked, 'A miller!'

The pendant swirls, faster, faster, round and round. What is it trying to tell me? With a shudder I creep nearer to the stones and toss the thing into the centre. There's a bump and a crunch. The millstones grind to an imperfect halt, hesitating, grunting like a great beast tasting something new. Seemingly satisfied, they pick up speed again, juddering, but inexorable.

Lucie

I wake late after yet another terrible sleep. Reuben has been discharged from hospital and Jane has whisked him back up north. I'm tormented by the things I don't know. Are they getting on? Has Reuben changed since the accident? Is he taking his pain meds? He would never even take a paracetamol before.

Floss pitched up yet again, as if she can sense my troubled thoughts, when I was taking a sly midnight puff under the pergola. It's chucking-out time, I told her, not visiting time. And anyway, I'm *not* going midnight walkies, not again. I'd been too weary to protest when she followed me through to the bedroom. She leapt lightly onto the duvet as soon as I snuggled down, turning around three times before settling herself into a snug ball. Three times, like a spell of protection.

That unmistakeable noise, that deep unearthly rumble, had shaken us awake just an hour or so later. I'd known instantly it was the mill wheel, but as I'd stumbled over to the window, the black gap between the curtains warned me that it was out of time and out of context. Not natural, and the not-natural made my mouth go dry. Floss was awake by then, sitting up, ears cocked. I'd grabbed my coat and a torch and taken a deep breath.

There'd been a late-night frost. The outside was monochrome; white ice dusting the black twigs, the black stones. The rumbling so deep I could feel it in my bones. The mill door was open. Standing in the shadows, I could see the mellow gold of its insides bleeding out onto the white ground. And there was Mac, standing in a pool of light, just inside the door. She was holding up her hands, like the wicked spellcaster in a pantomime.

Holding up her hands, and they were glittering with otherworldly frost, stained with something I didn't understand. Ghost blood. My brain was making pictures that weren't there. *Ghost blood*.

As I watched, in my confused, dreamlike state, Mac wandered off, back to her house. And I went into the mill. I hadn't meant to, but she'd left the door open. I should have locked up and returned the key, but instead I found myself standing on the threshold, in the gloom, letting my gaze wander over the rough surface of the walls, the complicated ups and downs of the machinery. I crept in deeper, shivering in the incredible chill. It was as if the frost had got into the walls. Playing my torch beam over the old timbers by the millstones, I spotted a snail trail of silvery lines. Some kind of list: *4 firlots, 2 pecks of barley, a quarter pound of nails*. A primitive pencil drawing: a flower, pansy petals, stalky leaves, scribbled on the wood. And beside it, a name. I peered closer. The inscription was faint silver, but the name was unmistakeable: *Bella*.

The mill den is the sisters' favourite haunt. The burn, brown as a tarnished coin, runs through the bottom of it, and the trees bow down in prayer towards the water. Some of the trunks are as broad as ponies' backs and the girls like to lean their spines against them and look up into the canopy of leaves and the fragments of sky beyond. Some days the sky is grey as stone; sometimes blue, like a bird's egg, and the hawks, black as letters, scrawl across it. Bella imagines her name etched forever on the sky.

They pick wildflowers in the den, or weeds, not knowing how to tell the difference, and slither down to the water's edge to toss pebbles. Their hound, Faithful, dives into the shallows and the water breaks around him as if you'd thrown in a handful of diamonds. Elspeth always pleads to be allowed to swim in the millpond, but it's very deep, and Bella is afraid to let her, in case anything bad happens.

I'm sitting at the table with Mac's notebook when a heavy knock on the back door pulls me back to the present, to the safe cottage kitchen. With a start I realise it's after ten in the morning, and I'm still in my pyjamas. Floss, who's been hiding under the table, gives a high-pitched warning bark. The poor dog is thoroughly freaked out. I bend down and rub her silky ears, then I open the door a crack, still smoothing down my bed hair.

It's only Arthur. I stand aside to let him in, automatically scanning for suspicious packages. He appears to be cake-free, for once. Arthur's white bakery boxes are piling up on the kitchen table. One is empty, the others are half-grazed, full of crumbs and cake corners, where I've done a Mary Berry on them, sampling bits and discarding them, unimpressed. The last box has to go. It's full of something that stinks of vanilla and I've had to tape the lid shut. The smell of vanilla makes me want to retch.

Max and Jethro pile in too, claws clicking on the hard floors. They smell of earth and cow dung. Under the table, Floss growls, as if she just cannot be bothered with them. Arthur raises his eyebrows.

'What's wrong with her?'

'Ask your mother!'

'What has she done now?' A flicker of fear passes across his face.

I don't answer straight away.

'She's losing the plot. Seriously. Started up the mill in the middle of the night. We thought it was an earthquake.' I glance at the little spaniel. 'No wonder Floss has adopted me!'

Arthur sighs. He pinches and rubs the bridge of his nose, so fiercely that he's in danger of dislodging his glasses. 'Ma is eccentric. I've learned to live with it, but I can see how she might come across as . . . odd. She likes to keep the mill ticking over.' He sighs. 'If it was left to me I'd lock it up and throw away the key.'

The spectacles fall back into place, framing the fear I can see in his bright blue eyes. I pick up the huge key from beside the kettle. 'Here. Knock yourself out. Do us all a favour.'

He recoils from it. 'Shit. She went away and left it unlocked?'

'She seemed really out of it.' Seeing his expression, I take pity on him. 'Come on. You need to walk this out. Walking is the number-one cure for whatever ails you.'

He gives a humourless laugh. 'That's what I was just doing, but I couldn't find Floss.'

'Sometimes it's good to have some human company.' I can't believe I just said that. I tweak at the soft leg of my pyjamas. 'Give me two minutes to get my jeans on.' Definitely not like me.

We walk to the millpond, falling easily into step. The track is still soft and damp, but the trees are mesmerising, new leaves like sparkly, bouncy hair against a bright sky. The last time I'd looked up at the sky it was littered with stars. Things seem so different in the daylight. Normal.

'My mother is worried about you,' Arthur says.

That gives me a warm feeling, that someone is worried about me. 'She's given me a week off.'

'She's far too easy on you.'

'You think?'

'You should come and work for me. I'm a slave driver.'

I glance at him and laugh. The sun has turned him all golden: hair, specs, skin. He doesn't look like a slave driver. He just looks kind and healthy and full of life.

'I don't believe it!' I'm grinning at him. He makes me want to smile. 'You're as soft as your mother!'

He's looking straight ahead, adopting a mock-serious expression. 'Don't underestimate the soft people. The soft, silent people are the ones who think.'

'So what are you thinking now?' I like his profile, the frankness of his mouth. He doesn't smile unless I smile, as if he's tuning into me.

'I think you're enjoying my company.'

'It's a walk, Arthur. Don't flatter yourself.'

We both chuckle at that, and then he gets serious again.

'Have you heard from . . . he who shall not be named?'

Thoughts of Reuben block out the sun for a bit, and I shake my head. 'No, not since Jane whisked him home. She's phoned with updates a couple of times, but no, I haven't had any contact.'

I want to tell him about my final visit to the hospital, the day Jane headed home to get clean clothes. I was yearning for clarity, a sense of direction, but Reuben's sister was there, and a friend who was giving her a lift. There was way too much talk about bus timetables and visiting hours, and all the time I was searching Reuben's face for clues. How I longed to see that special warmth in his eyes, the fire that kindles just for me. But he was cool, polite.

At one point Laura got up to go to the loo and the friend decided to grab a coffee. Alone at last, I turned to Reuben to say all the things that were crowding my head. They came out in a mad, breathless rush. *I miss you. I love you. When you're well, we can get back together* . . . and he's holding up his hand. I'm forced to look at his palm and that thread work of little lines I like to kiss. He's saying things too, all in a rush. *Things have changed. We need to cool it. I still value your friendship, but* . . .

We've reached the millpond. We pause and I stare down into the black water, half-afraid of what I might see below the surface.

'The last time I saw him, he said he valued my friendship.'

'Um . . . friendship can be undervalued,' Arthur says carefully.

I glare at him. 'This guy has been fucking me for months and he dares to label me a *friend*?'

There's an awkward pause. Arthur shrugs. He's gazing at the far bank, where two mallards are engaged in a noisy exchange. There's a lot of flapping and the water sprays silver from beneath their wings.

'Maybe that's the answer you've been looking for.'

I fold my arms across the lost place. 'I wasn't looking for answers.'

'You didn't want to make a decision, but you must have wondered how it was all going to end?'

I glare at him. 'Who says it's ended? Things are tricky right now. He needs some space, and so do I.'

'But he refers to you as a "friend", and that pisses you off.'

'I don't know! I don't know what to think!' I stalk off, waving a hand at Arthur, who follows in my wake. 'Change the subject.'

I feel suddenly weary. The lack of honesty in my life is weighing me down like a waterlogged winter coat. I am buttoned up and bound, plodding along the same old pathway, which never seems to end. I cannot work out how to throw off the coat, so instead I just burrow in deeper. *Change the subject.*

'So what do you want to talk about?' Arthur says, which isn't particularly helpful.

'Can we narrow it down?' My words sound unreasonably snappy. I let my breath out in a sigh. 'Let's talk about you. Tell me what happened – here. What happened to your dad?'

Arthur's face is carefully neutral. The path is narrow; he's looking straight ahead, and I'm walking slightly behind, so I can't really observe his expression, other than the tensing of his jaw. His voice is tight too, as if it doesn't want to give too much away.

'He was miller here for years, and his father before him. A real family-run business. I always assumed I would follow him.'

'But there was an accident?'

'Did my mother tell you? She doesn't usually speak about it.'

I try to recall if she had spoken of it. 'Maybe not. I think you mentioned something, in the hospital. Was it an accident?'

'Yes, a fatal accident, in the mill. About five years ago now.'

I'm not quite sure what to say. I never know how to be tactful in these conversations.

'What was he like, your dad?'

Arthur's face softens. We have passed the millpond without incident. I want to tell him about what I thought I saw. I want to share my panic, but that would mean revealing too much about myself. What would he think of me, wandering out in the moonlight to write poetry in my pyjamas?

I'm no longer sure where we are. The path is overgrown and the scent of the undergrowth fills me. It's green and wild and secret, and somewhere up ahead the dogs are crashing around in it.

'This is the way to the weir. Do you want to go on?'

I still feel exhausted, but I nod anyway. 'Your father?'

Arthur smiles, and we move on in single file. His voice floats back to me, warm with affection. 'He was a very gentle man, the sort of man you could always rely on. People talk about "rocks", don't they? Well, Dad was a rock, a big old river boulder, sitting in the stream, with all the crap of the day flowing past him. Maybe even with a bird or two on his head!'

'Dippers. Dippers like to sit on big rocks.'

Mac had pointed out the dippers earlier, big dark birds, bobbing into the water to fish. Their Gaelic name means 'blacksmiths of the stream', she'd said, and I'd remembered that.

'They remind me of little fairy folk, the dippers, ducking and diving,' I say. 'And the heron, the one that sits on the far bank of the pond – he's like a proper old fisherman!'

I realise Arthur's managed to body-swerve any mention of his father's accident. I suppose you don't want to dwell on it, or share the nitty-gritty with a stranger, but like a third-rate detective my curiosity has been roused.

Arthur flashes a grin back at me. 'See, you're starting to feel at home!'

Do I? Do I feel at home here? Walking behind Arthur, focusing on nothing but the track and his back, the damp at the hem of his jeans and the snag of the brambles and that green, summery smell – it feels good. Peaceful. As I examine that, he starts talking about something else: fairies and myths and old stories.

'Wait a second . . . what stories?'

He pauses and I half-collide with him. He's very tall close up, and this feels oddly intimate. 'The stories Ma is writing – they're all based on local legends.'

'All of them? Even the one about the two sisters?'

'The two girls did actually exist. They lived in a castle a few miles from here – Castle Binnorie. It's ruined now, but if you follow the course of the burn out to sea, you'll see it on the headland.'

'Whoa.' I pull up sharp. 'So what are you saying? It's not just a story?'

'Oh it *is* a story – myth, folklore, whatever you want to call it.'

'But with real people. In a real location. That sounds like more than "just a story".'

'Most stories are attached to reality somehow.' He pauses to look at me, the ghost of a smile playing around his lips. 'Think of …' His eyes search for inspiration among the leaves. 'Killiecrankie. The Soldier's Leap.'

'I'm pretty sure that counts as history.'

'Okay. How about the Loch Ness Monster.'

'Superstition. Fantasy.'

'But a real place.'

'True.' I consider this. 'Fantasy embroidered around a familiar location.'

'But is it fantasy? You can't say the monster doesn't exist just because you haven't seen it. You can say you don't *believe* in it.'

'You mean like if a tree falls in the woods with no one there to hear it does it still make a sound? That kind of thing makes my head hurt.'

Arthur laughs, pulls the blossom from a weed as he brushes past it. I'm still thinking, even though my head hurts.

'So "The Cruel Sister" is fact-based fiction set in a real-life setting . . . and . . . and I went into the mill last night. There's writing on the wall. I saw Bella's name.'

'Yup, this is the very mill that features in the story,' Arthur says, bringing me back. 'Don't even ask me about the miller. It's a spine-tingler. I don't want to spoil it for you if you haven't got to the end yet!'

But my spine is already tingling. I'm viewing a scary movie through my fingers, and I can't seem to look away.

Mac

May

Mint is a great balm for the tummy. I have three different varieties in the kitchen garden, all contained in pots of various sizes. You cannot let mint loose; it seeds itself with great abandon and spreads like a virus, but at this time of year the new growth is quite manageable and full of flavour. I've decided to make mint tea for Lucie.

I harvest a few fresh sprigs, the sharp scent taking me right back to my youth and those chewy white spearmint toffees I used to buy with my pocket money. The fragrance alone is enough to perk up the soul, and I hope it might work on the poor girl. I feel she's been very out of sorts lately.

Maybe I'm overreacting, of course. I've been feeling very down myself, if I'm honest. I don't like the dark turn my thoughts have been taking, and I can't seem to shake off the gloom. I'm not sure what's triggered this. Memories seem to have surfaced from nowhere, and all my fevered scribblings about the two sisters . . . I feel like a door has been unlocked. People never stop to consider how the consequences of their actions will reverberate through time: Bella and little Elspeth. And that woman . . . I haven't thought of her in so long, but her name keeps floating up from the depths of my consciousness. Anna Madigan. The name is etched on my brain these days, and every time I catch sight of it the green-eyed monster rolls over in its sleep.

As if she knows I'm thinking of her, Lucie appears in the

kitchen doorway. She still looks cold and grumpy, even though I've put the electric heater on in the study. I had suggested she do a little light hoeing in the kitchen garden instead of sitting at the keyboard (we used to have a chap from the village but he was hopeless), but she just glared at me. She's become quite difficult lately – either too tired, too poorly, or simply not in the mood for anything. Back in January, when she'd turned up at my door with her life in a wheeled suitcase, she'd seemed so meek. I suppose this is what happens when you get to know people better. You have to learn to live with their flaws.

We did have a small set-to, the day after I set the mill going in the middle of the night. I can't imagine what she must have thought. Probably thinks I'm going doolally. She'd brought Floss back, quite late in the afternoon. I hadn't been expecting her and when I opened the front door there she was, all in black like some sort of exorcist, with the huge iron mill key raised in one hand like a crucifix. *You forgot something. And please keep the dog under control – she's waking me up in the night and she cries like a baby and it's freaking me out.*

Quite overwrought, the poor thing.

I'd brought her in and sat her in the front room. Floss folded up in front of the cold hearth and judged me sadly. 'My dear,' I'd said, 'you look quite peaky.' Can I get you anything? I'd reached out a hand to her and noticed the faint tinge of blue sparkle still sticking to my skin. I'd rooted through the fresh-milled flour the previous night, to make sure that Anna Madigan's love token had been pulverised to dust. I saw Lucie edge away from the sparkle, like a wary Jack Russell about to bite. I waited for questions but none came.

Instead she said, 'I went into the mill after you left. I had a little look round. I saw Bella's name on the wood, and the flower drawing.'

'There are lots of names in there,' I told her. 'Arthur's father, grandfather, great-grandfather, they all signed their names for posterity. Some of the millwrights too, and the farmers. Even the customers! If you look very closely you'll see our initials, Jim's and mine, enclosed within a heart. Of course, we were very young –'

'Bella,' Lucie snapped. '*Bella* – written on the wall. Is that the Bella in the Cruel Sister story?'

'There are many Bellas. It's a common Scots name, short for Isabella –'

'Just tell me!'

'It has never been authenticated and it's a very old story –'

'YOU ARE A HISTORIAN.'

'Sometimes . . .' I'd picked my words carefully. 'Sometimes the past is reflected in the present. We see little glints of it now and then, like a broken mirror or . . .' I gesticulated with my hands. Miniscule filaments of crystal blinked in the lamplight. 'We are not separate from it. All that has gone on before is just a glint away.'

'*Beyond the civilised circle of light.*'

The phrase sounded like an accusation, and on the cold hearthrug the dog growled.

I come to her now with the mint tea steaming in a glass mug.

'What's this? Are you trying to poison me?'

I chuckle. Always so prickly! I press the drink into her hands. 'You keep saying your tummy's unsettled.'

'Indigestion, from your son's pastries.' She sips the tea and grimaces, whether from the heat or the taste I can't tell.

'How are you getting on, in the cottage?'

'Fine.'

'Do you find it a little lonely? You said you were a tad uneasy. "Freaking out", is the phrase you used, I think.'

She looks at me warily. 'I overreacted. I'm fine.'

'You could always stay here. You could have Arthur's old room, as long as you don't mind model aeroplanes.'

She looks appalled. 'No. I like my own space. No offence.'

I recognise my own words played back to me. Touché. 'Well, the offer is there should you ever want it.' I notice she's clutching my notebook in her hand. 'Which bit have you been working on?'

She remains silent.

I ease the notebook from her cold fingers, and motion to the table. We pull out chairs and sit, and I fish my spectacles from the breast pocket of my blouse. 'These are not children's fairy stories, Lucie. We must record them faithfully, whether we like the content or not.' Letting my specs slip just a tad, I observe her reaction over the rim of them. 'Myth reflects the human condition. Jealousy, betrayal, revenge . . . it's all there. We cannot escape it. These old stories sometimes make sense of the things we can't; they hold up a picture of ourselves.'

'There's something not right with the picture,' Lucie whispers. A solitary tear slips down her nose. I suppose she is thinking of her mysterious gentleman caller. Not for the first time, I wonder what she's hiding and why she seems so agitated about the Cruel Sister story. Have I hit a nerve? The idea gives me a curious sense of power over her.

She looks so forlorn. Something in me wants to poke at her with a sharp stick. I begin to read.

The sisters go down the mill den one last time. Elspeth is wearing her new kid gloves and that buttercup silk dress, and her hair is shining with a fresh gleam.

'I can't believe we will be separated,' she sighs, 'now I am to be Lady Musgrave.'

Bella doesn't reply. She is quieter these days, darker. The girls follow the path of the lade to the millpond. Elspeth is chattering about weddings and dresses and her young lord and how much he adores her.

There is no one else about. They stand on the edge of the deep, dark pool.

What happens next is a blur, and sudden. There is a single irrational moment, and Bella sees her hand pressed into the middle of her younger sister's back. She feels the yellow silk, the softness of it as she pushes, the lack of resistance. There is a splash, heavier than the splash of the largest pike, and the next minute Bella is plunging thigh deep into the water, clutching at her skirts. There are strong currents and deep channels; the yellow silk sinks out of sight. Strands of beautiful blonde hair . . .

She winds her fingers in her sister's hair, but the water is stronger, and Elspeth slips from her grasp, slick as waterweed. She finds a hand, then, unresponsive, in the softest kid leather. Clasping it in her own, she pulls with all her might, toppling backwards into the shallows. She's still grasping the glove . . . but it is empty.

Only then does she realise what she has done.

Lucie is weeping now, her wet chin buried in her hands. I move my chair closer and enfold her in my embrace, squeezing her narrow shoulders. I feel the stiffness of bone beneath my grasp. I close the notebook.

'Enough of the past. Let's think about the future, Lucie.' She is unresponsive under my arm. I give her a bracing squeeze. 'You'll meet someone, I'm sure. Someone who cares about you.'

She pulls away from me, wipes her cheek. 'I'm better off on my own.'

'Nonsense. We all say that. Humans are not designed to be alone.'

'It's a massive design flaw, then. And the chances of meeting someone buried out here are zilch.'

I clear my throat. 'Maybe you already have.'

'What?' She stares at me.

'Maybe you don't have to look very far.' I raise my eyebrows in a tantalising fashion, waiting for the penny to drop.

'What? Arthur?' She laughs in a way I find quite offensive. My brows sink and my mouth clamps into a thin line. What's wrong with Arthur? I don't want him to be disappointed again, not after Nancy. If things developed, could Lucie be trusted? I don't say anything, but I resolve to keep a closer eye on their friendship.

Lucie

June

There's something very comforting about a hot bathroom – all that just-out-of-the-shower steam and the shampoo scent. It takes me back to a time when things were okay, a time when the only thing I helped myself to behind my sister's back was her very expensive body lotion. We had the usual bathroom spats, the two of us, about who had used up all the hot water or taken the last of the big bath towels, but on the whole a hot bathroom smelled of excitement, of going out. Of happiness and hope.

I used to think that, anyway.

Now I stand on a damp bath mat in my underwear and try to see my reflection in the condensed mirror. I wonder what Reuben is doing. It's Saturday, and when he's home he doesn't get up until lunchtime. I'm thinking about Reuben, but I can't get past the scared look on my face. I am a bird on a wire in a strong gale, clinging on for all I'm worth. It takes a special kind of grit. Or stupidity.

I've always hated water, but since the millpond incident, and the nocturnal, creaking waterwheel, I seem to have developed a sharp new wariness. I realise now that it can be tame, like the hot shower I've just taken, or it can be feral. If I open the bathroom window, the sound of it will force its way inside – the lade surging underground, overground, hitting the still, silent wheel at speed and sliding around it. It is only the work of a minute to shift the lever and open the floodgates. Likewise, it only takes one little push to submerge a rival in deep, dark water . . .

This tale of two sisters. Is Mac trying to tell me something? Does she know how I've betrayed my own sister? It's hard to look her in the eye – this story sits between us like a pointing finger. When I'm in Mac's company I feel like she's waiting for me to unravel, to confess. Perhaps that's my own guilty conscience, although it's never bothered me much before.

Shivering, I write in the steam in the mirror. Automatic writing, almost . . . My finger feels numb, skidding over the cool damp. *February*. February, the last time I slept with Reuben. Four long months ago. Here, in the little bedroom. February, and the sun filtered in through the curtains and stained his skin.

I squeeze my eyes tight shut, touch my face, gently, with wet fingertips. Tears or condensation, I'm not sure. I grab a towel and swipe the steam from the mirror.

Break the spell.

Arthur is waiting for me in his car outside the cafe. He'd wanted to pick me up, but I'd said no, I'd get there under my own steam. To be picked up felt a bit too date-like. This bears no relation to a date in any shape or form, just two almost-friends having a little road trip.

'How far is this? I don't want to be out all day.' I snap my seat belt shut, and catch the tail end of his grin.

'Oh, you've got things to do and people to see?'

'Something like that.'

'Here's a map. You can navigate.'

A folded roadmap falls into my lap. I sigh heavily. This smacks of involvement. Fettermore is circled clumsily in pencil. The car revs slightly, and Arthur leans towards me. He smells of flour, mixed with a faint, fresh cologne. It's not unpleasant, but I shy away from him all the same. He doesn't notice, too busy tracing a short arc with his finger between the village and a tiny black tower at the edge of the sea, marked on the map as *Castle Binnorie.*

'Hope this isn't a dump. Bet it's full of weed-smoking weirdos. Or Satanists.'

'Or it might be full of the memories of the past,' Arthur says. 'I thought you were curious about the Cruel Sister thing?'

'Only as far as it's about a dysfunctional family.'

He sighs and puts the car into gear. We drive along winding roads in near silence, me staring out of the window, and Arthur commenting on passing landscapes. I realise a part of me has been looking forward to this, but the dark, brooding part won't let me go.

According to Arthur, who seems to have taken on the role of tour guide, the castle sits out of sight on a rocky promontory above the beach. It was built in 1539, although the era in which it was inhabited by the two sisters is uncertain; lost in the mists of time. Or the sort of sea fog that descends as soon as we park the car. Arthur calls it a haar.

We have to negotiate a steep and sandy path. More than once, my trainers skid on small pebbles and there's an awkward patch where a clump of tree roots has eroded everything and you have to pick your way over the knots and ridges. My canvas bag is hampering my ascent, and I wish I'd left it in the car. What was I thinking, bringing a picnic? Hearing my own loud sigh, Arthur offers me his hand. I ignore it. The place stinks of foxes and is littered with sheep droppings, bottle tops and fag ends.

The castle rears up in front of us. The sandstone is very red against the pale sky and threads of mist encircle what's left of the battlements. Only two parts of the fortress remain upright: a jagged tower to the left and a tumbledown curtain wall to the right. It's just a shell, the abandoned casing of someone else's past life, but I experience an unexpected thrill of excitement.

'So, what do you think?' Arthur turns to me, waiting patiently for my verdict.

'Mmm. I'm trying to picture them – the two girls. What it would have been like when they lived here. It's very isolated.'

The castle seems to be growing out of this place, the walls flush with the edges of the rock and the steepest drop that I have ever seen. I wander to the edge and the view takes my breath away. Way down below, the river loops its way through the mist. There are reed beds on one bank, ancient woodland on the other. Midstream, a pair of swans ride their own reflections. I can see a white crescent of sand, marred by the dots and dashes of pebbles and shells, and, in the opposite direction, the wide expanse of the sea.

Arthur appears beside me, making me jump. 'Look at the playground they had, right on the doorstep. And the mill too.'

'So the mill – our mill – is upstream?' I nod towards the river. *Our* mill. It sounds oddly intimate.

I can almost see them, the two sisters, picking their way along the riverbank, skirting the reeds, chattering and giggling as the swans hiss and rear up at them. They break into a run. I can see the hem of a yellow dress disappearing into the trees. Out of sight now, they are drawing closer to the mill – to our mill – straining to hear the telltale rumble of the waterwheel.

As I look down on the tops of trees, gulls swoop so close that I can see their mottled grey backs. I'm conscious that one false step could send me tumbling to my death. Just one step. All it would take would be the pressure of Arthur's hand in the small of my back.

'I've seen enough,' I say quickly. 'Let's go.'

Mac

There was a thick sea mist the day Jim died. The haar, the locals call it. A real pea-souper. You could barely see your hand in front of your face. The ambulance got lost on the way up the lane. They had to ask old man Clark for directions, and the rumour that my husband was dead shot round the whole village before they even loaded him into the ambulance. Sneeze at one end of Fettermore and you'll have the plague by the time you reach the other. Such small-town minds.

The time of death is on his certificate, but I've always pulled away from it. I don't want to know when that severance took place – the last breath, the fading of the light. Was he aware of my anguish? Could he see the next world forming, rising up, in the dark corners of the mill?

I look around the place now. I promised Arthur I'd stop coming in here. He'd threatened to take away the key that last time and I'd thrown a bit of a tantrum; told him not to be so patronising, treating his old ma like a geriatric. 'You'd love to lock me away, wouldn't you? Stick me in a damn care home and forget about me?' He'd winced. I'd taken a fit of coughing – another symptom that has presented itself in the last few weeks – and he'd gone to get me some water. His hand was shaking a little as he'd transferred the cold glass to mine.

'You need to stop this,' he'd whispered.

'Stop what?' I'd sipped the water and looked at him keenly.

'Tormenting yourself. The past is the past.'

I'd pulled a notepad from a pile stacked on the kitchen table. 'I'm an historian. The past is an open book. An ongoing case.'

'Just don't lose yourself in it,' he'd said.

Just don't lose yourself in it. Inside the mill, it's dark, but the dimness has a shifting quality about it, as if the mist has seeped in through the cracks. I don't put the lights on; I know the place off by heart. I know this steep timber staircase, the way the bottom two risers are unevenly spaced. In old houses, that was a device to trip up unwary robbers. Here, it's probably just a result of human error. As I slide my hands over the rail, my fingers recognise the familiar knots in the wood.

In the basement, the blackness is full and perfect. Its presence overwhelms me as I step down onto the stone flags. I move into the centre, circle carefully on the spot with my hands held out, letting the dark close over my head like water. My fingertips tingle. He's down here somewhere, the miller. I can smell him: the stink of stagnant water and old sweat. He'll never give this place up, not after all these years. There's still potential for mischief here. That's what he feeds on – potential. He just needs a weakness, and he'll find a way in.

Come on then. Finish the job. *You might as well take me too.*

There's a noise above me, the scrape of the mill door opening. My heart stops for a beat. Is that Arthur back already? What time is it? I'm not wearing a watch and even if I were, I'd never see it in this pitch black. I come slowly to my senses. What in the world am I doing down here? Arthur will be livid. What if she's with him? Lucie?

Anxiety tickles my spine. Lucie shouldn't be here. Lucie should not be allowed to come in. Remember what happened to the other two girls. I feel my way to the stairs, shuffle my toe onto the first step. Of course, Elspeth and Bella would have known the mill well. It would have been the centre of the community, back then. They would have known the miller, and he them. Oh, he would have known them.

One step. Two. Should I call out? Three. Four. I'll tell Arthur I was just spraying for flies again. Yes, that would work. Or perhaps I'll say I left my watch here the last time, and I had to come back. I'm at the top of the stairs and trying to figure out a reason why I would have left my watch here. That's a very feeble excuse. But Lucie must not come down here. She must be protected. I feel responsible for her.

'Arthur? Before you say anything . . .' Out of breath, I emerge into the almost-light of the main floor. But it isn't Arthur standing there in the doorway. I experience a little shock.

'Oh,' I say. 'I wasn't expecting visitors.'

Lucie

Arthur persuades me to stay a bit longer. We go and stand within the castle's broken corner, avoiding fallen masonry, nettles and empty beer bottles. Someone's had a barbecue and left a burned-out silver foil tray alongside the sodden cardboard box from their carry-out lager. I inspect the walls, leaning back a little to assess the ferns growing on the stone ledges, the solitary crow preening in a high arch. I try to imagine where the bedrooms might have been, the fine oak staircases, the tapestries, but the world of Bella and Elspeth is so far removed from mine that I cannot conjure it up. It is a story perhaps best written down.

Just beside me, there's a low window, a ragged hole in the wall, really, but the perfect viewfinder for the scene below. I lay my hand on the sandstone frame and drink in the landscape. *They* would have seen this same picture: the haar and mirror-dark river and the swans.

'Does your mother come up here?'

Arthur moves to stand beside me, leans in a little, and I shuffle over so he can enjoy the view.

'She used to. Before her health started to fail she would roam the countryside in her Volkswagen, collecting stories, interviewing folk. She visited all these old places. This was one of her favourite haunts.' He pats the stone window ledge as if it's a faithful old horse.

'I can *see* it.' I can hear the excitement in my voice. I root around in my shoulder bag and produce Mac's notebook, the one I'm working on. I'm not quite sure why I packed it. It feels slightly sticky and I hope the lemonade hasn't been leaking.

'She writes so well . . . I can see the castle as it was, the girls flying down the passages and –'

Arthur's looking at me, lips twitching. I smile back. 'Seriously. Listen to this . . .' I flick through the dog-eared pages. Mac says her handwriting looks like a hen's scratchings, and she has a point, but I've grown used to it. 'Here's a good bit. Listen to this . . .

The castle keep is a sprawling edifice, and there are no shortages of places to go. They visit the kitchen when it's cold, and stand before the great black cavern of the fireplace, where the flames eat up whole tree trunks and spit out the sparks. It's deep enough to roast an entire flank of pork, and Cook serves them up slivers of meat so hot they flip them from hand to hand like live minnows before wolfing them down. Bella takes care to wipe her sister's mouth and the grease spots from her gown. A little boy turns the spit, but he doesn't speak or meet their eyes. The servants' faces are red and sweaty, even when the snow is on the ground, and they never pause from their chopping and hacking and fetching and carrying. They are swarthy and suspicious, like the guards on the battlements. The girls climb up there too, at Elspeth's insistence. The younger girl leans out as far as she dares, with Bella clinging to her bodice, and the wind whips their hair into their eyes and carries away their laughter.'

There's something odd about reading aloud to someone. Again, that spark of intimacy surprises me. I look up to find Arthur's eyes tracking the movement of my lips. I'm not given to blushing, but the top of my chest grows a bit warm. I snap the book closed, slightly embarrassed by my own enthusiasm.

'I was enjoying that. Read some more.'

I hand him the notebook. 'It's all yours.'

I wander away, staring at the walls as if, miraculously, the cavernous fireplace might manifest. I want to hear the cook banging pots and sharpening knives and swearing at the spit boy. I want to see Bella's name carved in a lintel. I want proof that these two girls lived out their lives here, just like we live ours, doing the best we can.

Arthur wants to go to the beach, so we retrace our steps and find a way down. There's something about the space, the surf-sound in my ears, that soothes me. As we trudge along the shoreline I lose myself in my thoughts.

Can you talk yourself out of being in love? I suppose you can train yourself not to think about love. I've been aiming for a certain numbness. Numbness is good.

It really is beautiful here: the sandy beach, the endless water, the horizon a faint navy line many miles out. To my right, the castle, still wrapped in mist, stands on its gothic rock, observing me, just as I, minutes ago, surveyed this very scene. It's all a matter of perspective. The white-threaded waves make me draw back my toes.

I'm convinced there's a knack to being alone. There needs to be a blank page where the past should be, otherwise you drive yourself mad with the *what ifs* and the *might-have-beens*. Alone is okay. I need to do alone things and make myself enjoy them.

The numbness is slipping a little, a slow sliding that makes me flex my shoulders. I take a deep breath. I seem to have become a shadowy soul, bounded by stone walls and damp trees. I feel myself unfurling, just a bit. Arthur is kicking pebbles into the surf. He looks up, and we make eye contact. I don't know what he's thinking, and the not knowing is strangely delicious. I allow myself the fleeting, subversive thought that this might be my last experience of total aloneness.

'So . . . should we go back?' I say.

He picks up a smooth pebble and strokes it with his thumb. 'To Fettermore?'

His thumbs, his fingers, are strong. His hands always have a just-washed, wholesome glow about them.

'Well we're done here, aren't we?' I turn in the direction of the car. More of a flounce really, if I'm honest.

His voice follows me, and I hear the jingle of keys. 'I'm going to stay a bit longer. Feel free to sit in the car if you like.'

When I risk a glance, he's laughing at me. I can either complete the full flounce manoeuvre, or I can stand and fight. Battle can take many forms. I let myself smile, feeling the numbness crack around the edges.

'I actually have a sort-of picnic in my bag.' I tug the shoulder strap. 'Well, lemonade and biscuits.'

He catches up with me and brushes past, closer than he needs to be. It's a very big beach, after all. 'Sort-of picnics are the best kind. And flour-based confectionary? Sold. Come on then, let's find a good place.'

I take a deep breath and follow him.

Mac

'I'm sorry – the mill isn't open to the public.' I brandish the big key in his face and march him out.

'I haven't come to see the mill,' he declares. 'I've come to see Lucie. Sorry, we haven't actually met. I'm Reuben. You must be Mrs Muir?'

I look him up and down, noting the walking stick, the slight hunch to his demeanour. He's a good-looking lad, but there are lines in his face that shouldn't be there. I recognise pain when I see it. Beyond him, a grey car lurks where the blue car had been. Something whirrs and clicks in my brain. I stare at the car. I think about the crash in old man Clark's cow pasture. I think about Reuben's accident, the same day. I snap my attention back to him. He's got a definite attitude, coming here asking for Lucie. I turn back to the door to hide my thoughts.

'It's *Doctor* Muir, actually, and Lucie isn't here.' It takes me a moment or two to lock up; the timber has swollen with the damp mist and I have to wrestle with it. It buys me some time. When I turn back to Reuben he's checking his smartphone. 'Jane not with you then? Your *girlfriend*?'

He glances up with impatience. 'No. Is Lucie around, then?'

'No she isn't. She's out for the afternoon. On a date.'

I watch his face for a flicker and there it is. A wince, just as surely as he'd stepped awkwardly on the gammy leg.

'When will she be back?'

'I've simply no idea.' I no longer want to have any truck with this man, but he follows me as I head towards the lane. 'Looks to me like you should be at home recuperating. With Jane.'

'It's been a long haul,' he concedes. 'I'm a work in progress.'

Ah yes, any writer knows how troublesome those can be.

'Right. I'll tell her you called,' I say, in what I hope is a dismissive fashion. Maybe he'll just get in his car and go.

'I think I'll just wait.' He fixes me with a look that says *try and stop me*.

'As you wish.'

Damn him to hell. Why is he back now, making waves? No good can come of this.

Lucie

'Just drop me off at the cafe,' I'd said to him. 'There's no need to take me home.' As if the short stretch of road from the village to the mill would suddenly invite new depths of familiarity.

'It's fine,' he'd replied. 'Another mile won't make any difference.'

I'd thought that was a bit cryptic, but then I suspect that Arthur has hidden and unexplored depths. Something fleeting and treacherous rises up inside me. As the car bumps down the track to the cottage, I gather my things together: the sticky lemonade, the half-eaten packet of biscuits. I brush crumbs from Mac's jotter and stow it more carefully in a side pocket, making a mental note to ask her straight out why she's stalling with this when I want so badly to know the ending.

'Strange car,' Arthur mutters. I look up as we slow to a halt beside it. Pale grey in colour, some kind of Toyota, with a number plate I don't recognise. 'Looks like you've got visitors.'

'I'm not expecting any.' I pull the bag closer to me like a shield. 'That's not my parents' car, or Jane's . . .'

Then I see him, loitering beside the cottage. Reuben. He's checking his phone, and I wonder if he's been texting me. Today has been the first day in all these months that I haven't been obsessively checking my mobile. My stomach clenches like a fist.

'Ah.' Arthur has seen him too. The car rolls forward an inch, as if he isn't quite sure what to do. 'Are you going to be ok?'

'Why shouldn't I be?' My voice sounds tight, remote. I release my seatbelt.

'I just mean . . .' Arthur sighs and slips the car into gear as I open the door. 'Let me know how it goes.'

I'm out of the car, half-scared to attract Reuben's attention. To Arthur I must seem detached, cold, but inside my heart is beating fiercely and my hand is shaking on the door handle.

'I'll be fine.' I slam the door in Arthur's face, and then turn and walk up the steps to meet Reuben.

Once again, Reuben is standing in my kitchen.

He looks tired, and the way his eyes kindle when he catches sight of me . . . well, that seems to be missing. There's an absence, somehow, as if the real Reuben is still in the hospital and this is a pared-down version. The first awkward greeting, and the usual faff when you're unlocking the door and ushering in an unexpected visitor, has diverted my thoughts. But now, as I lay my keys down on the table and really look at him . . . now, I'm remembering that last time, when it was supposed to be over and we'd kissed and ended up in bed together. The possibility is still there, floating round our heads like pollen, waiting to land.

Reuben's once easy smile is flawed. I can see the pain in his eyes, and it pulls on my heart like a magnet. *Don't go there.* Don't hug him. Don't touch him. Instead I ask him about his leg, about his new car and what it was like to drive, after the accident.

'Pretty scary, at first,' he says. 'This is the furthest I've been, since.'

'That road . . . that must have been difficult.'

He nods. No trace of the old bravado grin. My hand comes to rest on my abdomen, which feels all tense and knotted.

'Are you back at work?'

'Not yet. We're discussing a phased return. I'll be office-based for a while, obviously.'

He raises the walking stick a fraction and lets it drop back onto the flagstones with a sharp rap. I rush to pull out a chair.

'Here, sit down. What am I thinking. Do you want a coffee?'

'No coffee. No, thank you. Your boss, she's a bit frosty, isn't she? Does she know about us?'

'Do you think she does?' Suddenly breathless, I slump down into the chair beside him. 'I thought she might have figured it out. She's writing this story about two sisters and I keep thinking she's playing games with me, pointing the finger. It's like she's saying this is *you*. This is what you're doing to *your* sister.'

'So what? It's none of her business, miserable old cow.' Reuben dismisses it all with a sneer that makes me angry.

'You just don't get it! How guilty I feel! Have you any idea what will happen if Jane finds out?'

'That's why I'm here.'

'What? She's not –'

'No!' Again he pushes my fears aside. 'It's just . . . Jane and me, we haven't been getting along. Has she been in touch?' He's staring at his trainers and my eyes take in the soft wave of his hair. *No*. Suddenly he looks up. His eyes are shiny, moist.

I shake my head. The knot in my belly tightens. 'Not lately. We don't confide in each other much.'

He rubs both hands over his face, his hair. 'We're in trouble. I think she suspects.'

'What? I knew it.' We're facing each other, our eyes level. There is no hiding place for this cold dread. 'About us?'

He shrugs. 'No . . . not us specifically. She's suspicious, though. Asking questions. I caught her reading my messages once. Things haven't been right since the accident.'

'Since the accident?' I repeat. I'm thinking of all the months before that, the yearning glances, the secret meetings. 'Things haven't been right for a long time, or you wouldn't have been sleeping with me.'

He looks shocked. 'I still loved her.'

'So where did that ever leave me?' My fingers are twisting together in my lap.

'You're special to me.' He reaches out and grasps my hand. The skin-on-skin contact is a shock and I pull away.

'Special?' The word comes out like a pistol shot. 'That's a

patronising word. That's the sort of thing you say to kids on their birthday. "You're special, so you're going to get a special present." Don't do me any favours, Reuben.'

'Stop.' He bangs his hand down on the table, stares at the cherries on the oilcloth. *Cherry trifle.* Does he even remember that tiny detail? 'I didn't come here to argue about who loves who the most –'

'No, you came here to find out if I'll keep your secret – our secret. If I'll lie to my sister if she asks me.'

He opens his mouth, and I wait to hear what he has to say, wait to hear him tell me I'm wrong, but he remains silent.

'Don't worry, Reuben,' I continue. 'I have no intention of hurting Jane any more than I already have. I won't tell her.'

He nods. 'The thing is, even if she doesn't find out, even if she never has any evidence, she knows there's something . . .' He sighs. 'I just want to know, if Jane and I split up . . .'

I think I know what's coming next. My heart is banging against my ribs, and there's only one question in my mind. Will he end it, or will Jane? But I already know the answer. Reuben will never have the courage of his convictions. He's never loved me enough to make the break, to put me first. Even now, he's just making sure he has somewhere to run to if the shit really hits the fan.

'Lucie.' He turns a little, to look at me full on, but he doesn't try and touch me again. 'Lucie, I've missed you. I had to come and see you. Do you think . . . do you think we could make a go of this?'

I can't meet his gaze. I get to my feet and I can feel his eyes on me as I pace over to the Aga. I make a great play of folding a tea towel that's already folded.

'All these months you've ignored me.'

'I was trying to get over you. It didn't work.'

He sounds so weary, but I can't let myself buy into it or I'll be lost. Yeah, it's been exhausting, hasn't it, my love? All the subterfuge, the heightened emotion? The rollercoaster ride to nowhere. My inner knot loosens.

'Can I ask you this . . .?' I can hear my heart pumping in my ears. 'Are you going to end it with Jane?'

He tries to bat the question away, but it's the most important question I've ever asked. *Will you make that decision?*

He shrugs. 'It's up to Jane, isn't it?'

'Why?'

'It's her call.' He is a schoolboy hauled up in front of the head. 'She thinks I've been cheating – no evidence, of course – but imagine if I end it with her and then start up with you. It'd be too obvious. No, it has to be her decision, and then we can sell our relationship to her later. You were comforting me after she broke my heart, something like that.'

I am momentarily speechless. 'You don't get it, do you, Reuben? This is just a game, isn't it? A game you're good at. That's why you do it.'

He starts to protest. I move closer to him, so close I can feel the heat of him, catch a hint of the Reuben smell that's in my DNA. I wonder if I can trust my voice. I have to say this. I have to say it and I have to mean it. He will always be my sister's boyfriend. He will always be the person who was willing to cheat.

'No, Reuben.' I squeeze his shoulder, very gently. 'You're not the person I thought you were. I did this to my sister because I fell in love with you, not because I wanted to hurt her. It would kill her, if she knew. It would kill her if I got together with you now or at any time in the future. And worst of all, you didn't choose me. You couldn't even make that decision.'

Mac

Bella returns to the castle alone. Elspeth is missing. Men and hounds are sent out, but the hunt turns up nothing. Of the younger sister, there is no sign. Their father's fury dashes the walls of the keep like the east wind in winter, but it is just as futile. Bella is shocked and mute and no one can say for certain what the truth is.

In time, the young Lord Musgrave recovers enough to put in a bid for the older sister. Bella accepts without enthusiasm. She rarely leaves her room now; every whiff of the outdoors reminds her of Elspeth, and her resentment has withered on the vine, to be replaced by a deep, dark guilt she cannot shake off. It plods at her heels like Faithful, the old hound. The wedding is arranged by her mother, who can barely focus through lack of sleep. Her face is shadowed by grief and the preparations are muted. The flowers that deck the great hall are past their best and the wedding wine tastes like vinegar. No one has thought about music.

I can't settle into the story. I'm thinking of Reuben, of his unexpected appearance. Lucie is with him now. All those clues ... they all fit together now. The strange man with Lucie, the car crash, the girl's obvious distress. It all fits.

I put down my pen and get up from the desk, kneading my neck muscles as I make my way over to the study window. Outside, the grounds are looking a bit forlorn, and I make a mental inventory: grass needs cutting; must find a reliable man to cut said grass; buy bedding plants. Pansies, probably. Yes, you can depend on a pansy to gladden the heart. My heavy sigh mists the glass, and I press my palm to that unreliable organ. My heart. It's skittering about still, which is probably a good thing. At least it's still beating.

I'll get Lucie to plant up the pansies. Maybe she'll have a view on what we can do with the garden. She generally has a view on most things. I realise I've been allowing myself to lean on her, but now I'm not so sure that's a good thing. My little exchange with Reuben has put a different colour on things. I thought I could trust her, but now? The girl's been sleeping with her sister's boyfriend!

Had Reuben been hovering under the pergola like a bad penny? If he hadn't shown up, Lucie might have invited Arthur in, made him a meal. It could have been the start of something, but the prospect now fills me with dread. Is that what I want for my son? Do I want him to go through all the misery that Anna Madigan put me through?

For weeks now I've had some instinct that I've been missing something. Call it intuition, but I felt it deep within my bones, that familiar feeling of the truth finally coming to light. And back there, at the mill, it all clicked into place.

Reuben's reappearance is a red flag – a huge one.

Now it makes perfect sense: Lucie's black moods, the way she moons about the house like some kind of gothic heroine. And the poem . . .

The poem must have been about him! Her sister's boyfriend. My brief flare of triumph at my own detective work is quickly doused. How could she? Her own sister?

No wonder all these old memories are haunting me. I thought I'd long since ground them to dust, but they're always there, just out of sight. There must have been signs, clues, which I chose to ignore. Perhaps if we'd communicated more, Jim and I. If I'd looked up from my notes once in a while, if . . . I sigh heavily, and then anger suddenly floods through me, fire in my veins. Lucie cannot be allowed to wreck her sister's life, as Anna Madigan wrecked mine. Maybe it's not too late. I get stiffly to my feet and call to the dogs.

I'm waiting for him on the road. The dogs have scattered, apart from Jethro, who is watching me nervously, because he hates roads and this is the one thing I keep warning them not to do. The grey car eases into sight, carefully avoiding the potholes on the track from the mill. Pity Reuben wasn't so cautious that last time he left, he could have saved everyone a lot of bother. Better still, he should have made a proper job of things. I imagine Reuben lying in the wreckage, life extinct, and a smile plays around my lips. I'm still smiling as I step out in front of his car.

He brakes abruptly. I can't see his expression for the light striping the spotless windscreen, but his window purrs down and, hands stuffed in pockets, I amble around to the driver's side.

'What the hell are you doing?'

His irritation is raw, aggravated by whatever exchange he's had with Lucie. Hopefully she's given him his marching orders. Enjoying the height advantage, I stare him out for a heartbeat or two. He looks very uncomfortable, fists white on the steering wheel. The new-car smell steals up to meet me.

'Nice car,' I say. 'You're obviously not short of a bob or two.'

'Do you actually want something?'

He revs the engine a little, just to make a point, but I won't be hurried. My fingers make contact with something in my right-hand pocket. Paper, folded into a thick wedge.

'I'm on to you. I want you to leave Lucie alone. You think you can roll up here, disrupting all our lives –'

'It's none of your damn business what we do!'

His tone wipes the humour from my face. I lean in, grip the car door. 'It's my business if you're having it away in *my* cottage! Under *my* nose! You have no idea of the hurt you've caused. The pain, the heartache . . .'

He mutters something and jabs at a button. The window begins to nudge at my palms.

'No! I haven't finished with you yet, you scoundrel!'

I grip the window, rattle it with all my might, and he's swearing and grappling with the button. The window glides down again, giving me room to lean in and grab the front of his shirt.

'You listen to me, you little shit!' My spittle lands on his cheek. He shies away from me, moaning about an injured shoulder, but I tighten my grip, shake him like Max worrying a rabbit. 'You don't realise what you've done, do you? Your brain is in your pants. You never once stopped to think what this would do to me. You broke my heart – made me into something I'm not, a monster, and I can never forgive you. Or her! Never!'

I realise Reuben is staring at me with his mouth open. I can smell fear, like old meat, on his breath. I relax my hands, smooth his shirt and pat him on the cheek. 'Anyway. I've said my piece. You'd better get out of here, laddie.'

At some point the engine has stalled. He squeezes the steering wheel again, guns the car into life. 'You're crazy. Fucking mental.'

My fingers caress the paper in my pocket, trying to remember what it is. As realisation dawns, I begin to smile. Lucie's poem to person unknown. But we know now, don't we?

'If you want to know what you've done, maybe you'd better read this.' I wave the slip of paper at him. 'This is what happens when you mess with a woman's feelings – with two women's feelings. You're playing one sister off against the other, just like young Musgrave . . .'

But I'm talking to myself. The car has already lurched forward, wheels spinning a little in the mud. I feel cold spray from the puddles on my ankles. Reuben is staring grimly ahead, but his window is still down. On an impulse, like posting a letter, I pop the poem through the gap. Fly, little bird. Who knows where you will land?

Lucie

It starts to rain as Reuben leaves, and I watch the first big watery splatters on the glass. What have I done? Those things I said . . . I never wanted to hurt him and now he's gone, angry and rejected, just like the last time. I see him again in the hospital bed and feel overwhelmed with guilt and sadness.

I go to the back window of the kitchen. There's a clear view of the track from here, and I'm surprised to see that his grey car has come to a stop at the end. Is he coming back? But someone else is there. Mac is leaning in to speak with him. What does she want with him? What can she possibly have to say? Alarm bells sound in the depths of my being. Something doesn't feel right. She appears to be arguing with him; I can hear her raised, angry voice, though I can barely make out the words.

Horror and shame flood through me. Has she figured it out? Does she know my secret? Surely not . . . I tell myself that this is just Mac being Mac, interrogating a stranger on her property, being her usual rude and irritable self.

Reuben revs his engine and the car shoots off in a spray of rainwater and pebbles.

Mac's left standing out on the road, watching the car disappear. I step back from the window. I don't want her to see me looking.

Despite the rain, I feel an unavoidable urge to get out of the house. I end up sitting by the pond, and remain there for a long time, taking root on the damp bench like a stubborn twist of ivy. The rain doesn't come to anything and I feel slightly cheated.

There's thunder inside me. As the shadows get longer, the landscape stirs into life. A fight breaks out in the high trees across the pond – crows flexing some black-feathered muscle – and beneath them the water splits into rings and spirals as the fish rise.

Mac will fire me, for sure. She's a very black-and-white sort. She won't approve of what I've done. She'll ask me to leave, just like my mother and I'll have to start all over again. No home, no job, no Reuben. It's almost too much to bear. Maybe I'm disappearing into the landscape. I'll end up as a smudge on Arthur's crumpled map. *Lucie used to work here.* Instead of a little castle icon, or a church cross, there'll be a hunched matchstick figure, sitting on a damp bench, smoking a fag.

Mac

Arthur arrives at two minutes to ten. I'm still in my study and his car headlights play across the glass, illuminating the desk, the notebook. My pencilled words spark silver and come to life for a split second.

In the middle of the wedding feast, a stranger comes to the hall. He is cloaked and dragging something heavy in a jute sack. When questioned, he says he brings the gift of music, for shouldn't every bride be blessed with music? He is given a seat at the table, and food which he doesn't eat. Bella thinks he seems familiar, although his hood obscures most of his face. She cannot see his features, merely the shadows cast by them, and she's suddenly afraid to look too closely in case that's all there is . . .

I hear the car door slam and a lot of bad-tempered jangling of keys at the lock. Oh dear. I sit back and wait for the darkness to enter.

'You were making no sense on the phone whatsoever, Ma.'

'I merely called to tell you that Lucie had a visitor.'

'That was hours ago, Ma, and anyway, I'm more concerned about the other stuff you were saying. It's the other stuff . . . that's why I'm here at bloody 10 p.m.'

'You didn't have to come. I don't know what you're talking about.'

We are nose to nose in the study, Arthur still twitching his keys as if he's in a hurry to get away. There's a smell of petrol and night air about him. But what's all this? He's repeating things I don't remember saying and my heart is juddering like an old locomotive. I feel taken aback. Surely I said nothing of the sort?

'You were banging on about the mill. Again.'

'I was not.'

'You were.'

'I never mentioned the mill, son.'

I hadn't. Had I? Something is lodged in my throat. It's hard to swallow, to breathe.

'You said Reuben had come to the mill. Just before we came back.'

'Yes. Yes, he did. That's why I called you.' I feel for my chair and lower myself into it. Anything to unhook myself from Arthur's hardest stare. I pick up my pencil and begin to doodle on the open notebook. 'I only went in there to get my watch. I must have left it there last time.'

'I don't really care why you were in there, Ma. It's what you said. You said you were very tempted to "fix Lucie's little problem, once and for all".' He makes quotation marks in the air. 'Do you remember now?'

A flower takes shape under my pencil. A child's flower: five oval petals and a round middle. The pencil is shaky. 'I would've sent Reuben packing. That's all.'

'You really don't remember what else you said, do you, Ma? I worry about you.' Arthur's eyes soften. He's looking not at me but at something beyond the window, something that makes him rather sad and pensive. He's still talking but I'm not really concentrating on what he's saying. I get bits of it. *See someone . . . mention it to the doctor next time . . . memory loss . . . dark thoughts . . .*

I'm staring at the notebook. Below the flower, a single name is printed in a careful, schoolgirl hand. *Bella.*

I don't remember writing that.

Lucie

It doesn't take long for the pond to freak me out. I don't like it down here when dusk starts to fall. I don't trust this landscape where the trees crackle with secrets and the water smells wild and the midges and the bugs and the birds take on a new urgency.

I get up from the bench. Walk, and keep on walking. The path is littered with snails that crunch beneath my feet, making me wince with every step. Maybe I should go and have it out with Mac, find out what she knows. If she only knows half the story, maybe I could fudge things. The rain starts up again. A sparrow swoops too close, the vibration of its feathers a frantic chord that tears at my nerves. It would mean even more lies. The lies are now following me from place to place. When will it end? The urge to keep moving is overwhelming.

Skirting past the cottage, I find myself heading up towards the road, negotiating the rough track in my unsuitable sandals. I'm hunched up, hugging myself, and the rain is slick and cold on the exposed parts of me. It's late. Maybe Mac will have gone to bed. But postponing the conversation until morning will just prolong the agony. I feel sick, a bit green around the gills, as Mac would say. But I've been that way for months. I close my eyes as I walk, tilting my face to the rain.

Light floods my vision.

Headlights, nosing out of Mac's driveway, and the rain floating soft and yellow in the harsh beam. I am a rabbit, caught, standing there with my hair plastered to my scalp, in my wet top and with my dirty toes. A car door bangs and Arthur is suddenly beside me, solid and warm, smelling of damp wool, holding out a folded umbrella.

'Are you crazy? First Ma and now you. What's going on tonight?'

'It's raining.'

'I can see that. Where's your coat?'

I don't have to answer that. Just because Arthur took me for a drive doesn't give him the right to treat me like a child. Or a friend. We're not mates.

'I'm just . . . taking a walk.'

'Get in the car, and I'll take you home.'

'You get in the car.'

He brandishes the umbrella at me. The rain is making his hair curl and he looks like he's missing his warm kitchen. I suppose he'd rather be anywhere but here, trying to reason with a crazy person. I relent and snatch the umbrella from him, make a show of pressing the little steel button and pushing up the shaft. Its black wings flop about uselessly, and I suddenly feel very weary. I thrust it back at him.

'I don't want it. I'm perfectly capable of making my own way home.'

'Take it anyway.' His face is set, determined. Rain dribbles from his long eyelashes like tears. I wonder what's wrong with his mother now.

'You take it. You're getting soaked yourself.'

The umbrella wilts as he realises I'm not going to cooperate. He changes tack.

'So what did Reuben want? I mean . . . how did it go?'

Guilt paralyses me. Should I tell him that his mother knows my secret? That my time here might be running out? Rain trickles down my neck and my brow feels tight. 'It's still over.'

'That's good. Isn't it?'

'Is it? Is it?' I give a harsh laugh which isn't a laugh. 'Go home, Arthur. Go back to your fairy cakes.'

I turn on my heel – difficult in thin-soled shoes. His sigh gusts after me.

'Don't be so friggin' prickly. I'm concerned about you, that's all. Aren't I allowed to care?'

I swing around to face him. 'No, you're not! That's how it all starts. Sympathy, caring, all that shite, and then you end up with a piece of your soul missing.'

'I know!' he snaps back. Then, softer, 'I know.'

We regard each other like two feisty mutts spoiling for a fight. I manage some kind of sneer to break the contact and turn back to the track, intent on heading back down it with as much sassiness as my limp shoes will allow. I know he sees a girl who's wet and bedraggled and lost. I don't want him to see me lost.

I take a moment to glance over the boundary wall. The land and the sea are invisible. Everything is obliterated by a clammy curtain of rain, and the breath of the wind stinks of seaweed. The insistent *peep peep peep* of an oystercatcher drills into my brain.

Last time I noticed the field it was as neat as an old man's corduroy britches, freshly ploughed. Now the bits that are visible are a rich, purposeful green. How did that happen? I've been sleepwalking: back and forth to Mac's study, hypnotised by my typewriter fingers, sucked into her imaginary fucking world. She's pulling me into it. My life is being played out by two sisters who don't even exist. All my rage, my jealousy, my shame is being re-enacted, courtesy of Mac's pen. I'm beginning to think it's deliberate, like she's punishing me. She's messing with my mind. How long has she known?

Peep peep peep.

The cry stabs at my innards. I experience a sick jolt – where has the time gone? It's gathering speed and I'm clinging on by my fingernails. I lay my hands across the lost place in my abdomen. I feel suddenly scared. Whatever crop that is, beyond the wall . . . it will flourish and ripen and then it will be autumn and I'm not ready. I'm not ready.

I think I hear Arthur call my name, but over the wall the bastard bird is still going *peep peep peep*.

'Lucie!' he tries again, just fierce enough to let me know he thinks I'm ignoring him. 'Lucie. I could murder a drink.'

I'm dithering in the middle of the path, pretending to gauge a particularly deep puddle. I risk a backward glance. He's standing in the car headlights, a dark lonely man-shape in a halo of gold and raindrops.

'The pub's still open,' he says.

I turn back. 'Go on then. I suppose we could have just the one.'

I begin to retrace my steps, walking back towards him just a shade too quickly. I hope he won't notice.

Lucie

July

I struggle to open my eyes. Light is pouring through the window. Why hadn't I closed the curtains last night? Frantically I backtrack, but something has forced me awake. My phone is ringing in the depths of the house. I sit up, but then the ringing stops, and I find that I don't care enough to get up and investigate further.

I sink back into the pillows and look at the man snoring softly beside me. Arthur.

After drinks in the pub that first night, we quickly fell into a pleasant routine, away from Mac and Reuben and other concerns. We'd meet in the pub after work, just talk. Or Arthur would talk and I would whine or find fault with things. I'd order pints, determined to out-man the baker with his gin and tonic. It suited me to think of him as shy and boring, and therefore not quite worthy of my attention.

But last night, something changed. Last night he was all I needed. We'd sat in a dark beery corner, under amber lamplight, shielded from real life by dusty tapestry curtains. I'd spoken about Reuben, about how much I hurt, cursing my fate while shredding beer mats. I couldn't bring myself to mention Mac. That was something I needed to process in my own time. Arthur just nodded and cradled his tall glass and gazed at me as if the words spilling out of my mouth were really, really important.

I'd soon moved on to wine, which went straight to my head

and made me think I was irresistible. Who doesn't want to be irresistible? I never stopped to consider the consequences.

I remember both of us dissolving into laughter, Arthur putting his arm around me. We were sitting side by side on the banquette and it was easy for him to hug me. I let my arm snake around his waist and we sat like that as a new awareness bloomed between us. We had definitely crossed a line, stumbling together into new territory.

The rest happened almost accidentally. We ticked off all the required clichés: he walked me home; I asked him in for coffee and discovered an unopened box of almond slices. We scooched up together at the table, heads leaning in, mugs aligned. He went all Paul Hollywood for a bit, holding his cake up for inspection, pointing out the delicacy of the base and banging on about Madagascan vanilla. Finally, bored, I leant over and took a massive bite of his cake, leaving him holding a mere stub. There I was, giggling and spluttering crumbs, with him glaring at me, mock fierce, and telling me I was in big trouble.

Like the best of fights, we took it to the bedroom.

It was different. Reuben was still in the sad bits of my mind. I think Arthur knew that, and worked hard to banish him for good. He almost succeeded. I almost lost myself in Arthur, but a bit of my brain refused to let go completely. It watched me from a corner of the room, standing apart like a shy girl at a party. Afterwards, I lay cradled against his hairy chest. He kissed the top of my head, cupped my breast as if I were some kind of goddess, and a slow, sad tear trickled from my eye. It must have landed on his bare skin, causing ripples like something falling into the millpond, because he gave a start, twisting round to look in my face, determined to see the things I don't want people to see.

'What is it?'

'Tears of joy.' I stuck my tongue out at him. 'Are you staying?'

The look on his face told me he'd never considered otherwise. 'Fine,' I said, rolling over to switch off the lamp. 'Just don't snore.'

I consider him now with something like sadness. I can't afford to let him in.

When my phone rings again, a little later, I scrabble for last night's T-shirt, haul on yesterday's knickers and stub my feet into flip-flops.

My phone is doing that curious little jig in the middle of the kitchen table, disturbing all the crumbs. The inevitable cake box is still sitting there from the day before, and two empty coffee mugs. I grab the phone. I see that it's Jane and my heart misses a beat. I think about not answering, but what good would that do?

'Jane? Hi.'

'Hi, Lucie. Is this a bad time? I know it's early but . . .'

She sounds friendly enough. Her voice is tight, but not angry. 'It's as good a time as any. Are you okay?'

I know what she's going to say. I know I have to pretend not to know. I've been waiting for this phone call, this conversation, since Reuben's visit two weeks ago. She dissolves into tears, and I find myself trotting out all the usual crap. *Maybe it's for the best. Some things aren't meant to be. Plenty more fish* etc., etc. She ended it, finally – not him. But she doesn't tell me why.

'Will you come home, Lucie. Just for a bit? I know you're busy, but I could use a friendly face. That's what sisters are for, right?'

I take a deep breath. 'You know I'm always here for you. I'll see if I can get away this weekend.' It would mean not having to face Mac. The idea grows very appealing.

'Okay. Stay as long as you want. Surely you can take a week off? You're entitled to holidays.'

This makes me smile somehow. I have a vague memory of Jane kicking off about rates of pay when she took on a paper round at fourteen. She always had a strong sense of right and wrong. We make arrangements. Jane promises to pick me up from the train station. I break off the call and stand for a moment, gripping the edge of the table.

I hear a subtle cough behind me. No doubt Arthur was disappointed to wake up to discover the bed cold and empty, but he's found me now. I lean on the table, listening to his approach, stiffening as his arms come around me, fearing his heat against my back. I stand passively as he hugs me.

'Are you going to see your folks?'

'My sister, yes.'

Last night, his breathy words in my ear made me catch fire. Now, I detach myself. I step out of his embrace and he lets me go. He's standing there in just his chinos, barefoot and bare-chested. Unlike Reuben, Arthur has thick fur on his chest. I'd combed my fingers through it, rubbed myself against it.

'Yeah. I'm going home.'

'You are coming back though?'

I let the silence speak. He gives a stilted laugh. *Offer him a coffee. Smile at him. Don't be such a bitch.* Still I stand there, paralysed. He shrugs, defeated.

Mac

The stranger carries with him the smell of bone fires and the east wind. Beneath the damp dark cloak, all that he might be is concealed. All but the thin hook of his smile and the claws of his fingers on the jute sack. His fingernails are as yellow as sheep hooves and rimmed with something white, like flour, and when Bella asks where he's from his voice is too low to hear. The answer falls to the ground, to be crushed by her father's boots, by the stamp of his laughter.

'What have you in the sack, traveller? A gift for the bride?'

A rare gift indeed, the man might have said.

I barge into the cafe.

'She's gone! I knew she'd leave. Women like her can't be trusted.'

Anita, wiping down the table nearest the window, looks at me with something like alarm. I brush past her, aware of the door slamming in my wake. The framed prints rattle against the wallpaper.

'It's the east wind. The east wind never brings any good with it. The bible says it blows from the direction of God, but I've never believed that. Quite the opposite, if you ask me. But no one asks me. No one asks my opinion. Why didn't she tell me she was going, instead of leaving a note? She's good at that, isn't she? Leaving notes about the place. I would have said to her – now is not a good time. There's work to be done, before the east wind comes. And now it's too late. It's getting too late.' The two old biddies who seem to live permanently in the corner are looking at me, whispering into their teacups. I give them an evil stare. 'Mind your own goddamn business!'

Arthur has been busy behind the counter, but now he drops everything and shushes me. He seems very tense.

'Don't shush me! She left me a bloody note. A note! Not even a by your leave!'

'Mother, not here.' Arthur holds aside the bead curtain, and I blaze around the counter. The kitchen is heavy with the smell of dough. Three seeded loaves sit on the worktop like a trio of bunched-up tabby cats.

I brandish the note at him. 'This is just typical of Anna Madigan. She never came straight out with things.'

'What are you talking about? Look, Lucie got a call from home. Family business. And what the hell is wrong with you? You can't come in here kicking off like that.'

'Since when did her family show the slightest interest in her? We're in the middle of important work. I have a deadline! Is she coming back?'

'You're not even listening to me.' He turns his back, tosses a checked tea towel over the bread. I can see Anita through the curtain, hovering. Her eyes are huge and watchful.

'Is she coming back?' I grab at Arthur's elbow, but he shakes me off, rounds on me with a violence that is uncalled for.

'I don't know, Ma! I'm not her keeper. She's got a lot going on right now.'

'I've got a lot going on! What is wrong with people? No sense of loyalty, decency. Always out for themselves. I'd thought better of Anna, but it seems she's just as treacherous as the rest of them!'

'Lucie.'

'Yes, Lucie. She's just like –'

'You called her Anna. Twice.'

'I didn't.'

'You did.'

Did I? Fear throbs inside me. Anita is holding out a glass of water.

'Come and sit down,' she says gently. I follow her through into the cafe, docile now.

'I can't believe it. She wouldn't desert us, would she? I'd grown used to having her around. And things aren't *finished* yet.'

No one answers me. I sip the water. It has a cold bite to it and I shiver. My teeth are chattering. The bloody east wind never blows any good.

Lucie

I take the early train north, sharing a table with a woman who looks up only briefly from her glossy magazine. I don't make eye contact, just lean into the window and watch the sea roll by for the next twenty minutes. The train is a good place to think. Maybe it's the gentle rocking, the landscape whizzing past . . . everything receding, making way for all the things that loom large in your mind in the middle of the night.

Like losing your new job, and being made homeless and destitute. And ending up in bed with Arthur.

Am I really so needy, so desperate? No, that's unfair to Arthur. The guy is sweet, kind. He doesn't judge me. He makes me smile with his endless cakes and his twinkly eyes. He doesn't take me too seriously. But why did I have to take it too far? How can I be with Arthur when Reuben is still in my bones?

Sighing, I let my head loll against the back of the seat. The scent of coffee and the clink and rattle of the drinks trolley comes to me from some way off. The thought of a caffeine hit and a packet of ready salted perks me up, pokes me with a little needle of excitement. I can imagine I'm speeding away from it all; taking a minibreak of blue seas and open sky. The light is different. Everything it touches, the clouds, the water, the grass, shimmers with some kind of eagerness.

My thoughts latch onto the mantra of the wheels. *Arthur is behind me. Mac is behind me. The mill is behind me.* All that darkness, and concealment and the suffocating, dripping greenery – all behind me. Stone cottages loom and disappear in the blink of an eye. Perfect gardens, ponies. Wooded glens. Free and fleeting. Nothing sticks.

Jane is waiting for me at the station. We don't hug, because she's parked on double yellows and we have to rush. When we get home, she abandons me in the hall, claiming that her bladder is about to burst. The place feels smaller, darker and smellier than I remembered. My mother emerges reluctantly from the kitchen, as if she's been skulking in there since I left. Her hug is brief and chilly, and I think she's lost weight. Beneath a string of amber beads, her collarbones are razor sharp, and her blow dry is limp.

'How was the train?'

'Fine, thanks.'

I follow her back into the kitchen, watch her as she bustles about, switching on the kettle, laying out cups. China cups and saucers, as if I'm a guest – a visiting committee member or someone from the Women's Rural. Normally we'd have mugs pulled from the pine stand in the corner beside the bread bin. It'll be biscuits on a plate next, rather than straight out of the tin.

'Did you have a snack?'

'I had a coffee. It was disgusting.' I'd been too preoccupied to snack. How was I going to deal with Arthur? I didn't need this new complication. I should never have let myself get close to him.

'I'll make tea,' my mother is saying, as if this will counteract the bitterness. She bursts open a packet of shortbread fingers and fans them out on a delicate plate that once sat in my grandmother's display cabinet. It's decorated with blue poppies. I've always loved that plate. My gaze wanders round the kitchen, picking out all the things that are so part of the fabric of home that they barely register any more: the pale green colander hanging beside the cooker, the spotty milk jug with the superglued handle. Yesterday's mail stashed behind the radio and a tea caddy from Harrods, stuffed with odd keys, receipts and all those things you don't want but think you ought to keep. I go over to it, remove the lid. Near the top is a receipt for a dress I bought for a cousin's wedding four years ago, and the memory stick with my college essays.

'What are you doing?' My mother glances at me with suspicion.

'I'm just . . .' What am I doing? I'm a child cast out in some ghastly wilderness. I want proof that my life is still here, that a bit of me is still here. 'Nothing.'

My mother shakes her head a fraction and I replace the lid. She hands me a cup and saucer.

'We'll sit in here. Dad is just catching up with his emails. He'll be in shortly.'

My father hadn't come to greet me. I'd assumed he was out. The fact that he is actually here, squirreled away in the front room, feels like a snub. Does he know? Has my mother told him about Reuben and me? The secret is hovering between us. She can't look me in the eye because of it.

The Station Hotel has always been our go-to place. Dad likes the steak pie and my mother meets her friends in the coffee lounge every week. The scones are always freshly baked, apparently, and not reheated in the microwave. Arthur would approve. The place hasn't changed much since the heyday of steam, and the landlady (who, for some reason, Jane and I long ago christened the Bar Lady) is of a similar vintage.

'Do you remember when we came here for your eighteenth?' Jane says, as we browse the big menus, bound in burgundy leather. There's a spark of devilment in her smile, and I roll my eyes and smile back.

'Oh yes. I was mortified!'

Jane is chuckling now. 'Dad made a big thing of ordering you a "legal" wine, and the Bar Lady just looked at you with that *face!*'

I join in her laughter, mimicking the landlady's soft Highland lilt. '"I think you'll find that the young lady has been eighteen for the past two years!"'

'Of all the places to do your underage drinking . . .' Jane looks mock stern.

'Probably not one of my best ideas.' I gaze around the dining room. Everything is deep purple, from the velvet curtains to the flock wallpaper. The walls are dotted with rail-related oil paintings in gilt frames: steam locomotives, viaducts, handkerchief-waving Victorians. The paint looks wet and glossy in the subtle lighting. I take a sly peek at Jane. She looks hollowed-out. Her face is full of shadows. Reuben's name hasn't come up so far. Perhaps he'll become one of the many things my family aren't comfortable talking about. Despite our reminiscing, Jane has been distant with me. I've put it down to misery, but the alternative is too grim to contemplate. It occurs to me that I've run away from a confrontation with Mac to a potentially more painful one with my sister.

'I think I'll have the fish,' Mum says, closing her menu and laying it down on the white cloth. She's completely ignored the underage-drinking anecdote, and Dad is still browsing, even though everyone knows he'll choose the steak pie. I sip my Coke. Although I'm longing for a big slug of wine, I've deliberately chosen a soft drink. There are too many undercurrents, and I need to be able to swim.

'What are you having, Dad?' my mother prompts. I hate it when she does that. Why doesn't she call him Angus? A hundred vintage grievances boil under my skin.

'I see they have a lamb hotpot. That sounds nice, doesn't it? Hotpot.'

'Mmm. Hotpot.' Mum picks up her menu again and leafs through it. I grab a pale mauve serviette and spread it over my knees. I badly want to shred it.

'I think I'll just have the steak pie.' Dad closes the menu firmly. Jane catches my eye. Normally we'd share a sly giggle, but she remains unmoved. I catch sight of something in her gaze before it slides away. The serviette grows hot and sticky in my fist. I need air.

'I'm just going to the loo,' I announce, pushing back my chair.

Mum looks at me sternly. 'But we're just about to order. We don't know what you want.'

'Scampi and chips,' says Jane. 'Lucie always has scampi and chips.'

'That's right,' I agree. I'll have what I always have. It feels like some kind of statement.

Outside, in the car park, I light up a cigarette, one eye on the back door in case my mother should pop out unexpectedly. That won't happen, of course. She'll be too busy bitching about me, until the Bar Lady rocks up with her order pad and it will be all fake smiles and happy families.

Clamping the fag between my lips I rake in my handbag for my phone. I'd heard its insistent beep back at the table, and my mother had heard it too, glaring at my bag as if I was up to no good.

Two messages. The names flash up: *Reuben. Arthur.*

I click on Reuben first: *In Dundee, babe. Miss you. Want a visitor for old times' sake?*

Once, my heart, my gut and all the other bits of me that responded to Reuben would have grown hot at the very sight of his name. Now my critical self tries to decode what he's written. He's working away. He's bored. He wants sex. With a resolve I didn't know I had, I consign Reuben to the trash.

I click on Arthur's message: *Hope all going well up there. See you when you get back :)*

No hidden agenda. No demands. I hit reply. *Cheers. Just about to have scampi – could be worse.* My thumb hesitates. *See you soon.*

The door bangs behind me. It's Jane. 'What are you doing? Mum's freaking out in case you're not back in time for the food. Are you smoking? Seriously? She's not going to be happy about that either.'

I make a face and the fag wobbles in my mouth. 'I'm an adult. I don't give a shit what Mum thinks.' The words have a satisfying power. I add a smiley face to my text.

'Who are you texting?'

'Arthur the Baker Boy.'

'Oh really?' Jane peers at the screen, so close I smell her wine breath. 'See you soon? Is there something you want to tell me?'

My heart skips a beat. I add a kiss, just the one, and press send. I can't be sure if that's a loaded question, so I paste on a smile.

'Come on then, let's get this over with.'

I drop the phone into my bag and grind out the cigarette beneath the heel of my shoe. Jane follows me back into the building.

I'm lolling on my old single bed. Two days at home, and I've had to unzip my jeans to accommodate my bloated belly. My parents seem to have bread with every meal and cheese on toast for supper. Resting my palm on the place just above my pubic bone, I think of Reuben until the soft skin there blooms warm, and I feel a corresponding tug deep inside. Reuben slipping into my room, softly closing the door, reaching for me. His hand heavy in the place where my hand is, fingers sliding under the lace of my knickers, and me half-rising from the bed to meet his mouth, kissing him fiercely.

And my mother walking in with a pile of ironing.

My whole body cringes at the memory and I sit up, as if by moving I can dislodge the shame. I slide my feet to the floor, feel the chill of the old floorboards. My gaze swings around the dimensions of this tiny room. Once my sanctuary, and now what? It's never been allowed to change, this room. The duvet cover is a relic of my school days, soft cream with virginal pink roses. The walnut dressing table is festooned with cheap beads and scarves and dayglo nail polish. In the bookcase, *Harry Potter* and Roald Dahl gather dust alongside CDs of McFly, Girls Aloud and Good Charlotte (my little act of teenage rebellion). This room is all about the child me, the teenage me, as if I've packed up who I really am and taken her to Fettermore in my suitcase.

I get to my feet, observing the adult me in the mirror on my wardrobe door. My hair needs a trim. I smooth it all to one side so that it cascades over my left shoulder. Tilt my head and search my eyes. They look sad. A chill prickles the suddenly exposed part of my neck, and my belly, where my jeans are still flapping open. Instead of attempting to haul up the zip, I just tug down the front of my baggy T-shirt. The wardrobe is a dull, dark wood, the sort you'd find in an old-fashioned B & B. My parents have never done Ikea. Opening the door releases the smell of lavender from one of the many bags my mother buys from church fundraisers. I run my hand along the hangers of familiar clothes: skinny jeans, tiered skirts, dresses I've barely worn and, at the back, my school uniform – black trousers and a white shirt scrawled with adolescent last-day graffiti, the striped tie looped around the metal hook.

None of it fits any more. Not the uniform, not the jeans. Not this bedroom. Not this life.

The door opens a fraction. Jane's elegant fingers appear, followed by her face. A twist of a smile. 'Can I come in?'

I hoist up my jeans, tug my top down some more. 'Has Mum sent you up to get me?'

'Well, no, it's just that . . .'

'She can't leave me alone for a second.'

'She's made cherry trifle.'

'Ugh.' I flop down on the bed. I can still hear the crack of my mother's disapproving spoon on Reuben's trifle bowl. 'I'm *so* full. I couldn't eat another thing.'

'It's what we always do, isn't it? We always have a pudding when we have visitors.'

I lie back, picking at one of the fat pink roses on the duvet cover. 'I'm not a visitor. I'm still part of the family, aren't I?'

There's a distinct pause. 'Of course you are.' Jane's voice is sharp. She's still hovering on the threshold of the room, gripping the open door. New lines of disappointment are visible around her mouth, and I see a glimpse of a future Jane, a mature, harder

Jane. We still haven't really talked about Reuben. I get up, rummage in my bag for my purse.

'I'm going back in the morning, Jane. I'll check my ticket, but I'm pretty sure I got an open return.'

'You've only been here two days. We haven't had time for a chat.'

'Mac needs me. She has a deadline.'

'Let's skip the trifle then. Let's hole up with a bottle of wine.' Jane backs up a step, as if she's planning on zooming down to the fridge.

'I shouldn't . . .' I shake my head, but she's talking over me, bright and determined, as Jane always is.

'We haven't done that for ages, and . . . I need to tell you something.'

Christ. Something in me plunges to the ground. What? Is she seeing someone else? Is she pregnant? The idea cuts a swathe through my innards. As she slips away, I try to stop my imagination bouncing off the walls: Jane pregnant, a little piece of Reuben shrapnel burrowing into our future. *I need to tell you something.* At least she doesn't need to *ask* me something.

Jane returns with a bottle of chilled Chardonnay, gripping a pair of Waterford Crystal glasses by the stems. She bears a stern warning from Mother: 'We *must not* stay up here all evening, she says. It's anti-social.'

'Tough shit.' I take a glass from Jane, hold it by the stem as she splashes wine into it. The scent teases me, makes me long for dark nights and someone to hold. Arthur, maybe? She sweeps aside a porcelain trinket box and sets the bottle down on my dressing table, remaining there, her hips braced against the furniture, rather than lounging next to me on the bed. We used to lounge a lot as kids, swapping confidences, making jewellery, writing stories. In laying our bodies open to periods and spots and boyfriends, a coldness must have seeped in. And now I'm afraid to share anything with my sister, in case I let my guard down and the secret escapes.

'You've never asked about me and Reuben.' She swigs her wine in a most un-Jane-like way. An angry way.

I gaze at the carpet. 'I – I wasn't sure what to say. I didn't want to – add to your pain.' *Add to your pain?* Jesus, I sound like Jane Austen. I sound fake. A big fat fake.

Jane gives a harsh laugh. 'Believe me, you couldn't make it any worse.'

Oh, I could. I sip from the crystal glass. The rim is chipped and I feel the sharp, warning edge against my tongue. I swallow. Take a deep breath. 'So what happened, exactly?'

'This fucking happened.'

This is not good. Jane seldom swears; her language is teacher-perfect. She leans forward a fraction and produces a piece of paper from her back pocket. I take it from her and the plunging sensation gets so bad I can barely breathe.

It's folded into four neat squares. The creases are sharp, the paper smooth, warm from her body. When I open it out, it wants to cling to itself. I proceed carefully, as if this is an ancient, precious manuscript.

It isn't. It's my love poem, the one I scribbled in Mac's study with her husband's old pencil.

Scanning the first two lines, I go weak with horror. I recognise my own handwriting. I experience that sick jolt you get when you see the boy you've fancied for ages snog your best friend. Betrayal. I have betrayed myself.

Hot shameful sweat pools in my armpits, under my thighs. My top lip beads with it, and the wine glass in my hand grows slick. In my other hand, the red-hot note begins to shiver with a life of its own. In my head it is vibrating, like the papery wings of birds. It has its own music, singing my guilt. *This* will betray me.

Silence stretches out between us. My thoughts tumble over themselves. How did she get this? Hadn't I tossed it in Mac's bin? What's it doing here?

On my birthday, you wish me all the best,
and I act restrained,
as if I couldn't care less,
but inside
I am waiting for another chance to be alone
with you, to memorise you all over again.
That's still love, isn't it?

'What do you think?' she says eventually.

She's watching my reaction. And I, unable to lift my eyes from those mortifying scribbled lines, can only manage a weak shrug. Has she recognised my handwriting? I try to recall all the times she will have seen it – birthday cards, Christmas cards, school jotters – but my brain refuses to compute.

Jane makes an irritable move away from the dressing table, as if she can't bear to be still. She pauses beside the window, staring out, arms clasped tight about her body, her wine glass poised. Beyond her, the sky is growing dark, and the top branches of the apple tree bluster violently. As if by stealth, the season is changing; the year is drawing in on itself. She puts the glass down on the sill and hauls at the sash window with so much force I can see every muscle straining in her back beneath her striped Breton top. Evening air floods in. It smells bitter, like bonfire smoke.

'I knew it,' she's muttering. 'I knew it.'

I place my glass on the carpet, rest the paper on my knee. If I breathe slowly enough, my heart might stop banging. 'Knew what?'

She swings back to me. 'That he was seeing someone else! Didn't I say that? When I was staying with you? I told you I thought he was cheating on me.'

'You had no proof.'

'But I do now.' Triumph flares briefly in her eyes.

When did I write the poem? It's hard to think, skewered on

the end of my sister's rage. And how did she get it? Could she have gone into Mac's study and found it? There's only one way to find out.

'Where did you get this?' I smooth out the note across my sweaty thighs.

'I was in the car with Reuben, shortly before we broke up. I dropped my phone down the side of the seat. At first, I thought it was a receipt – maybe from a hotel or something – and I started thinking all kinds of crazy things. I was scared to look at it in case it was – oh, you know, a double room at a place where we'd never been together. Such a cliché, isn't it? But I was expecting something. After all my suspicions, I was waiting for something to blow my world apart. And it did. It's worse than any hotel.'

'Has Mum seen this?' It matters. Mum would certainly recognise my handwriting. Fresh waves of dread wash over me.

She scowls at me as if the question doesn't make sense. 'Don't you think she worries about me enough?' The 'me' pricks me like a needle. 'No, I haven't gone into any detail with her. I just said that it wasn't working out.'

'The best thing you can do with this' – I hold the note by a corner, as if it disgusts me – 'is destroy it. Burn it. You know, the ritual flame. Cleansing and all that.'

'Mmm.' She takes the paper from me, refolding it carefully, like a treasure map. 'Get rid of the evidence, you mean? Maybe. Or perhaps I'll just keep it for now. Something might come to light.'

Black letters form in the dark spaces. A nightmarish word search that won't keep still. I struggle to read the words, reciting them in my head like a child with a difficult book. I can't make out the meaning. And there's water, too; so much water, a deluge from above, and I realise I'm underneath the waterwheel. I can see the creaking elm buckets beginning to tip. I'm in danger. I need to get away, but I'm trapped in the wheel as it starts to move. I begin the clamber round the wheel, like a hamster or a rat.

I need to collect the words but they elude me, always just out of reach. The wheel is gathering pace and I can't climb down. I'm in a world of water and wood, of groaning and creaking and thumping. Gears and cogs whine in my ears, snap at my limbs. If I look down I can see blackness, and something else in the corner. Eyes. Blood-red and unflinching. The dark is gaining on me, and I'm out of my depth.

I wake gasping, as if I've surfaced from some cold, dark pool. The dream tastes rank in my mouth, like day-old bedside water. I sit up, scrabble for the lamp. The sudden light brands my eyes, and I press the heels of my hands tight against them. The cold has got into my bones and I'm shivering so much my teeth chatter. Jane must have left the window open and the breeze is tugging at the curtains.

Pushing back the jumbled covers, I pad across the cold floor. Rain coats the windowsill. I struggle to bring down the sash, to block out the elements. As I turn back to the bed I catch sight of wet footprints on the floorboards. For one terrifying moment I think they look like hoof prints, but not those of a horse – more like a cow or a goat, with that deep cleft between the two halves. The breath leaves my body. I can't look at them. I dive back beneath the duvet and will myself back to sleep. When I wake up, it's fully morning. Everything is dry. Everything is normal. I'm no longer sure of the division between waking and sleeping.

Jane hugs me at the station. It's unexpected and catches me off guard. I submit to her soft *pat pat* in the region of my shoulder blades, holding my chest, my belly apart from hers. I can smell shower gel and breath mints. Even for an early morning station drop-off she's thought about lip gloss and a selection of thin bangles. They jingle as she steps back and briefly drops her hand to mine.

'Take care, Lucie. Keep in touch.' My eyes slide away from hers. She's thinking things I don't want to see.

My train snakes into view. We watch it, falling silent as it crawls to a halt. Travellers surge forward. I pick up my bag, breathe in the diesel fumes, let myself be caught up in the urgency. Jane and I become separated, limit ourselves to safe waves and promises, and then I'm on board, alone, squeezed into a single seat beside the toilet. I keep my bag on my lap and close my eyes. As we depart, another voice, another tannoy: *This train is bound for King's Cross, stopping at . . .*

I have a sudden urge to stay put, to remain on the train and wash up in some strange, anonymous place.

But I know the mill hasn't finished with me yet. And neither has my sister.

Things have altered in my short absence. The track down to the mill seems narrower, the trees loom larger. Standing water shivers in the ruts, black as oil.

'We've had a lot of rain,' Arthur says, shifting down a gear. The car slops through the puddles. Long grass chafes the under-carriage, and I stare out of the window, my fingers knotting together in my lap.

I hadn't asked him to pick me up from the station. I'd ignored his last few texts, but he was there anyway, standing on the platform, eating a KitKat. 'You needn't have bothered,' I'd said, and he'd shrugged and reached for my little suitcase. Suddenly unburdened, I'd fallen into step beside him. He didn't ask how things had been. We didn't speak until we got to the car. Arthur had stowed away the case and closed the boot, and he'd turned to me and said, 'It's good to see you.' Nothing fancy; no expectations. Just the truth. My throat had closed up, tears building behind my eyes. When he opened his arms I bumped against his chest, letting him hug the breath from me. I hid my face in his shirt, escaped chest hair tickling my nose. I felt more at home than I'd done in a very long time.

We pull up in front of the cottage. It's only lunchtime, but everything looks dark, as if the light has gone somewhere else. The mill is brooding, its windows carefully blank. When I get out of the car I can hear the faint creaking sway of the wheel, the twitch of something not quite extinct. Arthur hears it too. He's unwound himself from the driver's seat, but he's still clinging to the door. He seems in a hurry to be off.

I look at the cottage, rummage in my handbag for the key. I don't really want to be alone, and I turn to him and smile stiffly.

'Do you want . . . a coffee?' As I'm saying it I'm remembering the slick heat of him in my bed, smooth skin, searching lips. He's remembering too. His eyes gleam hot and quick and when he grins back it makes my insides curl deliciously.

'Later, perhaps. I have to get back to the cafe.'

'Of course. Later then.' I watch him take my case from the boot. He sets it at my feet, pulls up the telescopic handle so that all I have to do is curl my fingers around it. I meet his gaze. 'Thank you.'

'You're welcome.' He kisses my brow. 'I've put some milk in your fridge. Ma would have done it but she's not very well, actually.'

'What's wrong with her? Is she pissed off with me because I left in a hurry?'

'She thought you'd gone for good.'

'It crossed my mind.'

'But something pulled you back.' He winks at me. He's hoping it was him, and I wish it was. But there's something more, something deeper at work here. I squeeze his arm and turn to go.

Even though I've been gone for only a couple of days, the cottage feels cold. There's a smell of sour milk and mildewed logs, and when I rest my hand on one of the chair backs, it comes away clammy. A primal urge to re-establish myself hits me, a need to take the place back. I make myself busy – switch on the heating, light an almond-scented candle, fill the kettle. The radio is soon blasting out chart music.

My favourite mug, abandoned in the sink, has been rinsed and placed upside down to drain. There's an unopened packet of digestives on the table. The fridge yields a carton of fresh milk, wafer-thin ham, some tomatoes and a couple of bridge rolls. Everything will be okay. Arthur thinks of everything. I take a deep breath, let it out slowly, relax my innards. It's okay. But something is niggling at me like a remembered headache.

The love poem. The study. How did that piece of paper get from the bin to the floor of Reuben's car? Logic tells me that Jane must have recognised my handwriting, that she's playing with me, enjoying watching me squirm. Then I go into denial, tell myself that the thick, clumsy pencil would disguise my true hand, and anyway, your writing alters over the years, like your politics or your dress size. I try to recall the last card I sent her. A birthday card, probably, with a brief greeting and my name scribbled in haste. No resemblance to any love poem I might have written . . .

I wander to my bedroom, full of memories of a few nights ago. The duvet, which probably still smells of Arthur, is turned down and the window ajar. My laundry is scattered around the floor and the bin is full. There are tissues and a condom wrapper beside the bed. My body floods with heat. Sighing, I sag against the windowsill.

The wind has changed. It's forcing its way in with an exasperated sigh, bringing with it the tang of wild green things. The great trees behind the mill breathe in and out in some mesmerising dance. Their light and shade flickers across my vision.

I'm bone-weary. I stretch out on the bed and find myself thinking about Mary Poppins, who could only ever stay until the wind changed. In my head I recite the lines from the film: *Wind's in the east, mist coming in, like somethin' is brewin', and 'bout to begin* . . . I adored Bert the chimney sweep; didn't care about his dodgy accent. I still love that film. Jane, who disapproves of the Disneyfication of literature, loved the books.

A memory comes to me: Mum sitting on Jane's bed, reading *Mary Poppins*. Jane is about six. Their heads are bowed, Mum's voice low and soothing, Jane cuddling her pillow. The glow from her My Little Pony lamp is as cheery as Christmas tree lights. I'm standing in the doorway, clinging to the handle, half-in, half-out of the room. I'd been sitting on the bed too, but I'm a fidget. I wasn't listening. I was spoiling the story. *If you can't behave, Lucie, then leave. Just go.* The china doorknob is sweaty beneath my hand. I want to twist it off, hurl it at them as hard as I can.

I close my eyes, swallow hard. Memories jumble into dreams.

Mac

Floss is the first to hear Lucie. I'm still in bed, although it's past noon; covers pulled up to my neck, with a hot water bottle at my back and the spaniel tucked into the well between my knees. I don't encourage the dogs on the bed. Beds are for humans, and there's nothing worse than a bottom sheet full of grit and dog hair. However, it's keeping her quiet. The other two are curled up on the rug.

I rose early to let them out, dissolving against the door frame in my insubstantial nightie as they rootled through the weeds in the kitchen garden. I still haven't found a man to do the garden; the rosemary is waist-high and you can't see a damn patch of soil between the nettles. Still, another month and it will all start to die back. The thought made me shiver. There's a change coming. I can feel it.

I boiled the kettle and filled a hot water bottle as I contemplated all my various niggles: lower back, right hip. My left armpit – was that glands, or something sinister? And the old ticker, of course, skipping away like a vintage clock powered by a cheap battery.

I let Floss up on the bed because she knows she shouldn't be there. It keeps her docile. She's afraid to sniff the sheets or lick her paws or wriggle around with a full bladder in case I remember that she's there and ditch her unceremoniously onto the floor. I hear Lucie coming up the stairs. She seems more hesitant than usual. Her steps are measured, almost reluctant, as if she knows I've rumbled her. She'd seemed such a quiet little thing. I have to be careful how I play this though – I suspect my son has a soft spot for her, and I don't want to antagonise Arthur, to cause a rift. Besides, we have unfinished business, Lucie and I. Time is marching on, and the miller's story is bursting to be told.

'I'm in bed!' I call out. My voice is pleasingly frail. I realise Lucie hasn't been up here before, but the door is open, and sure enough, the footsteps pause and her face appears. She looks glum.

'I'm not well, Lucie.'

'I know. Arthur told me.'

So she's seen Arthur already? This little intimacy makes me wince. The girl is unreliable, dashing off like that.

She checks out the room. It must seem very grey to her: dull velvet curtains, dusty furniture, worn-out carpet. Those huge, inherited mirrors, on the dressing table and the wardrobe, magnify the greyness and cast it into infinity. I can see myself in them; pale hair, pale skin, drab blankets, waiting to be cast heaven knows where.

Shy as a parlour maid, Floss beats the eiderdown with her tail until dust motes rise into the air. The girl comes to stand at the foot of my bed. She's wrapped in an oversized cardigan I don't recognise. Maybe she's been swapping clothes with Jane, and confidences, the way sisters do, and all the while she's been having it off with the boyfriend. I experience an intense burst of anger. I motion the girl closer, coughing as I struggle to sit up.

'You might get me some water. Or tea. I think I could manage a cup now. Very weak. Just milk.'

'All right.'

'And a biscuit. A water biscuit. They're in the bread bin. Better make it two. And a couple of slices of cheddar.'

She quirks her mouth at me in a way I don't like and then turns to leave.

'Wait a minute, missy.' I wonder if it's still going on, this affair with Reuben? 'Are you here to work? I can't have you running off like that.'

'It was a one-off. I'm back now.'

We'll see about that. I don't want her near my son, not now, knowing what she's capable of. I raise my voice, a little querulously. 'You did get my phone message, didn't you? You could have answered.'

'I did get your messages. All of them.'

What is that look she's giving me? Distrust? Suspicion? She's regarding me like Floss does sometimes, waiting for me to yell at her, or smack her with a rolled-up newspaper. But I'm not sure what I'm supposed to have done. Things are getting hazy. I decide to ignore it.

'So the notebook is in the study. You'll see the story has progressed. So let's get it typed up – chop-chop.'

'But first you want a cup of tea and a water biscuit with cheese?'

'*Two* water biscuits.' I wave her away. I try to recapture my concerns of a moment ago, but they've disspated like mist. I seem to lose the thread of my thoughts continually these days, while the past remains sharply in focus. 'Thank you, dear. It's so good to have you back.'

That doesn't ring true. There's a reason I don't want her back, but at this moment I can't quite grasp it. I settle more comfortably on my pillow and wait for my cup of tea and chocolate digestives.

Lucie

The house feels strange without Mac bumping around. I hadn't realised how much noise she makes. Even when I'm working in the study, I'm aware of her presence, her muttered conversations with the dogs and her off-key humming. She's either pottering from room to room with a blanket wrapped around her like a plaid, or she's busy in the kitchen, lumping dog food into earthenware bowls or scraping mud off her boots or banging the back door.

The house is too quiet, as if something has just left. I remember being a teenager, bunking off school, faking illness, everyone else going about their day. I remember the feeling of the house settling around you, sussing you out – the imposter.

I make tea, splodging the bag about for an extra three seconds, just as Mac likes it, and spread the water biscuits, licking butter from my thumb. For once, the dogs have not followed me, but still I feel like I'm being watched. The hairs on my forearms prickle. When I take up the snack, Mac is asleep, her head thrown back on the pillow. Floss fans her tail and looks up at me with pleading eyes, careful not to move too much. Mac's skin is translucent, her mouth slightly open, lips vibrating with a soft, purring snore. She looks vulnerable, not the sort of person who would leave all those weird messages on my voicemail. I place the mug and plate softly on the bedside cabinet and tiptoe downstairs.

I'd turned my phone off last night and gone to bed, anxious to separate myself from the rest of the world and what might be brewing with Jane. I'm almost willing my sister to see the light.

I'm waiting for an explosion, a reckoning – anything to end this torment. Unable to drift off for hours. I'd woken in the morning with the feeling that I'd spent the night caught in that hazy place between waking and sleeping. Feeling hungover and cranky, I'd switched on my phone to discover Mac had left endless voicemails. *Anna, I haven't seen you for ages . . . Anna, we have a lot of work to catch up on, chop-chop . . . Where are you? I really need you here . . .*

I listened to them all, poking at my Weetabix with a spoon, but unable to eat. What the hell was going on? Anna? Who's Anna? With each message the mood got darker and the tone more frantic until it no longer sounded like Mac's voice. That was the most chilling thing. I could hear the dogs barking frantically in the background, as if she'd shut them in somewhere.

Panic gripped me as I realised I'd just swapped one unbearable situation for another. Should I phone Arthur? He'd want to know, wouldn't he, if his mother was having a breakdown? In the end I'd tossed my cereal bowl into the sink, unable to make a decision.

Even now, back at work, I'm unable to focus. The study is freezing; I can see smoke-breath when I open my mouth. The smell is overpowering, a weird bouquet of damp woodland and dirty carpet. I wonder if one of the dogs has peed in here again. I mentally go through the motions of opening the solitary window, visualise clambering on the desk, shuffling through piles of crap. It's too much bother. Instead I stand there, paralysed, and after a few moments I realise I'm staring at the wastepaper basket.

Had I crumpled up the poem and chucked it in there? I rack my brains, but it's useless. I'd been upset, disturbed. You do things and then you don't remember them. Or had I held on to it, dropped it somewhere in the Miller's Cottage for Jane to find? Maybe Mac had fished the poem from the basket. Liked it, perhaps, and decided to keep it. But neither of those scenarios explain how it got into Reuben's car. Had I done that myself? Was my mind playing tricks? But given recent developments, maybe it's Mac whose mind is playing tricks. I'd been waiting all morning for a confrontation which never came. Maybe she'd been arguing with Reuben about something else entirely, but it seems unlikely. Either she's had a mental lapse about the whole situation, or she's biding her time, waiting for me to crack. Maybe she's sending me subliminal messages through the Cruel Sister story, playing with me until I finally confess and leave for good. I can't escape the notion that Mac has an axe to grind, although I can't quite see what connection it has with me. And Anna. Who the hell is Anna?

Sighing, I turn my attention to the desk. There are at least six jotters scattered across the surface, vying with electricity bills, invoices and newspaper cuttings for space and attention. The mess has blossomed like hogweed. There are yellowing recipes clipped from old newspapers, receipts for grain going back to the eighties. One black corner of the laptop pokes out from under the debris.

Sighing, I pull it out, and the crap collapses like a tower of Jenga blocks. Dumping the computer on the chair, I gather up a collection of random notebooks and loose pages from the floor. I flick through each jotter, a bad habit of mine. I've always been hungry for other people's writing. I've read Jane's diary, attempting to assess her relationship with Reuben. I've read and re-read his texts to me, trying to second-guess him. I even scour Arthur's menu, in the hope of uncovering what he's really trying to sell. And now the tables have turned. My writing has fallen into the wrong hands. My sister's hands.

I follow Mac's frantic scrawl through several books, trying to piece it together, realising that she's been scribbling the story of the Cruel Sister on anything that's come to hand. I open book after book. The tale of the Cruel Sister has cut loose. It's rambling, disjointed – spilling like ivy over every scrap of paper, dark tendrils reaching for me, wrapping around my wrists, my arms, up to my throat.

'You bring me a gift and yet I don't know you.' Bella cannot take her eyes from the stranger. Her imagination is lost in the black folds of his cloak. The hall spins away; her father, her mother, her new husband and the babble of the wedding party. 'I do not know you.'

'If you don't want my gift, then I will go.'

As suddenly as that, in the blink of an eye, the stranger picks up the jute sack and strides away. She hears the slither of his cloak across the threshold and the bang of the hall door. He is gone.

The bride runs after him, flowers falling from her hair. She follows the scent of him, one of fields, old hay and dung; of gunpowder and something she can't quite recognise. Something stagnant and sickening, like water that has been stopped up for too long.

I place the laptop gently on the floor and sink onto the chair, clear desk space for my elbows and allow my head to sink into my hands.

Where on earth do I begin to find an ending?

Lucie

August

The fluttering starts low down in my belly. It twists and blooms; the *thrip thrip thrip* of beating wings. Beating wings, beating heart. Discordant fluttery notes vibrating through my bones. I jerk awake. I can hear the stop-start stirrings of the sparrows in the ivy. The window is open a crack, and the fresh scent of dawn lures me.

We are still wrapped up in each other, Arthur's arm around my back, cradling me to him. I press a kiss into the hollow of his throat and raise my head. I need to disentangle myself. Under the duvet our legs are a jumble, and even though he's still asleep, his arm tightens around me when I move. His damp penis grows hard against my thigh. My head is full of the night. Not the sex, not the feel of him inside me, but the intimacy; the gentleness of his hands on that lost place. The place that is no longer lost, but full.

It is too much. Too soon. Stealthily, I retreat, letting the cold air seep in around us, two separate beings once again. I slip from the bed and pull on some clothes, pad through the silent chill to the back door. Jamming my feet into borrowed wellies, I let myself out into the dawn.

The mill looks unusually mellow, the stone stained pink, the black trees behind it haloed in red. Raucous crows jostle and bully each other. Up ahead, on the track, a large dog fox slinks about his business. On a sudden impulse I climb the boundary wall and drop down silently into the field.

There is a path of sorts, dividing the weedy margin – hawthorn and nettles and docks – from the crop. It's barley, I can see that now. That last time, when the sky was low with rain and mist, only the green edge of it was visible, but now acres and acres lie before me. A vast tawny fur, shifting in the breeze, and beyond that the sea. It's tipping over into full, golden ripeness. Not long now. The tall, fibrous stalks are straight as soldiers, and there's a sharp edge to the path, where the plough scored the earth just six months ago. Only six months ago I'd arrived here, intent on breaking new ground.

Goldfinches dart in and out of the hawthorn. Their wings go *thrip thrip thrip* against the leaves, a noise like someone plucking strings. It unnerves me. I should go back, but I'm mesmerised by the rise and fall of the barley – it's like the whole field is breathing. I want to plough into it, feel it surround me. But instead I take a step back and fall heavily over the plough rut.

I feel the fall in every part of me: my jaw, my nose, my teeth, my buttocks. I lie there, stunned. Black is creeping in. I don't know if my eyes are open but I can't see the light, just the nodding ears of barley; whiskers scraping my face like fingernails, jabbing my lips.

The barley is burned. Gold has tipped over into russet and the sun is hot. I see yellow at the edge of my vision, the lazy trail of silk through the field. *The mill. We must go to the mill.* A child laughs. I struggle to sit up, but dizziness overwhelms me, and I'm coughing, spitting feathers of barley from my mouth.

But he'll be there. The miller will be there.

Don't be afraid.

I must swim to the surface, choking in the black water. I must come up for air – find the voices. Yellow silk brushes my skin, the scent of lavender and smoke and candle wax.

Bella, don't leave me with the miller . . . Bella . . .

I sit upright with a huge gasp. My head feels twice as heavy as it should and I have to hold it in my hands as I scan the field.

The meadow is empty, a vast swathe of near-ripeness, the only sound the soft swish of its breathing. I try to pull together the frayed edges of what happened but it's all falling away.

Embarrassment overwhelms me. Falling and banging your head – it's a childish mishap, or something an old lady might do. I scramble to my feet, wincing and clutching all the bits that feel jarred, disjointed: my belly, my right elbow. For a moment I can't get my bearings. The barley field has turned into a skein of wool; I'm knitted into it and stumbling over the threads, the rows and ruts of the land.

I can hear barking a long way off. It gives me something to fix on, and I follow it, scrambling over the stone wall and finding myself once again on the familiar track that leads to the mill. What the hell am I doing? It's Sunday morning. I should be in bed with Arthur right now, waking up to a kiss and maybe more, looking forward to a leisurely breakfast. I imagine him wearing my purple robe, knocking up pancakes and listening to Radio 2. That's all he wants, to be with me, to look after me. It should be simple.

When did I start making *normal* so complicated?

Everything aches. I could have broken a leg out there, been lying for hours, and Arthur would have been frantic. He's got enough to cope with, with the way his mother is at the moment. Splinters of a story jab at me: yellow fabric, the scent of candles. Have I been sleepwalking? The sky is brightening into full daylight. The mill is still in shadow. The barking is getting louder. Floss is standing by the old shed that houses the waterwheel, and even from a distance I can see the outline of her slight body heaving with the effort of making her voice heard.

I hear the scrape of the cottage door and Arthur comes into view around the corner. 'Floss,' he's saying. 'Pipe down.' His voice is low, as if he's afraid of waking up the world. He isn't wearing my robe, but his feet are jammed into some ridiculous pink flip-flops, long discarded in the utility room. His shirt is flapping open and his glasses must have been left in the bedroom. He squints slightly when he catches sight of me. It's cute. A surge of something hopeful takes my breath away.

'Where have you been? I was getting worried. Are you okay?'

No, I'm not okay. I want to talk to you about the past, about how it always has a hold on the present, no matter what you do. It's waiting there, just out of sight. It's waiting to take over. But I don't know how to start such a conversation. I stretch my lower back against my hands and wince.

'What is *wrong* with that fucking dog?'

Arthur's attention is diverted. He crouches down at the bottom of the cottage steps and slaps his thighs and makes encouraging noises in Floss's direction. She stops barking and creeps from the shadow of the wheelhouse. She looks thin, battered, and she's panting in a stressed sort of way. I suppose life, for dogs, is a constant dreamlike existence, living in the present moment, feeling your way through a jumble of impressions: sights, sounds, smells.

I crouch down too and the dog slinks between us, troubled seal eyes searching our faces. I fondle one ear and she licks my wrist.

'She's probably been chasing rats.'

I make a face. 'Ugh. I hate rats.'

'They tend to nest under the wheel,' Arthur says. 'There's a pit beneath it, and an inspection tunnel that runs underground from the wheel to the burn.'

'Really?'

'Yes. I'll let you see it one day. If you wade into the burn, you'll see an old iron gate. You can walk into the tunnel from there, right into the wheelhouse. It's quite a feat of engineering, but only Ma goes in there now, to put down rat poison.'

'I hate water. I think I'll pass.'

'Probably wise.' Arthur straightens up, adjusts his jeans. Floss still looks miserable, so I stay a moment longer, running my hands over her soft coat. She's trembling from head to foot.

'I never go near the place. It stinks down there, once the poison starts to work and the rats start dying off.'

I hold up a hand. 'Enough, thanks. So does Floss do this a lot? Bark at nothing?'

'Dunno. Like I say, I don't come down here if I can help it.' Arthur casts a bleak look at the silent mill. 'And when I do, I'm either rescuing Ma or . . . well, let's just say I have a new reason to visit.'

I move closer to him, and he reaches out, kisses me on the mouth – a soft, butterfly kiss – and I lace my arms around him, hold him tightly. Floss nudges my knee and whines, but we're no longer listening.

Mac

Precise details of the reduction process of bones can be hard to find. Typically, the bones were first boiled to make them brittle and to remove the fat. The fat would be skimmed off, and used for such things as coach and cart grease. More primitively, the bones would be burned to achieve the same effect. They would then be either chopped by hand or put through a toothed cylinder. Either process would reduce the bones to smaller, more manageable pieces. In the final process, the millstones powered by the waterwheel would grind the bone to dust.

Anita sets a glass of something steamy in front of me. I snatch my papers away from it and tap the vessel with my pencil.

'What's this?'

'It's chai, with steamed milk. It's very . . . settling.' She smiles, but doesn't look at me, just sweeps some crumbs from the table into her elegantly manicured hand.

'Didn't I ask for coffee?' It's not a complaint. I really cannot remember.

'You told me you hadn't been sleeping well after your recent illness.' She glances at the wall clock. 'It's after four. Maybe a break from caffeine might help. Chai contains spices – cardamom, cinnamon, ginger . . . all very warming and soothing. It promotes a sense of wellbeing. Try it.'

'Has Arthur put you up to this? He has, hasn't he? He thinks I'm going doolally. What tosh! I'm a very busy woman, and I've been missing in action for a week. I have things to catch up on. Deadlines. Good heavens!'

'Try it,' she says, with just a hint of frost. She walks away, swinging her tea towel and I take a sip, face already puckered in anticipation of such rancid foreign muck. But it's surprisingly pleasant, warm and spicy. I dash away the froth from my lip and turn back to my papers.

'You'll be interested in this, Anita.' I raise my voice so that it carries across the cafe. At an adjacent table, a couple are tucking into something that smells of sausage. They look like ramblers, with matching blue cagoules draped over the backs of their chairs.

Politely, Anita returns to my side, her face like that of a poker player.

'Bones.' I indicate the notes spread across the table. 'That's your bag, isn't it? I bet you didn't know that at one time the country was full of bone mills. They spread it on the land, you see. Bone meal. We still use it today, although I had to stop my gardener spreading blood and bone meal. Tremendously pungent stuff – used to drive the dogs bonkers.'

'Is this to do with your story, the one Lucie is typing up?'

'Not at all. This is cold, hard fact. We had bone mills all over the place, for processing animal bone. Dundee revolved around the whaling industry, you see. Think about whalebones – used for corsetry, of course, but nothing was ever wasted. And there was cash in it. We used to have rag-and-bone men here. They'd go around the houses with their carts, collecting old clothes, dead dogs . . .'

Anita pulls a face. 'My only interest in bones is anthropological and forensic.' She bundles up her tea towel and turns to go. Piqued at losing her attention, I rap the table.

'You can mill *human* bones, girl!'

The other diners look up. Anita glances briefly towards the kitchen, as if she'd rather be there than here.

'You can grind human bones?' she repeats.

'Fee-fi-fo-fum!' I deliver this with the aplomb of Brian Blessed. 'I smell the blood of an Englishman! Be he alive or be he dead, I'll *grind his bones to make my bread!*'

The ramblers are arrested in the middle of their fry-up. The man – an Englishman, perhaps? – lays down his knife and fork and looks around for back-up. I spy their wholemeal soda bread, one of Arthur's specialties, and point to it, laughing uproariously.

'I'd check out the origins of that flour, if I were you!'

Arthur replaces Anita at my side. His face is rosy from the oven. He is not smiling.

'I think we've all heard enough, Ma.'

'But it's part of our history. I visited a bone mill in Norfolk a few years ago, and in the 1800s they actually rendered down exhumed skeletons imported from Germany. Can you imagine the outcry if we did that now?'

'Enough.'

'"One ton of German bone-dust saves the importation of ten tons of German corn." That was the maxim.' The gentleman at the next table is glaring at me, and I wonder vaguely whether he might be a German tourist.

Arthur picks up the nearest piece of A4. I can see my scribbles projected through the back as he holds it up, as if I've been writing with a stabbing, urgent passion. Have I? His face creases as he scans it. The lamplight bounces off his trendy specs, so I cannot read his thoughts.

'Is this to do with your collection of stories? It's gruesome.'

'History is gruesome, son. We don't progress by being nice to each other.'

He replaces the paper in front me. 'Are you sure you're well enough to be out, Ma? Let me run you home.'

'If that's your clumsy way of getting rid of me, don't bother. I will get home under my own steamed chai, thank you very much.' I shuffle my papers together and drain the last of the drink. Perhaps they've put something in it, to calm me down? I think of the pills I still have in my bedside drawer. I must get rid of them. History is predicated on evidence. I must put them down the loo. Flush them into fertiliser.

'I just think you've been overdoing things.' Arthur's tone softens, but I brush it away, busy packing my notes and pens and books into my holdall. I get stiffly to my feet.

'Well, I'm up and about now, but I'll go and have an early night, if that will make you happy. No doubt Anita's concoction will put me out like a light.'

Arthur is distracted. He's gazing out of the window and I can see his eyes clearly now. They gleam with that rare warmth that manifests when you catch sight of someone you love. I once caught Jim gazing with that sort of warmth at Anna bloody Madigan. I want to warn him off, but I know he won't want to hear what I have to say about women like this. I confine myself to a hard stare as the girl crashes through the door, but she doesn't even notice.

She always seems so distracted, as if her head is full of thoughts she's bursting to share – but she never does. Even after all these months, Lucie remains a closed book. To me, at least. Perhaps she opens up to Arthur, which is a worry. I'm not quite sure how far this relationship has gone.

'I'm just going,' I say pointedly. She looks suddenly awkward, as if she's not sure of her welcome. I put on my coat and leave, lugging the heavy bag along with me. I've taken my eye off the ball. Things are definitely progressing between the two of them, I can tell. I feel a loss of control which makes me all too aware of my own pressing and very mortal deadline.

Mac

September

There's a nip in the air now. I'm used to shivering in big woolly cardigans, but Arthur chides me for not putting the heating on. I refrain from pointing out that the walls here are so thick, the window frames so crumbly, that the cast-iron radiators barely make a dent in the chill. Far better to keep to one room and make yourself as warm as you can.

In the front room, I assume a prayer position on the hearthrug and build a fire in the draughty grate. First, twist greasy old newspaper into fat croissants; next, add a firelighter that makes your fingers stink of paraffin; build a little tent of kindling, paper-white slivers of pine and ash. Always keep your axe sharp for the kindling. Don't leave it embedded in the block – the sap will rust the edge. Chopping kindling with a good, sharp axe should be effortless, like slicing through a Viennetta.

There's something timeless about building a fire. It's a meditative act. I could be my mother going through these motions, or my grandmother. You can stand outside of yourself, watch your fingernails turn black with soot, let the flames warm your innards as well as your extremities. I've given up on my extremities, to be honest. The old ticker has forgotten how to pump blood and I've been reduced to wearing fingerless woollen gloves when I write.

My notebook is balanced on the arm of the leather armchair. I slant a waspish eye at it. I can hear the miller's voice, critiquing my every word: *That's not how it was. You have the details all wrong, old woman.*

'I'm doing my best,' I tell him.

Sometimes I think I should like to chuck the damn notebook on the fire. Watch it curl and blacken and ignite. You'd hate that, wouldn't you, my friend? You're desperate to have your voice heard. His voice is in my head all the time now, until sometimes there is no space for anything else.

The dogs bring all manner of slobbery sticks into the kitchen, abandoning them as soon as treats are produced. Their offerings invariably find their way into the kindling basket. I snap bits of ancient willow into pieces, strike a match with damp, grubby fingers, observe the flame lick around the paper, take hold, burst up through the twigs. The bleached withies are like bones, human ribs, poking out of the darkness, hissing and spitting and succumbing.

I make it back to the armchair, my knees and feet protesting mightily. Pick up the notebook and my pencil.

Lucie

Since the weather changed, Mac has taken root in her sitting room, pulling her battered leather armchair as close as she dares to the hearth. She sits there for ages, feeding the fire with bits of twig and old magazines. The log basket has somehow been supplemented with chair legs and broken pictures frames, and once I walked in to find her tearing pages from an old diary – 1997. She was watching the whole year go up in flames, one day at a time.

I'm about to leave after yet another day of editing, of dusting, of sifting through the debris of someone else's life. I've started locking away all the notebooks, just leaving her the black, hard-backed one, in the hope that she'll actually write in it.

I knock gently on the door. I know Mac is in there, but there's no answer. I'm about to turn the handle when I hear her, deep in conversation. The dogs are in the kitchen, but I've been pestering Arthur to arrange a GP visit. Maybe the doctor has popped in, and we can get to the bottom of her erratic behaviour. Mac's GP is old-school, a man with a waxed moustache, a knowing twinkle and bad breath. I met him one day in the cafe and made a mental note never to ask for him in the event of thrush, cystitis or anything below the neck.

Now, however, relief makes my shoulders sag. I wait, ear pressed to the pine panels. There's a short silence. Mac starts up again.

'She fell asleep. Out like a light. I tucked her up on the very couch you're sitting on. No, don't move, dear. You look very like her. Must be the red hair.'

There's another silence. My hand grips the brass knob. The hairs on the back of my neck prickle. A new unpleasant word unwraps itself in my head: *evidence*.

'She was guilty as charged. Blame will find you in the end. There's always one bird that starts off the dawn chorus. The bird with the most persistent song gets people to listen. You can never hide from blame, Bella.'

I burst through the door. The sofa is empty. There is no one here apart from Mac. She's perching on the edge of her leather armchair, stoking the fire with pages from a children's picture book. She regards me with surprise.

'Anna? What are you doing here?'

Mac

After Lucie left, I came across a photograph frame at the bottom of the log basket. I don't know how it got there. The glass is cracked right across but it's otherwise intact, a Sunday-best smiling family group.

I blow the sawdust off and trace the faded faces with my finger. It was taken outside the Miller's Cottage, our home for many years before Jim's parents died and we inherited this sad pile. Perhaps Jim senior was the photographer that day. There's my mother-in-law, Patsy, seated at the front with the baby on her knee. She's beaming, the proud grandma. And behind her stand Jim and myself, close together, arms touching, as if nothing could come between us. Arthur would be about eight months there. Patsy passed away when he was a toddler. What a sad loss. How I missed her help and sage advice. We enjoyed a special relationship, Patsy and I, as you do when you love the same man.

There's a stinging irony there. Anna Madigan loved that same man too, though our relationship could hardly be described as special.

I let my mind drift back to that bitter confrontation.

Christmas Eve, 1997. The turkey is in the oven, Arthur's Nintendo carefully wrapped and hidden away. I am feeling neither festive nor full of goodwill. I snatch my keys from the satsuma bowl, gun my Volkswagen into gear and head for Dundee.

Anna Madigan opens the door and we're face to face for the first time in months. I'd been wondering why her social invitations had stopped. Now I know. I wipe my feet fiercely on her doormat and push my way inside. Her house is neat magnolia. There are no draughts, there's no dog hair. Everything is carefully cushioned with fabric; the soothing tones of some carol concert echo from another room. Anna Madigan's ginger mop is all over the place, as if she just got out of bed, and my gut twists.

'Where is he?' My gaze swings to the staircase, follows the line of each beige Axminster step.

'I don't know what you mean.' Her skin is pale, freckled. Not a hint of a flush.

'I think you do.' We are eyeball to eyeball. Her brows have a bold arch to them. *'Where is my husband?'*

'He isn't here.' She gives a small, slightly victorious smile and I want to knock her perfect teeth in. But I believe her. I don't think he is here. We probably passed on the road – he'll have gone home to wrap up my non-stick pans. I've left the oven on, and I fleetingly hope he checks on the turkey.

But I've spied something else, a carefully concealed glint at the neckline of her blouse. Like her smile, it is victorious, and I reach out and grab it, yank the sapphire pendant from her white neck, snapping the chain. She squeals. I snarl words of abuse and we tussle for Jim's gift of love.

She wins. Triumphantly, she stuffs the evidence into the back pocket of her tailored slacks.

'I found the receipt for this in his wallet, you . . . you *shameless whore*! I knew it!'

'Oh, that's sad – such a cliché!' she sneers.

I've suddenly had enough of her. I feel weak, but I have to have the last word. *'You* are such a cliché, madam,' I tell her, as I let myself out, quietly. 'And you're prepared to put up with it. That's the saddest thing of all.'

I place the photograph gently on the mantelpiece and lean in closer, despite the fire's fierce heat. It depicts the sealed family unit I want: never to age, never to betray each other. Never to grow sick and die. Never to stop loving. How I wish we could all be protected under glass, like tender plants. A single cool tear tracks its way down my heated cheek.

All I can do now is protect the living, protect Arthur. He doesn't deserve to be hurt, and that would most certainly be on the cards if he throws in his lot with that girl. It's not going to happen – not on my watch. The thought stiffens my spine. I may have been sadly lacking as a mother, but it's never too late to make amends. I can make up for all the times I neglected him. Poor Jim, waiting for me to spare some time for him. I never realised how lonely he was. But Anna did. There's always an Anna or a Lucie waiting for you to take your eye off the ball. I suddenly sweep the old photograph from the mantelpiece, snap off the sides of the frame and feed them into the fire. A movement on the sofa catches my eye.

'Don't look at me like that!' I toss the photo into the flames. The glass bursts and the faded photo curls into tongues of blue. 'You're about to get your comeuppance too.' I tug the black notebook out from where it has lodged itself in the side of the armchair and hold it aloft. 'The bird of blame will sing its song for you in the end, Bella.'

Lucie

I traipse back to the cottage. It's only four thirty, but the light has that wintery quality that makes people turn up their collars and moan about the nights drawing in. As I hit the mill path, Floss appears from nowhere, tongue lolling, bits of undergrowth sticking to her fur. She looks overjoyed to see me. I fumble in my coat pocket for my phone and she wags her tail.

'No biscuits,' I tell her. 'Come home with me and I'll smuggle you a Hobnob.'

I have a text from Arthur: *Busy day. Just cashing up. Fancy some pecan brownies?* He just can't help himself and it makes me chuckle.

I text back: *Maybe. But we need to talk about your mother.*
I know.

I feel suddenly cold, and button up my jacket.

Floss has raced on ahead. As I emerge into the mill den and head towards the cottage, I can see her at the waterwheel, staring through the iron grill. Her head is slightly tilted, as if she's waiting for it to move, and she pretends not to hear me calling her, even when I mention biscuits.

'Floss! Come on, it's getting cold.'

I walk over to her. The steady flow of the diverted water fills my ears but there's nothing to see; the wheel remains motionless. On a sudden whim, I head for the bridge behind the mill. Its walls are short and stout; Mac told me once that it was built with stone appropriated from much older buildings that once stood here. I've no idea what the buildings were: tumbledown cottages, perhaps, or the village inn, or the bakehouse, or the church. The place has a timeless quality; I can see the past in layers all around me, and the bits I can't see are buried in silt, just out of sight.

If I lean over the bridge, just a little, I can see the brown swirl of the burn far below, and the meeting place where the lade hurries from the wheel to join it. Downstream, the dippers bob from bank to boulder. If I lean a little more, I can see the entrance to the tunnel that Arthur was telling me about. Curiosity creeps up out of nowhere. I have a sudden, irrational urge to investigate, even though my hatred of water makes me hold back. I'd have to clamber into the burn and walk under the bridge, but it can't be that deep.

Floss nudges my knee. I glance down at her. 'Want to go walkies?' She wags her tail and smiles at me in the way dogs do.

It takes me five minutes to nip back to the cottage and don my wellies. We have to go upstream, a good bit past the mill, to find a place where the bank is low enough to clamber into the burn. Floss plunges into the water like a duck, but I have to summon all my courage to follow. I plod through the shallows, breathing hard, boots sliding on the pebbly riverbed. Several times I nearly lose my footing, and I start to panic, but Floss's enthusiasm drives me on. I stagger under the cavernous stone arch of the bridge, until we come to the place where the waters meet.

Floss is belly deep in water, barking at the tunnel, but I have to take my time wading through the strong undercurrent. The eddy coils around my wellies like a serpent, and Mac's stories have never seemed so alive. It's easy to imagine kelpies and trolls and other strange beasts on an evening like this, when the light is fading. It's easy to imagine that something is watching from the high, dusty windows of the mill.

Floss begins to whimper. The iron gate that seals off the mouth of the tunnel is heavy and resolute.

Mac

I need to keep an eye on Lucie. I'm not sure why she's being so odd with me. Does she know I've guessed her dirty little secret? I bet she's in my cottage right now, getting her claws into my son. I can't have that. I just can't. I leave the fireside, closing the door of the sitting room firmly. The phone on the hall table explodes into life just as I'm leaving the house. It's one of those horrid digital affairs that sits bolt upright in its cradle, and the ringtone jangles my nerves. I dither, half-in, half-out of the front door, irritated by the notion that it's probably someone wanting to sell me a new boiler. Or maybe it's Arthur. Sighing, I let the door swing shut and snatch up the handset.

'Yes, what is it?'

The caller clears his throat. 'Hello there, Margarita. It's Doctor Mackay here – um, Henry.'

'Hello, Henry. Is everything all right? Did you get my latest test results?' My heart beats a little faster. My hand grips the phone.

'No, no. Everything's fine, Margarita – um, Mac.'

The good doctor obviously can't decide whether this is a social call or a professional one. I decide to help him out. 'Did Arthur ask you to call me?'

A beat or two of silence. 'We did have a few words, last time I nipped in for a latte, yes. The thing is, Mac – the thing is, he seems to think you are a little . . . stressed. Do you think that could be the case?'

I suppress a tight smile. 'Well you know how it is, Henry. Publisher's deadlines and so on. I expect I've been a little short with him recently. My head is full of my work in progress.'

I press the phone closer to my ear. I hear him grunting in agreement, swallowing loudly – no doubt swigging a little afternoon brightener. 'Of course, my dear woman. We all get a bit tetchy at times, but if you have any concerns, any concerns at all, don't hesitate to –'

'And how are you, Henry? How's the golf?'

'Oh, still playing a round, you know!' He gives a leery laugh.

'And how's Kitty? I hear she's been made president of the Horticultural Society. Bad business about the treasurer. I always suspected he took too many holidays.'

'Oh, a bad business.' He clears his throat again, takes another gulp of his firewater. 'Pleased to hear you're keeping abreast of things, though. Jolly good.'

We wrap up the conversation and I drop the phone back into its cradle. Arthur and the doctor are obviously in cahoots. How dare they check up on me? Imply that I'm not the full shilling? Damn cheek.

I let myself out of the front door. I need to find Lucie. I hope Bella won't follow me. She's really getting on my nerves.

Lucie

I test the iron gate with both hands, as if I'm an inmate trying to escape. It won't budge, but flakes of rust fall like dandruff into the swiftly moving current. Floss whines impatiently. I peer into the darkness. I can just make out the barrel vault of the stone ceiling before it peters out into solid darkness. There is no light at the end of this particular tunnel. The air smells rank and earthy and I'm quite glad the gate's locked.

'Looking for something, dear?'

The unexpectedness of Mac's voice makes me reel back in surprise. She's directly above me, leaning on the parapet, looking down as I had done just thirty minutes before. The odd, steep angle alters her appearance. She looks unfamiliar, her face half in shadow. Puffier, older, darker. Her hands blend with the stone, become part of it. Gargoyle claws. My heart, already alarmed, starts up a steady bass thump.

I back up a few steps, the water welling around my boots, threatening to tip me off balance. Floss deserts me, scrambling up the steep bank and flattening herself like a cat as she melts into the undergrowth. I can hear the angry chirruping of a bird downstream, but other than that, silence stretches out between us.

'Floss has been barking at the wheelhouse, so I just thought I'd have a look for the inspection tunnel.'

Mac smiles, and the shadows creep up to her eyes. 'Just rats, dear. Just rats. They nest under the wheel. I have to put down poison. Such a damn nuisance.'

I retreat further. Mac has the height advantage and I don't

like it. I feel intimidated. 'Do you want to have a look?' she offers. 'I can fetch the key?'

The dense black of the tunnel yawns in front of me. I've had enough of the cold, swirling water. I need to get out. I shake my head, begin to retreat. 'Another time, maybe.'

That night I hear the now familiar crying. Half asleep, I creep through the silent house and let the little dog in. She bolts into my bedroom and burrows into my back as soon as I lie down. She stinks of river water and nettles, but I'm too exhausted to care. I wrap the duvet round us both and eventually her soft doggy snores kick in. Her entire body twitches from time to time, and I can't decide whether she's chasing dream rats or trembling.

'There's something going on with your mother.'

Arthur lifts his gin and tonic. The cardboard mat sticks to the bottom of the glass, and I peel it off, mopping at the scarred tabletop with a serviette. I pick up my own glass of soda water; the ice chinks and the slice of lime pops up to the surface like an exotic fish.

'Are you sure you don't want a wine?' asks Arthur, wiping his mouth.

'Too much to do.' I'm already rooting through my bag, hauling out jotters and sheaves of paper and piling them onto the dry bits of the table. 'I don't even know where to start. She's talking to herself. Her study is a *mess,* and she's been writing the story in different books and stuff. This is her original notebook.' I hold up the black hardback. It's dusty and dog-eared. 'This is what I've been working with. It contains all the folk tales that she wants to include in her new book, but halfway through "The Cruel Sister", she's suddenly gone off on a tangent. It's like the story got away from her. Look . . .'

I pick up an exercise book and open it. Mac's scribbles disappear off the page. Arthur takes it from me and reads.

'"The yard is dark. The cloaked figure is some way off, and by the light of a full moon" – Jesus, there's always a full moon – "Bella can see the tracks that he has made in the dirt. She follows the trail of the stranger's boots in the earth, thinking about the jute sack, wondering what's in it. She looks at the footprints without seeing the very thing that should have sent her running back into the hall . . ."'

There the writing peters out. Arthur glances up. 'What? What is she not seeing?'

I choose another notebook, spiral-bound with red tulips on the cover. I've been through them all. Silently he takes the book from me and reads on.

'"The footprints are not solid like the prints of a normal man. Each one is distinguished by a deep cleft that runs from toe to heel."' The writing stops, and Arthur stops too. 'What is this guy? And where's the rest of the story? This is the ultimate cliffhanger.'

I produce a third book. This one is a reporter's notebook full of meaningless calculations and meter readings. There's a shopping list too: potatoes, spring onions, Winalot. I flick through until I find a few more paragraphs of narrative and read them out loud.

'"The stranger stops, as if he can feel her eyes on him. 'Who are you?' Bella wants to know. 'You seem familiar . . .' The man pushes back his hood. The shadows about his face remain, as if they have always been there. His eyes are the fathomless black of river pebbles. Bella gasps. 'I do know you. You're the miller!' He does not reply. Instead he asks the girl a question; a question she does not want to answer. 'Tell me. Did you drown your sister in the millpond?' Lucie remains tight-lipped. Her eyes grow as black as his. 'That,' she says, 'I will never tell.'" *Lucie*? What the hell am I doing in there? What's she trying to say?'

Arthur scratches his head. 'A misprint, obviously. Secrets never to be told. Where's the rest of it?'

'Do you think she's guessed, about me and Reuben? She

must have. That's why she's writing all this stuff, about secrets and sisters and betrayal.' I wave at the books. 'I'm still piecing the rest of it together.'

I'm haunted by the fear that my secret is about to be exposed. I cannot sleep for it. I am both the dark older sister and the golden child entangled in the waterweed. But that anxiety has been overshadowed by something else. I slip an old newspaper cutting from my pocket. It's yellow and criss-crossed with knife-edge creases from being folded between the pages of *The Scottish Miller's Tale*.

'You need to see this. What do you know about Anna Madigan?'

My question catches Arthur off guard. He takes a sip of his drink; frown lines gather above his spectacles. 'She and her husband were friends of my parents. I remember she had red hair and baked really good brownies.'

I allow myself a smile. 'So they were quite close then?'

Arthur sets down the drink and leans back in his chair. 'I suppose so. I remember Ma and Dad going to dinner parties at the Madigans', but only because my babysitter let me stay up to watch *Twin Peaks*. It must have fizzled out. I don't think I remember the Madigans being around when I was growing up.'

'*Twin Peaks*?' I tilt my head and fix him with a look that makes him chuckle. 'You must have been a strange child. Anyway, Anna Madigan. Over the last few weeks, your mother has sort of lost interest in what I'm doing, like she's in her own little world, but I've been trying to sort out all the mess. There are cuttings everywhere, but these ones . . .'

The clipping is from five years ago. I spread it out on the table and make a dramatic gesture with my hand.

Arthur peers at the newsprint. 'Anna Madigan disappeared? Was she ever found?'

I lift my shoulders and make a face. 'Not that I can see.'

Arthur blows out a breath. 'I've never heard about this.'

'These cuttings chart Anna's disappearance over a period of years. Every time a body was washed up, the papers rehashed the whole thing. Must have been a nightmare for the family. If your mother wasn't close friends with this Anna, then why has she kept them all?'

'Maybe Ma just had a passing interest in what happened to an old friend. Wouldn't you?'

'Depends who the old friend was.' I'm thinking of Reuben. If they were dragging the river for him . . . yes, I'd want to know. How would I feel if they found a body? My mind refuses to go there. I would be bereft, of course. But it would be a freedom of sorts. The thought is so unwholesome I push it away. 'You need to read it.'

Mac

Anna Madigan came to see me.

It was about a month after Jim's death; three weeks, perhaps. There's an old Irish quip – *would you take my coffin so quick?* – a jibe at those who move in rather too rapidly on something that belongs to you. Horribly apt, really. But this time, there was nothing left for Anna Madigan to take.

I was in the hall with the dogs when she knocked. They went berserk and I had to hold on to their collars while fumbling with the door and shouting through the crack. 'Step back, whoever you are! And don't put your hands in your pockets!' Eventually I got the door fully open and there she was – Anna Madigan, standing like a schoolgirl in the dinner queue, hands by her sides and her handbag gripped under her oxter. Max sniffed her cowboy boots, and Jethro continued to bark for no reason whatsoever. I gave him a warning dunt with my knee.

I stared at her, but her gaze slid away from mine.

She was younger than us, Jim and me, but she was pushing sixty by then. She looked like she'd hardly aged. Down to good genes, perhaps, or a damned expensive night cream. Fifteen years had passed since I'd last confronted her in a hallway. The red hair was duller and shot through with silver, trimmed and straightened and coaxed into a longish bob. She was wearing a cute little fawn trench coat and a silky blouse with butterflies on it. We spoke at the same time.

'What do you want?'

'I came to offer my condolences.'

I turned to go back into the house. 'Don't bother. I don't want them.'

'Please . . .' She followed me, lingering rather determinedly on the threshold so that I couldn't close the door. The dogs had disappeared into the garden.

I gave a shrug and she followed me into the hall. She didn't fit this house. She was too colourful and modern and I didn't want to hear what she had to say.

'I know you probably don't want to see me, but I felt I had to come.'

I wasn't comfortable facing her here in the hall; I had nothing to hide behind. I asked her if she wanted a cuppa, because the making of it would give me something to do, and she smiled, as if I'd forgiven her, and we went through to the kitchen.

She plonked herself, uninvited, at the head of the table.

'Richard doesn't know I'm here,' she said. 'He thinks I've gone for a walk with the dog.'

'You have a dog?'

'She's in the car.'

I hadn't heard a car, but then I noticed the set of keys in her hand. The key ring was adorned with a ridiculously oversized, furry panda. Classic Anna Madigan. I busied myself with the tea things. 'So you're still dissembling. Still hiding things.'

She looked at her hands. She was wearing a very pretty shade of polish on her nails. Coral, I think you'd call it. I noticed something else too: that sapphire pendant, Jim's love token, obviously mended after our tussle and now reinstated around her brass neck. I saw a glint of blue, cunningly concealed beneath the lapels of her blouse.

'All that is done with. I wrote to you. I tried to explain, to apologise.'

'Yes, I got your letter.'

She looked at me as though she was expecting something. Her eyes matched the pendant, bright sapphire, like they'd never known heartache, or anything dark and sullied. What did she want me to say? What was she seeking – absolution?

I looked right into those blue eyes. 'I also found the emails you sent to Jim shortly before his accident.'

She hadn't been expecting that.

There is nothing more dangerous than a silently smiling woman. Anna sits there, smirking at me. She almost stole my husband, my child's father. She was thwarted first time around – my threat to tell her husband put paid to her game – but she came back a second time! I found those emails, just before my husband's death, telling him she'd never stopped loving him. She wanted to see him again, after all that time. That's what hurt me the most, that passion could survive such absence. At the time of the affair, Arthur had been a teenager, and Jim was afraid he'd go off the rails if he left. He needed his father, and that's why Jim had stayed. He didn't choose me. He didn't stay for me.

I read my husband's replies to this woman's entreaties. Jim was in love with Anna Madigan until the day he died.

A splash of milk and the tea is ready. I've chosen a rather nice cup and saucer for her: vintage fine bone china, patterned with yellow roses. I place it in front of her. She makes a little start as if she's lost in thought, and takes a sip, still smiling politely.

'You know, few of us stop to think about fine bone china,' I say. When I have her surprised attention, I continue, 'It actually contains finely milled cow bones. You can distinguish it from porcelain by holding it up to the light.' I lift my own cup, which is empty, to the kitchen window. 'It has a translucent, ivory colour, whereas porcelain appears very white.'

She doesn't quite know how to reply, gently replacing her cup on its saucer.

'Of course, Charles Krafft, an experimental American artist, has taken it to a whole new level, with the introduction of human bones. He makes little bone china trinkets out of exhumed skeletons – a keepsake for the loved ones left behind. Human bones can be burned and milled to form a very fine ash. Ashes to ashes. Dust to dust.'

Anna Madigan is still smiling, but very faintly now. The nervous pulse in her neck makes the sapphire pendant glint brightly for a second. I smile back.

'Drink up your tea while it's still hot.'

Lucie

Dundee woman Anna Madigan has not been seen for over a fortnight. Mrs Madigan, a fifty-nine-year-old office manager, was reported missing by her husband, Richard, on 9 September, when she failed to return from walking the family dog at Tentsmuir Forest. Her car was subsequently found close to the area, but no sightings of Mrs Madigan or her dog, Floss, have been reported. Police are keeping an open mind, although the area has become notorious in the last few years as a suicide hotspot.

After a few minutes Arthur looks up. 'From the way you're looking at me – is there something I'm missing?'

'The dog. Floss.'

He glances back down at the paper. 'There are loads of dogs called Floss.'

'When did your mother get *her* Floss?'

Arthur sits back in surprise. 'What are you saying? It's a coincidence, that's all.'

'When?' My eyes are burning into him. I can't help it. Unpleasant thoughts are uncoiling in my brain. 'How old is she – Floss?'

'Um . . . well, we got her from the kennels in Dundee. About . . . God, I dunno. She must be about six or seven.'

'Did you go with your mother to pick her up?'

'No, she just –'

'Appeared?'

'When you put it like that, yes, but –'

'Did your mother ever speak about getting another dog? Three dogs is quite a handful for a woman who's always moaning about her health.'

Arthur swigs the last of his gin and tonic. A bit angrily, I think. 'I don't know what you're getting at.'

'I don't know what I'm getting at either, I just thought it was all a bit strange. But then your mother is very strange.' I shake my head like a bewildered child. Arthur's face is sullen. When he's annoyed, his lips become thin. Lines appear, between his brows and around his mouth. His friendly golden glow fades as quickly as if someone pressed a dimmer switch.

'It doesn't even say what type of dog Anna's Floss was.'

'Okay. Let's just leave it.'

'Let's not. You brought it up. What's your point?'

'Don't make an issue about it.'

'You're the one with the issue. Why bring all this up?' He swipes a hand towards the cuttings. 'My mother is a hoarder. That doesn't mean she knows anything about *this*.'

I let out a sigh. The weirdness of Mac's world is getting to me. My head is making connections it probably shouldn't and I feel guilty, but I have to have the last word.

'I just think your mother is getting really . . . unhinged.'

It's not a nice word to use about someone's mother. There's a pause, and Arthur stares into his glass. I long to take it back. I wish I could be gentle with him. He looks up, fixes his gaze on one of the pub's twinkly amber lamps.

'She phoned me. About Reuben,' he says eventually. He rolls his shoulders, takes a breath. I get the feeling he didn't mean to speak of this, but it's one of those things that has to be held up to the light. That's why I write rubbish poems. Secrets need an airing from time to time, whether it's a good idea or not. 'She hinted that she – that she could have killed him, there in the mill.'

'What? When was this?'

'The last time he turned up looking for you. She said she'd thought about pushing him down the basement stairs, but when I confronted her about it she denied ever saying that to me on the phone.'

I stare at him, my breathing suddenly shallow. 'Seriously?'

He frowns at me. 'It's not something I'd make up.'

I look away. 'I think . . . I've noticed a change in her. When I started she was rude and messy and eccentric, but I got used to that. But there's a *line,* isn't there?'

Arthur nods. We make troubled eye contact. 'I don't know what to do.'

'The doctor, maybe?' I'm thinking Alzheimer's, early onset dementia and all the other things I don't want to mention. 'When was the last time she saw a doctor?'

'I did mention it to her GP.'

'Make sure he takes it seriously, Arthur. Okay, maybe I'm out of order with the cuttings. They probably mean nothing but, to be honest, your mother isn't making sense a lot of the time.'

He holds up his hands. 'I know. I know. I haven't done anything about it because . . . I don't want to lose her, too.'

His face is very still, taut. He snatches off his glasses and pinches the bridge of his nose. He looks vulnerable without the glasses, as if he's removed a piece of armour. I reach for his hand. I try to imagine it being my mother unravelling, but I can't. My mother is far too buttoned up.

'Mac – she's a writer, someone who trades on her imagination. Perhaps we're reading too much into this. Try not to worry.'

We seem to run out of words. Arthur replaces his specs and drains his glass. I take that as my cue and gather up my stuff. The newspaper cutting I fold carefully and slot into an old envelope. We get to our feet simultaneously and I hug his side, sliding my arm around his back when he just stands there, unresponsive.

'Are you coming back to mine?' I give him a squeeze, but he moves away.

'I could,' he says. 'But I'm not going to.'

I find it hard to do affection. Even though I half-expected the rebuff, it stings. I stomp away. It's already almost dark outside, and spitting rain. As the heavy pub door swings shut, we fumble about for a moment, buttoning coats, securing scarves. We have no answers: not about Anna Madigan, not about Mac, not about us. I am dissatisfied, and pissed off with Arthur.

'You need to decide what you want,' he says, as we exit the car park. 'Stop drifting. Stop letting things happen to you.'

I bristle. 'I don't know what you're talking about.'

'Yes, you do. Reuben and you just "happened". You drifted in here because you'd run out of options. And now you've drifted into me.'

I want to bite back, but he's on a roll.

'I'm not a stopgap. I'm not your comfort blanket. I really care about you, but I don't know where I stand.'

I look down at the tarmac. 'In a pub car park, right about now. You think too much, that's your trouble.'

'If you want me, Lucie . . .' Arthur's words are clear and cold, pebbles dropping to the bottom of the millpond. 'If you want to be *with* me, it has to be a *decision*.'

He looks like he might say more, but instead raises his shoulders, then drops them with a sigh.

I turn to face him. I'm not sure what to say. I do care about him, but the words won't come out. It all feels a bit premature. I'm not sure how long it takes to get over someone, even if they're never truly yours in the first place. I'm shivering. Arthur comes closer and takes my cold hand in his warm one. His heat seeps into me, makes me take a jagged breath. I'm scared I'm going to cry.

'You have to decide if this is right for you. I know what I want,' he says. 'Come on. I'll walk you home.'

We stroll up the hill, barely talking, but it's easy all the same, like I don't have to try. I wish I had space for him. When we reach the cottage door, he turns to me and kisses me lightly on the mouth, tells me he'll see me soon.

I've left the heating on, and the cottage is warm. I drop my bag, my keys, on the table and stand there, not moving, listening to the clock ticking. I take out my mobile and automatically check it for messages, but the screen reveals nothing. Reuben has stopped texting me now. He's moved on. My stomach flutters once, twice. Loneliness is a solid lump inside me.

It's in that moment that I make my decision.

Lucie

October

'Let me see my gift,' says Bella, and the miller smiles like a wolf, like some creature that shouldn't possess a smile. He makes a slight bow and gestures towards the door. 'Not here in the yard,' he says. 'Let's return to the hall.' Bella hesitates before beginning to retrace her steps. She can feel his eyes on her. Her spine drips with ice.

The guests are excited by the reappearance of the jute sack, and press themselves into a rowdy, wine-soaked circle, which the candlelight doesn't quite reach. The miller places the sack in the centre and his gaze touches every face. One by one the revellers fall silent. With a trickster's sleight of hand the miller whisks away the covering and reveals the most exquisite harp. There is a collective gasp. Bella presses her cold hand to her throat. The instrument is beautifully fashioned. She cannot look away from the curved bow of it, pale as moonstone, or the spun-gold, gossamer-fine strings.

Of its own accord, with no human agency, the harp begins to sing.

The miller smiles.

The harp sings like a bird at first light, pure and sweet. It vibrates with a sound like the thrip thrip thrip of wings in the hedgerow. The music is wistful, an unearthly humming that vibrates through the oak rafters and the stone walls. The wedding guests can feel it shivering up the backs of their legs, through their ribcages.

Just as Bella thinks she can stand its sweetness no longer, the frail notes begin to change. They become discordant. They take on a *whining tone. As she listens, the tone becomes a voice, and the notes become words. Harsh words, full of blame. And their message is unmistakeable:*

'My sister! Killed by my own sister! Killed by my own sister! My sister! Killed. Killed. Killed.'

The guests look at each other with horror. The father bellows in rage and the mother wipes her eyes. Bella is paralysed. She claps her hands to her ears. 'Make it stop!' she cries. 'Make it stop!'

The miller is still smiling. Bella begins to understand then that nothing on earth will make the harp stop.

So this is how it ends. My fingers drop from the keyboard and I ease myself back in Mac's chair. My head hurts, and a dragging pain has settled in my lower back. I feel like I've been standing for too long on a cold stone floor in a draughty hall. I'm part of that strange ring of wedding guests, beyond the civilised circle of light.

The computer programme issues a prompt: *Do you want to save changes to The Cruel Sister?* Do I have a choice? Things are changing so quickly that I can't keep up. October has slipped into my bones, and I still don't have a plan. I should have a plan by now. I click save and the document fades to black, and I sit looking at the blank screen for a long time, until my bladder finally forces me to act.

There's a tiny toilet off the hall. It's unheated and old-fashioned, with chipped white porcelain and one of those high cisterns with a pull flush. The oak toilet seat is so old I swear it has woodworm. I sit down to relieve myself with Mac's tartan blanket still slung around my shoulders. Perhaps I am turning into Mac, mooching about these corridors and ignoring all contact with the outside world. A few weeks ago, I'd received mail from my mother – news from home in a modest notelet with pansies on the front. It smelled of the manse, and her handwriting was as familiar to me as her Sunday shoes, or her pink dressing gown. I wonder if Jane has revealed the love poem and my own traitorous handwriting. Have either of them identified my distinctive strokes and loops, like miscreants in a police line-up? I'd checked her news for passive aggression but there was none, just a mention of my father's dodgy knee and something about the Friendship Circle. Mrs Black has put the hardware shop on the market and my old school pal Becky just got engaged. Jane has been on a date with a new man, a head teacher she met at a conference. Shortly after that I had two missed calls from Jane. Her voicemail message was brief: nothing to worry about, just hoping for a catch-up. I suspect she wants to tell me about the new man, now that Reuben is off the scene. If only we could parcel the past away as neatly as our old dolls.

I cannot reply to my mother, or chat with my sister. To do so would be to invest in the future and I don't dare let myself expand any further than the present tense. What I am is right here, right now. I am the cold toilet seat pressing into my buttocks, the irritating drip of the cold tap. I am the green tiles, the balding loo brush. I cannot think beyond my own griping pain, the stuck-fast pressure that has been building in my belly all day.

Mac

I come downstairs to find Lucie exiting the WC. She's as white as a sheet and biting her lower lip.

'Good heavens, girl. Got a gippy tummy? You look like death warmed up.'

She smiles weakly. The only bits of colour in her face are the livid dents in her lower lip made by her teeth.

'Not feeling great. Maybe I'll go –'

'Just go! Yes, indeed. Take yourself off to bed.' I hope she isn't going to be sick. She has that clammy look, and her fringe is sticking to her brow. Whatever's wrong with her, she deserves it, but I try and come up with a pleasant expression. 'You'll feel as right as rain after a nap.'

She nods. 'I'll take home the laptop and your book and type up the rest of your story. Is that it? Is that the end?'

I glance at the canvas shopping bag leaning against the coat stand, trying to think back to what I wrote last. 'The harp is singing? Ah yes, proclaiming Bella's guilt for all to hear!'

Lucie shivers. 'It's never going to stop, is it – the guilt? The voice isn't going to stop until she takes responsibility for what she's done.'

I don't answer. *Sometimes you have to be made to take responsibility.* But I don't say that to her. Instead, I move over to the stand and unhook her khaki jacket. It's unlined and insubstantial. 'This is very light, dear. Do you have a heavier one for the winter? You might catch a chill. We don't want anything bad to happen to you.'

She looks alarmed, and I wonder, not for the first time, if she'll stay, or if she'll up and leave like the wild geese as soon as my manuscript is finished. For some reason the thought disturbs me. It makes me feel cheated. Wrongdoers simply can't be allowed to up and leave.

'I haven't planned that far ahead,' she says.

I proffer the jacket and she shrugs into it, meekly. Again I wonder if I'm making her nervous.

'That isn't the end,' I say quickly. She darts me a look and I press home the point. 'Aren't you wondering about the miller? And about how the harp was made? Oh, there's more to come.' I tap my temple, as if it's all up there, waiting to gush forth.

She buttons her jacket, slings the bag over her shoulder. 'Write it down then. Let's get it finished.' She opens the door, steps out into the cold.

Her attitude makes me bristle. 'Hold on a minute. Don't dismiss it all like that.'

She swings around. 'Like what?'

'Like these stories have no consequence. Oh they do. They do. You'll find that out.'

She snorts, bats my indignation away with her hand and continues walking. How dare she?

'How dare you, Anna Madigan?' I yell from the doorstep. 'You slut! How dare you come in here upsetting everything?'

The girl stops dead in her tracks, turns around slowly. She's a distance away now. I think she might be saying something but I can't hear her. I can't stop the words coming out of my mouth. I fire every vile insult I can muster at her, and she hunches her shoulders and hurries off into the distance.

'There are consequences, Anna!' I yell after her departing figure.

I remain on the front step until she disappears from view. Anna? Why is Anna always in my head? I shake her away. Despite my winter woollies, an icy breeze does its best to raise gooseflesh on my upper arms. Lucie. I must concentrate on Lucie now. The story is nearly finished.

There isn't much more to tell, but what's left is the shocking part.

It's the bit that changes what you think you know.

Lucie

I go for a lie down, but I can't get comfortable and end up sitting on one of the hard pine chairs at the kitchen table. I figure I should probably stay close to the bathroom, since I seem to have developed the frequent urge to pee. The pain is restless, gripping me from time to time like a bad period. I make tea from Mac's garden mint, munch on some dry crackers and watch *Friends* on my laptop. Rachel and Ross are on a break, although the terms and conditions of it seem a bit muddy.

I'd had to finish with Arthur. 'This isn't going anywhere,' I'd said, as gently as I could. 'It *can't* go anywhere.' *I won't let it.* That last bit remained unsaid. There were a lot of really important things left unsaid in that conversation. *You'll understand. Soon.* He took it so well I think I hate him. I wanted him to fight for me, for what we could have had, but instead he was strangely passive. I think he'd been expecting it all along.

But that was weeks ago now. I've tried to give up visiting the cafe, or the pub. I sit in the cottage and watch *Friends* until the light fades. Then I close my curtains so I don't have to look at the mill. Floss has stopped coming around because I refuse to let her in. The particular mystery of her background is too much for me to handle at the moment, and I'm not sure where I found the energy to get wound up about it in the first place. I can't bear to walk beside the pond either. According to the story, Bella took her sister's life there. I'm just as guilty. I took something just as precious from Jane – not just her boyfriend but all the things she'll never get back: her trust, her hopes for the future, her peace of mind. Guilt is indestructible. I know there'll be a reckoning, some day soon.

I have distanced myself from everyone who cares. It seems easier that way. I am shrinking in on myself, but that's not the whole story.

Mac

There's something timeless about building a fire. I could be my mother going through these motions, or my grandmother. It's a meditative act. You can stand outside of yourself, quite separate from it. You can watch your sins turn black as soot.

I should have made this particular fire many months ago. Before Lucie came. The girl is responsible for stirring up old memories. All this carry on with Reuben – the girl is another Anna Madigan, stirring up trouble, causing grief. Perhaps it's a good thing that she did. There are things I need to deal with before I become too frail. This bonfire will be a cleansing. A ritual flame. A way of getting rid of those things I have held onto for too long.

In the dark, I assume a prayer position among the mud and dead leaves. As I crouch and steady myself I feel earth beneath my knuckles; damp, peaty mould. Something crawls across the back of my hand. My nose stings in the cold air, as though I've been dunked in icy water. My ears find every chirrup, every last squeak in the night. The old ticker is pumping so furiously I think I might collapse right here on the bare ground. They would never find me out here. My body would disappear beneath a coverlet of organic matter. I would become a rotted layer of the past. I'd simply dissolve and everything would right itself.

But I can do this. I am here to build a fire, a fire bigger than any grate or chimney will allow. It will be uncontained. Yes, there's something timeless about building a fire.

First, twist greasy old newspaper into fat croissants; next, add a firelighter that makes your fingers stink of paraffin; build a little tent of kindling, paper-white slivers of pine and ash. Always keep your axe sharp for the kindling. Don't leave it embedded in the block – the sap will rust the edge. Chopping kindling with a good, sharp axe should be effortless, like slicing through a Viennetta.

I've already prepared the kindling. Disarticulated it. The axe was sharp. It was a lot like slicing through a Viennetta.

Lucie

Sleep comes in fits and starts. I wake up after only an hour and take myself through the house to glug down two paracetamol at the kitchen tap. The water is icy, freezing a track down into my deepest parts. I can't stop shivering, and have to boil the kettle to make up a hot water bottle. After twenty minutes the pain in my back starts to subside and I wander off to bed. I miss Floss. I miss her undemanding presence. I doze. Some time in the night, the pain creeps around to my front, a foreign ache that grips me low in the belly, and I have to lie with my knees drawn up. I clutch the hot water bottle to the sore place, but I start to sweat and fretfully throw off my covers. The gap in the curtain is still showing midnight black. Sleep vanishes, and, cursing, I get up again, feel around for my slippers and stagger back to the kitchen. Thoughts of tea and toast make me nauseous. I could go outside for a fag, but I gave up smoking around the same time I gave up Arthur.

I'm worried about Floss. Pulling a smelly old quilted coat of Mac's over my nightie, I stick my feet into wellies and unlock the back door. Thoughts start to whirl around in my brain. Could Floss really be Anna Madigan's dog? Perhaps Anna Madigan wanted to leave her husband, to just disappear. You hear about that all the time; people getting so overwhelmed with life that they take off, leaving no trail. Jesus, I thought of it myself, on that Aberdeen to London train. Anything to get away from the guilt. It would be classic Mac, to take the dog. I can just imagine *that* conversation, in Mac's draughty kitchen: 'Well, you run off if you want to, Anna, but don't abandon the damn dog!'

Although I call her name softly, there is no sign of the little spaniel. I look up at the sky, a deep navy blue, speckled with stars. I wonder where Anna Madigan is, whether she and Mac ever kept in touch.

Far off, a bird of some kind sets up a piercing alarm call. I can smell smoke. I sniff the air sharply, like an animal – the acrid bonfire scent is unmistakeable. My first thought is the mill, with all that dodgy wiring and rotting timber. I hurry round the corner. Smoke hangs in the gloom, and the stone walls hover in and out of focus like ghosts. Off to the left, a good distance from the building, flames leap and crackle. A dark figure, witch-like in the fiery glow, is doing something with a rake. Sparks pop and scatter like champagne bubbles. I release my tightly held breath with a groan.

For fuck's sake, Mac. What next?

She greets me from across the bonfire, as if this is a normal autumn garden tidy-up; as if I'm not standing there in the pitch black, bewildered, in my nightclothes.

'Hello, Bella!' she says. 'What a blaze!'

She appears to be burning a vast quantity of branches and leaves. The heat is so fierce I have to shield my face with one hand as I edge closer. I can only see her top half, arms bunched as she brandishes the rake. Her face is a waxy orange 'O', wavering and reforming in the heat haze. I think she's grinning, but the smoke gets in my eyes and everything blurs.

Without warning, something cracks in the centre, and the blaze caves in, flinging burning embers my way. I jump back. White-hot heat engulfs me, and my streaming eyes make it impossible to make sense of what I'm seeing – noirish impressions of things that shouldn't be there: twigs that look like ribs; a charred twist of something long and bony; black fingers set into claws. Painted nails. I recoil, rub my eyes. *What?*

Something pops inside. Inside *me*. Water soaks my thighs,

gushes into my wellies. Liquid splashes to the ground and the hot ash sizzles where it falls.

'Oh dear.' Mac is beside me, even though I hadn't seen her move. She's surveying the wetness with a profound sadness. She smells otherworldly, of smoke and soot. I'm mortified, clamping my legs together, tugging at my sodden nightie. Her hand shoots out, finds the hard swell of my abdomen beneath the borrowed coat.

'How long have you known?'

I shake my head, still in denial. Real tears now, not smoke tears, trailing down to my chin. I can taste the salt.

Mac is still speaking. 'Go inside. Go back to bed. Nothing will happen before morning. I've a few things to do here . . .' She's looking at the bonfire, which is starting to die down. The blackened rib-like things . . . She hefts the rake into the heart of the blaze and they disappear from view. 'Go to bed, dear. We'll sort things out in the morning.'

She moves away, whistling a strange little tune. Sobbing, I stumble back to the cottage.

The plastic curtain around the bath is brightly patterned with polka dots, red, green and yellow. As I sit on the toilet, waiting for the shower to run hot, waiting for my body to empty itself, they dance before my eyes. In my head I'm joining up the dots; a child immersed in a puzzle, biting my lip, unable to figure things out. As steam billows around the curtain I force myself to my feet, strip off my sodden T-shirt, release each welly with a dull, wet plop. I climb into the bath and let the spray batter me. It's scalding, but I don't care. I'm numb.

For the first time in a long time I look down at my naked self. I splay my hands on either side of my abdomen and inspect my round football of a belly. The skin is taut and smooth, the water bouncing off in rivulets. It looks like someone else's skin. My breasts are someone else's breasts, larger than mine, pale and solid and blue-veined. I cup one of them, cautiously, as if it belongs to another woman and I'm not sure of my welcome. The nipple is hard and brown and my palm comes away wet with milk. Everything is draining from me. Everything. My legs can no longer support me and I sink slowly down into the tub, sink down until I'm on all fours, watching everything spiral down the drain, out of my body, beyond my control. I can no longer hide from myself, from what I've done.

I remain there on all fours, like an animal, wounded, trapped. The hot spray pelts down on my neck, on my back. I focus on the plughole, come to know it intimately, the brown plaque around it, the soap scum and the trapped hair. Pain and fear overwhelm me. I am naked and shivering and exposed. Eventually, I sit back on my heels, close my eyes, hold my face up to the gushing water.

The past has caught up with me.

Mac

Well, this is a bit of a pickle.

Lucie has been pregnant all along. That's put a dampener on my bonfire, that's for sure. She was acting the innocent, but surely she must have known? I've never believed all those stories about women popping out infants without an inkling that they'd a bun in the oven. It doesn't add up, but Lucie is very good at hiding things. Would she ever have confessed? Well, regardless, her body has decided to end this charade. Some things simply cannot remain hidden.

Poking gently at the hot, powdery ash on the margins of the blaze, I wonder how best to proceed. I cannot allow myself to worry about Lucie's predicament right at this moment. I am consumed by my task. I've started, so I'll have to continue, to paraphrase *Mastermind*.

Magnus Magnusson would know what to do. Or I could have asked Anita, guru of all things bone, for advice, but instead I turned, against my better judgement, to the Google. Too much information can be as unhelpful as too little. One Californian fire chief was almost poetic in his graphic descriptions of how the process works: *Body fat can make a good fuel source, but it needs material such as clothing or charred wood to act as a wick.*

Five years rotting in a water-soaked tunnel have denied me a fuel source, and the clothing I disposed of before things became too unpleasant. That nice trench coat, the silky cream blouse with the butterflies on it, the too-young-for-her jeans. I had thought to donate them to charity, since they were of such good quality. Some poor soul would have been glad of that coat in this dreich weather, but I thought better of it. I cut them up and burned them too. The pendant I squirreled away in my study drawer. I had almost forgotten it was there, until Lucie brought to the surface all those horrible memories. It seemed very fitting to feed it through the mill. I recall a fragment of poetry – Longfellow, I believe: 'A millstone and the human heart are driven ever round; if they have nothing else to grind, they must themselves be ground.' That about sums it up. Love is just a power play, with winners and losers. The Bellas and the Annas and the Lucies might enjoy a moment of glory, but Elspeth and Jane and me – we've still got a tale to tell.

The disposing of the clothes – that was a bit of a low point. That was when I let the embittered voyeur in me untwist, slick its way sickeningly to the surface. After the outerwear, the bra and pants had to come off. Matching undies, wouldn't you know? Such a cliché. Pale cream with ecru lace trim. I'd peeled them away as a lover might – as Jim must have done – gently unhooking the bra, sliding the knickers down over her ankles. The fabric was dank; her skin like hard candle wax. So, so cold. I imagined how my husband would have traced her once-warm breasts with his hands, her narrow waist, and I wept hot, thick tears – bodily fluids dripping onto that sparse mat of pubic hair in some ghastly subversion of what my husband did to her.

Assuming there is sufficient wick material, the body can sustain its own fire for around seven hours. Given that I was dealing with skeletal remains, I estimated that four to five hours would suffice. It gave me a good deal of unwelcome thinking time. There had never been any satisfaction in the deed. A fleeting moment of exultation, perhaps. But I had misunderstood, about the ending. Jealousy acts as a wick; it just keeps the hate burning brighter.

I poke at some of the top timbers. They haven't quite taken hold – too green, I should have used seasoned logs – but underneath, the flames are flickering nicely. As the green wood shifts, the heart of the fire pops and sparks and cracks open like an egg, molten innards searing my face. There's something black in the centre, a nucleus, like that dark, bloody fleck you sometimes find in an egg yolk, repulsive and nauseating. You know it shouldn't be there, yet you still have to deal with it. The black thing flexes and unfurls, reaching out beyond the flames: a curled fist, with one charred pinkie cocked, as though taking tea from a bone china cup. The fist is defiant. I push it back into the blaze with a hasty jab of the rake.

How like Anna Madigan not to give up without a fight.

Lucie

The now familiar swoosh and grind of the mill rouses me, and I surface from sleep with my heart already bumping. How could I have slept? The noise of the waterwheel rattles me into full wakefulness, and I struggle to sit up, praying that what happened in the night was just a bad dream. The full hardness of my belly reminds me that it was not, and that there is more to come. Dread washes through me all over again, but for now, there's no pain, just a dull tension. My body smells comfortingly of shower gel.

The curtain gap reveals a strip of just-about-there daylight. I reach for my phone to check on the time. It's just after eight. I thought Mac might have come to my aid, but she's obviously totally involved with whatever she's doing. What the fuck is she doing? The fire, her unhinged behaviour, the grinning, the singing . . . the stuff on the bonfire. What did I see? I was in pain, panicky. It was dark, but . . .

Should I call Arthur? I've invested so much energy in keeping him away, keeping him from finding out about this fix I'm in. It wasn't a choice I wanted to make, but how would he feel about a pregnant me? Sure, he'd be kind and supportive and no doubt encourage me to eat enough cakes for two, but he'd get sucked in, and I'd never know the truth. I want him to choose me because he can't bear to live without me, and not because I'm some idiot charity case.

I glance back down at the phone. He's texted me a couple of times in the last week: *How are you doing? Pop in for a coffee. The scones are just out of the oven.* I'd kept my replies brief and discouraging. To alert him to his mother's odd behaviour would alert him to mine. I'd done a damn good job of concealing this baby, even from myself. The more I hid it, the more I pretended this wasn't happening. This *couldn't* be happening to me. Only the pain compelled me to face up to the inevitable.

Reuben. I could call Reuben, but I have no idea how he would react in a crisis, especially one such as this. I've never seen that kind of Reuben, and he's never seen that kind of me. How would he cope with a vulnerable, scared, needy Lucie? I don't want to find out. Grief drenches me down to my toes.

What do I do? What do I do?

Eventually I text him. Eventually he texts back. I pace around the room, tapping my mobile against my chin. I don't want anyone near me, but I can't do this alone. I pause by the window to haul back the curtains. Pain knifes through me. The phone clatters to the floor. I'm gripping the window ledge with all my strength, gripping until my fingers turn white. The contraction overpowers me. I am helpless.

Breathe. Just breathe. Isn't that what they tell you to do? Jane pops into my mind. I exhale, eyes screwed up, concentrating on my out-breath. It mists the cold windowpane. Jane and I used to watch *One Born Every Minute*. It had become one of those cult things with us, required viewing after a wine or two, when we were in the mood to be entertained, alarmed, freaked out. *Look at the size of that bump! Oh my God, I can see the head! Seriously? That's gross.* I wish I'd listened more to the midwives, delivering solid-gold words of wisdom, despite that extra flick of mascara for the cameras. I wish I'd sneered less at all the panting and the groaning. I wish I hadn't covered my eyes during the scary parts.

The vicious squeeze subsides and I get to breathe normally again. It's grey outside, but all the mill lights are on; the place looks like an advent calendar on Christmas Eve, open and expectant. The incessant trundling of the machinery grates on my already shredded nerves.

I thrust my feet into my slippers, drag a blanket round me

and waddle towards the kitchen. My bump had been slight, easy to hide, easy to ignore, but now it has expanded to fill my entire being. It is all I am aware of. Every fibre of the house has altered to accommodate it. The walls tilt under my questing hands, the chair groans beneath my weight. The clock ticks louder and the old-house smell makes me gag. I have entered some kind of otherworld where nothing is quite the same, and there is no going back. This new knowledge shakes me to the core. Soon I will split into two, like some exotic species. I have no baby clothes, no cradle, no experience. I have no one to rescue me. No place to go.

The laptop sits folded on the table in front of me. If I Google 'labour', it might give me some pointers. On the telly they time the contractions, but I don't know how long this limbo lasts. I flip open the computer, press the button. Surely Mac will come? I think of my mother as the screen bursts into life. She hated us watching *One Born Every Minute*: 'You'll know all about that soon enough. Switch it off.'

She's always been like that about anything dodgy. Sex was something we never, ever discussed. When she walked in on Reuben and me, I thought we would both die of embarrassment, but we didn't. There were consequences, but nobody died. I won't die of this either, but somehow I have to get through it and come out the other side.

The contractions are coming every ten minutes. I'm timing them by the digital display on the computer while simultaneously revising childbirth. I'm sticking to the NHS site because it has nice images of serenely pregnant women and freshly laundered babies in hats.

Contact your midwifery team if:
- your contractions are regular and coming about 3 in every 10 minutes
- your waters break

- your contractions are very strong and you feel you need pain relief
- you're worried about anything.

If I had a midwifery team.

I cope with the spasms by getting to my feet and leaning on the table. The table is solid, unshockable. It absorbs my tears, my swear words, my sweat. My nails make marks on the underside. I'd chew it if I could. But each time I think I cannot take any more, the pain eases off and I breathe and wipe my eyes. An hour passes in this way, two, and I'm still holding off. I can't commit to this. I can't make a decision. I want Mac to come and take over.

For all her craziness, I still want Mac, with her calmness and her logic and her unvarnished version of everything. Her notebook is sitting to the left of the computer. In a calm moment I flick it open to her latest words.

'She killed me! She killed me! My own sister!'

The hall has fallen silent. There is no sound but the soft vibration of the strings. The words are as crystal clear and ice cold as the water gushing from the mill wheel. There is no escape, no going back. All eyes are on Bella.

'What trickery is this?' their father roars. His sergeant reaches for his sword. 'That is my little Elspeth's voice.' The mother weeps into her hands.

'No trickery at all,' says the miller, smiling his wolf's smile. 'Do you not recognise your child? She is altered, true. She has been put back together differently, shall we say.'

He told them then, the wedding party, about how little Elspeth had been washed downstream. She was dead by the time she reached the mill, of course. At this Bella lets out an animal wail. The miller finds her gaze and she feels the black, choking water closing over her own head. The utter darkness. The end of everything.

'She came to rest beneath the wheel. I rescued her but it was too

late. That lovely girl . . .' His heavy sigh gusts through the company; hair rises on pale necks. 'I laid her out on the mill floor, tried to put the pieces back together. Do you not recognise her?'

The miller steps back and indicates the harp with a flourish. He trails a dirt-engrained finger down the elegant white curve of it, plucks the glinting strings. The song becomes more fevered: 'Killed. Killed. KILLED!'

Bella feels an answering chill travelling up her spine.

'Do none of you recognise the graceful arch of her backbone? The soft strength of her golden hair?'

The father barks a sound of utter disbelief. He is wordless with grief. There is the dangerous ring of drawn steel, but the miller just laughs.

'From the remains of your daughter I have crafted something as indestructible as it is beautiful. Her bones, her hair, her very voice. A work of art.' His gaze swings back to Bella. She is impaled on it. 'Your sister has a story to tell, a song to sing. I'm sure you'll recognise it!'

With the last laugh, the miller sweeps away out of the door, his cloak swirling around him, black as grave dirt. The bride stares at the bone harp. The strings ripple again, preparing to give voice to her guilt, and Bella screams a denial. He father turns on her as her mother, sobbing, falls to the ground.

'What have you done?' he roars.

Bella is in the centre of the circle. Bella and the bone harp and a ring of cold steel. Her father's men-at-arms are ready with their weapons, awaiting the word. The harp strings shiver. 'Sister . . . sister . . . how could you?'

There is only one thing she can do. The bride bursts through the circle and races for the door. She has a feeling the miller will be waiting for her.

Another contraction takes hold of me: a great seismic rush sweeping me away. I do not have the energy to move, but double up where I sit, gripping the chair as if both of us are being hurled across the universe. Stars ignite behind my eyelids. Bone, hair, voice – a union of all the parts of me, all the parts of Reuben, growing inside me. Our baby.

After an eternity, my body starts to relax. The contractions are coming thick and fast now. I need help. I need to find Mac.

Mac

It's a fallacy that the skull, when exposed to heat, bursts open like a boiled egg in a microwave. It's nonsense, and I'm sure Anita would back me up on this. Merely one of those urban myths that's arisen from the aftermath of fires. The skulls of burn victims quickly become brittle from the heat – they only have the thinnest covering of tissue – and so are easily broken. Like hearts.

Jim's toolbox lives in the miller's office, a small, square room just big enough for the miller. It has a half-door, like a stable, and an old-fashioned sloping desk that may have belonged to some long-dead schoolmarm. Lifting the desk lid takes you back through two world wars to a less complicated era; all those old ledgers, invoice books, dry fountain pens and bottles of ink. You'll find foam pads and stamps that bear the legend *Jim Muir: Purveyor of Fine Oatmeal*. There are drawing pins and rubber bands, rolls and rolls of fine jute string for tying up sacks, and Jim's very own Swiss army knife, right where he left it.

Even though Jim is no longer with us, the toolbox remains untouched – a mark, I suppose, of how little anyone cares to come in here now. It sits under the desk, the lid closed on a resourceful, hardworking life. It's a stout wooden crate, with rope lugs at both ends and a hasp for a padlock which has been missing for as long as I can remember. I grab the rope handle and haul the thing out into the light. The lid is sticky with layer upon layer of oil and grease and dust; that accumulated black grime that finds its way into the lines of a workman's hands.

My own hands are shaking a little as I ease open the lid.

The tools within have settled into a pattern, generation upon generation of awls and chisels and drill bits. It seems a sacrilege to disturb them, as if I'm breaking the seal on something that might be better left undisturbed. Nonetheless, I deliberate over them like a surgeon, selecting, testing, replacing, choosing afresh – junior hacksaw, claw hammer, pliers, tin snips. There is a delicious irony in this, the using of Jim's tools to dispose of Anna Madigan. Bones become calcified after burning. They go white and crumble. I scissor a pair of secateurs in my hand. Sometimes the process needs a little outside help.

Once I divert the water to the wheel, the machinery rapidly gets up to speed and the millstones gallop around at a rate of knots. The bump and rattle of the stones excites me, which hasn't happened for a very long time. Since Jim, my sorties here have been brief and craven. Today I feel like I'm taking my power back.

In the night, as my bonfire took hold, I nipped along to the pond with my flashlight and spanner to make sure the sluice was open enough to allow the water to surge forth. I became disorientated on the way back, the world flitting by in the torch beam like a magic lantern show: white stones and silver water; leaves beaded with jewels; black frames and fissures and shadows that made no sense. It was easy to imagine myself not an historian but an alchemist, the elements at my fingertips – water and fire and the cool, midnight earth. The air was spiked with something raw and magical. It was easy to imagine things floating downstream: white fingers, hair like waterweed. Sodden yellow silk. The miller striding ahead of me in the dark. In the bushes the goldfinches flexed their sleepy wings, *thrip thrip thrip*, and the breeze wept. Every story I had ever learned was about to be distilled into something significant.

I decide to use the first pair of millstones. These are the shelling stones, quarried from solid sandstone and used for breaking the husk from the whole oats. There is a hard, rough edge to them that suits my purpose. The second pair, the millstones proper, are more refined, intended for producing a fine-grade, civilised meal. Long, long ago, the shelling stones would have been the only stones available, and I suspect that this was what would have been used in the bone mills of old.

I begin to chant as I snip up Anna Madigan's skull and feed it into the eye of the stone.

'Fee-fi-fo-fum, I smell the blood of a red-haired woman! Be she alive or be she dead – I'll grind her bones to make my bread!'

'What the hell are you doing?'

Too late I realise that Lucie is standing behind me.

No sooner has she spoken the words than she doubles up in pain, sinks to her knees on the dusty floor. I had quite forgotten her predicament.

'Get an ambulance!' she gasps. 'This fucking baby is coming!'

'Oh dear, dear. Let me get you comfortable.' Hastily I drag some sacks from a pile in the corner and try to pack them under her, as you would a pony that's slipped in its stall. She slaps me away.

'Get help!'

'I will. I will!' I sigh at this interruption. Anna Madigan lies crumbled in a tin pail at my feet. I'm so near to closure. The girl is moaning through gritted teeth. 'Tell me. The baby . . . is it Arthur's?'

She sucks in a breath, glares at me. Her eyes are on fire. 'Does it matter? If I had the father now I'd cut off his dick.'

My mouth gives a prim little twitch. 'No need for that. I was only asking.'

The moaning is very distracting, so I can't quite follow my thoughts. Dogs whelp in stoical silence and all this humanity is too much. Lucie's voice turns wheedling.

'Please, Mac. My phone – I left it in my bedroom. Please could you bring it to me?' Sweat glistens on her upper lip. Her cheeks are as red as poppies.

'Of course.' I head for the door.

'Ring for the ambulance,' she calls after me. 'And Arthur. Please call Arthur. He'll know what to do.'

'Hmm.' I don't look back. Phone Arthur? To help with another man's baby? The minx. We'll see about that.

I find the phone easily enough. It's lying on the bedroom carpet, as if it's been dropped in a tremendous hurry. It seems to be none the worse for its ordeal, and everything lights up when I press random buttons. I have a mobile phone, which I rarely use. It infuriates Arthur no end when I turn it off and slip it into my sock drawer. *What's the point in that? You should take it with you at all times, in case of an emergency.* I tut in the phone's direction. Yes, Lucie – you should have your phone with you at all times, in case of an emergency. The display has a bar across it with Reuben's name, large as life. There seem to have been a lot of missed calls and my clumsy swiping makes an unopened message pop up. It's a rather terse reply from the man himself.

What? Why tell me now and not 9 months ago? Jesus. I'm in fckin Amsterdam. Call me.

So this is Reuben's reply. Oh dear. Clutching the phone, I wander through to the kitchen. The truth seems to have been withheld from those who should rightly know. I feel cold inside when I think of Arthur. He's been taken in by a floozy, just as his father was. Are we doomed to repeat mistakes across the generations? I swore I wouldn't let him be hurt like I was. No, it must end here. That girl cannot be allowed to foist her illegitimate child onto my son.

I wonder if the sister, Jane, ever found Lucie's poem. Reuben never spotted me posting it through the window of his car. I hope she found it. Someone had to do something, and I'm the only one in possession of all the facts. I imagine the betrayed sister discovering the poem, examining the handwriting. Putting two and two together. You don't want to believe an unpalatable truth, that's the problem, and when you *do* find out . . . the truth is like a cancer, impossible to dig out. The more you come to know, the more the pain spreads.

I find myself looking down at the phone. Something is hovering at the edges of my mind. There's a call I really should make. It has something to do with Lucie, and, oddly, with Arthur, but I just can't quite make the connection. Ah well. I slip the phone into my cardigan pocket and head back to the mill.

Lucie

My head is full of calculations. I try to work out the distance between the hospital and the mill; the ETA of the ambulance; the number of steps it will take Arthur to get to my side. I count breaths. I count the space between breaths. My body is consumed with effort. The pressure in my lower back is immense; this baby is threatening to cleave me in two. I'm feverishly picturing my spine as a long bow, drawn back, each vertebrae a hair's breadth from piercing my skin. I can see the polished white arch of my own backbone bursting from my body, my hair, lank with sweat, strung across it, taut and keening. *Thrip thrip thrip . . . help me help me help me . . .* Anguished wailing shudders through the mill, but I'm no longer sure whether it's harp music or the sound of my own voice.

I throw my head back, my face screwed up tightly with the pain. When the wave subsides and I open my eyes, I see the silvery writing on the old timbers by the millstones. From here, I can't make out the words strewn across it, or the childish flower, but I remember what it says: *4 firlots, 2 pecks of barley, a quarter pound of nails.* A name, etched in silver, flickers in and out of my line of vision. *Bella.* The name fights to be understood, and in the space between one pain and the next, it all becomes clear. Bella, standing on this spot, bargaining with the miller. Her name is a promise, a pact. *Make it stop.* A plea. *Make it stop. Make it stop.* I understand her desperation, the endless, grinding guilt. Carving her name into the wood like that. What did she sign away to him? Anything to stop the unstoppable voice of the bone harp.

Another contraction makes me suck in my breath. The grumbling of the millstones is making my head hurt. Where the hell is Mac? Where is the ambulance? I strain to hear an engine noise, or the wail of a siren, but the constant rumble blots out everything. I sit up, attempt to knead the pain from my back. As I shift position I kick the tin pail I'd seen Mac with earlier. A little puff of smoky ash rises into the air, and it distracts me for a moment. I nudge the bucket again with the toe of my welly, and a charred, bonfire stink rises up to meet me. The contents are white and flaky; broken, brittle shards that seem familiar, but I can't make sense of what I'm looking at.

Fresh agony seizes me, and I sink back onto the grubby sacks. The pain has altered; I feel an out-of-control urge to push this baby out. *Shit*. I hadn't read that part of the NHS website. I struggle out of my wellies. My thighs are wet and my questing fingers come away scarlet. I'm not sure if this is how things should be. I'm weeping now, just as Bella must have been weeping as she carved her name on the timber, as she sold her soul.

I'll do anything, just make it stop.

I feel so alone. The mill is cold, impassive. As I lie on the floor, my body labouring to expel the baby, the walls fade to black. The miller is gathering strength, taking shape in the corners, in the hidden parts of the place. An awful clamouring cold descends, and I'm trapped. I can no longer visualise the time beyond this. I'm vaguely aware of a shadow passing across the open doorway behind me. Mac has returned.

I open my eyes. I'm not sure how long I've been out of it. Everything feels unfamiliar. The memory of a sharp, smarting agony is still fresh between my legs and the sacking is wet. I move, tentatively, probingly. Everything is fuzzy, but I recall Mac's cold hands touching my belly, her calling my name, my own low animal moan, and a slow, slithering end to the pain. After that there is only blackness. I must have sunk down into my own exhaustion, overcome with the most delicious relief. I'm burning up but I can't stop shaking. My mouth is parched and sour. I need a drink but my teeth are chattering so hard I can't even speak.

I'm missing something here. The silence is deathly. There's no sign of Mac, and the millstones have stopped. With growing horror, I gather up what's left of my energy and shout into the emptiness of the mill.

'*Mac! Where are you? Where is my baby?*'

Her head appears at the top of the basement stairs. I'm still drifting in and out of whatever place I'm in. I cannot get warm. I cannot get up. My breasts are hard and tingling, waiting for a cry that hasn't come. I should have a baby in my arms by now. I sniff the air like an animal; it smells of blood and birth. I hear a snatch of that weird little song Mac was singing around the bonfire.

'*Mac!* What have you done with my baby?'

She completes the climb, slowly, like an old woman, and comes to stand over me. She's towering above me, a shadowy figure blocking out the light. She doesn't speak, and for an awful minute I'm not at all certain that this *is* Mac. It's someone else; someone I don't want to know. In my peripheral vision I can see the tin pail. It comes to me now, just what those splinters are. I recognise them now.

Bone.

That's what I saw on the bonfire in the split second before my waters broke. Skeletal fingers reaching out from the flames.

'My baby?' My voice is weak. The floor is spinning like a kiddies' roundabout and I'm barely clinging on.

'Lucie.' The figure crouches down. 'I'm afraid . . . Oh dear.' She takes a shaky breath. 'You had a little boy, but I'm afraid he – he wasn't breathing.'

I struggle to sit up. I want to jump to my feet and slap her, but I'm so weak. I feel hollowed out. 'I want my baby! What have you done with him?'

'Don't shout at me like that, Lucie.' Her voice is patronising, like she's talking to a cross child. 'I thought it best that you don't see him until . . .'

'I want to see him! I want my baby!'

'. . . until the paramedics get here and . . .'

'I don't believe you. I don't believe you even called the ambulance! Where's my phone? You're fucking crazy.'

'I don't have your phone, Lucie.'

'Right.' I roll unsteadily to my knees. Something slips inside me. The sacking is sodden with blood – my knees, my calves, my feet are red. They don't look like my legs.

Mac moves quickly, shushing me, trying to get me to keep still. I fall back, panting. 'Just relax. I think you may be haemorrhaging.'

She is so calm. She's so fucking calm, rolling up my bath towels from the cottage and packing them between my thighs. I'm sobbing now, wild with grief and fear.

'Do you want me to die too? Is that it? I know what you were burning on that bonfire!'

'Stop it now. Stop it,' says Mac. She tries to grasp my hand, but I don't want her anywhere near me. 'You don't know what I've been through, Lucie. Jim and Anna Madigan – they betrayed me. It's not something you can ever get over. And the grief . . . it stays with you. It grows into something else. You don't understand, Lucie, because you're on the other side. You're the other woman. You'll never understand what we've been through, Jane and I. How our hearts have been ground up so you can get what you want. Anna Madigan had the nerve to turn up here and beg for forgiveness. The guilt was eating away at her, you see, and it will do the same to you. I did her a kindness, really, because I made it stop.'

I understand now. I understand whose bones are in that bucket.

Mac

There's a back door in the basement. It has five locks: three bolts, a long iron hook and a big old-fashioned deadlock. Jim used to leave it open when he was milling, to keep the flour dust at bay, but it hasn't been opened for years. To the left is the window where we have the bluebottle problem. It has a wide stone sill, although I've never figured out why such a feature was necessary. It seems more suited to a dairy perhaps – a place to leave your cream to settle, or your cheese to ripen. I have used it in the past as a convenient ledge on which to store my home-grown onions or bunches of herbs. Lately, it's put me in mind of an altar; a space where you might leave votive candles, or an offering of some kind.

Today, I place the baby on the ledge.

Having arrived in the world so unexpectedly, the baby had appeared stunned. And, even allowing for the coating of blood and gunge, it was not a good colour. It never uttered a cry. I knew that this was a bad sign. I'd brought some towels from the cottage and I rubbed its black hair and its blue limbs. I swaddled it in a soft peach-coloured bath towel. Then, I took it down to the basement and laid it on the cold stone ledge.

I begin to sing as I climb back up the stairs. It seems fitting somehow. Just a few bars of an old tune that's been humming round my head since last night. It's the 'Lyke-Wake Dirge', an old country charm once chanted around a coffin. The old belief is that a departing soul must first traverse the Bridge of Dread, a link between worlds where your fate can go either way. Any misstep will see you tumble into the fiery abyss beneath the bridge, where the miller is waiting. It seems a fitting lullaby.

From Whinny-muir when thou mayst passe,
   Every night and alle;
To Brigg o' Dread thou comest at laste;
   And Christe receive thye saule.

If ever thou gavest meat or drink,
   Every night and alle;
The fire will burn thee to the bare bane;
   And Christe receive thye saule.

This ae nighte, this ae nighte.
   Every night and alle;
Fire and sleete, and candle lighte,
   And Christe receive thye saule.

Lucie is distraught, of course. But I feel divorced from it all, as if the blood, the weeping, all this drama is happening on the telly and I'm just an observer. Reality is that tin bucket and its contents. I have to mill the rest of those remains, grind them to powder, or things will go very badly for me. I should have done it years ago, and now the girl has complicated things, bringing her own story into the mix. I really don't need this interruption. Not now. I still have so much to do. I long to finish my task, but something tells me the moment is gone.

'Perhaps I'll tell you the rest of the story, while we're waiting. Did you read the last bit, about the miller making the bone harp out of Elspeth's corpse? Yes?' Lucie's eyes have closed. The lids are flickering, as if she's dreaming. I suppose she's exhausted – who wouldn't be? Perhaps the story will soothe her while we wait, although I'm no longer sure what we're waiting for. 'Yes, it's quite fitting to tell the story here, beside the place where Bella carved her name. I've always wanted to be a proper storyteller, Lucie. I once wanted to hold sessions here, in the mill. How atmospheric to tell the sisters' story here, where they are just a few layers away from us. Are you listening, Lucie?'

There is no response from the ground, although the girl's limbs are shaking. I bring an old travelling rug from the office and drape it over her, wrinkling my nose at the smell of birth. There's no dignity in delivery or death. Life is a messy business. As I step back, the silvery writing catches my eye.

'She had to come here, to bargain with the miller, Lucie. You see, the harp wouldn't stop, not for anything. It would not stop its accusations. Her sister's voice was always in her head, accusing her, day and night, and she thought the miller could make it stop. The miller is always waiting to help us. We only have to ask. But the price is steep. Bella bargained her soul for silence. I don't suppose that went well for her.' I run a tender finger over the inscription. *Bella*. 'The miller is here with us right now.'

I can feel my shoulders prickle. I glance at Lucie, but she is dead to the world.

This is when he is strongest, when you're at your most vulnerable, when you're fearful and angry and heartbroken. There's always a point of no return. A rash decision, a slippery slope, one push too far. There may be a moment of suspension, a hitch in time when the needle wavers between good sense and momentary gratification. In that moment . . . in that moment, the miller diverts the dark waters and floods your mind.

He was at my shoulder when I turned on the water that killed my husband.

The miller told me to do it.

I'm surprised when Arthur bursts in the door. It's unusual for him to move so fast – and he looks so agitated. His hair is all over the place, his face flushed. I'm not sure what he's doing here. Did I call him?

'What the hell is going on? Lucie!' He spots the girl there on the floor, barges past me to kneel beside her. Stroking her hair, clutching at her hand. Such tenderness. And then he looks at me.

239

I don't like the way he's glaring at me. You shouldn't look at your mother like that, with those haunted, distrustful eyes. I try and make the situation a little clearer.

'She's just given birth!' I tell him. 'Isn't that a surprise! I'm just here, trying to help.'

No sooner have I spoken than he's on his mobile, giving out our postcode. He's crouching over Lucie, her hand tightly clasped in his. Their grasp is shaky; I can see Arthur's whole body trembling with shock. Arthur is usually so steady, so calm. He'd taken a look under the towels and come to some conclusions. He's blaming me, and Lucie has gone strangely quiet. Arthur thrusts his phone into his jeans pocket and stands up. He's glowering at me, suddenly bullish, demanding to know where the baby is, and when I nod towards the stairs he almost bowls me over in his haste to get there. I hear him taking the stairs two at a time.

'It didn't cry. The baby didn't cry,' I say to the mill in general. The darkness in the corners grows deeper. Something scuttles across a beam, dislodging a little shower of rubble. Lucie doesn't answer, but I know the miller is listening. The miller has been with me for a long time now. He's always there in your weakest moments; those moments when you take a decision that alters your life forever.

Since his father's accident, Arthur's never set foot down there, in the basement, never offered to fix anything for me, never helped with the fly problem or put down rat poison, but now – for this girl and her brat – he can overcome anything. He can face his demons, go down into the dark. I hover at the top of the stairs, monitoring his actions by the movements of his feet. Squares of lights from the window illuminate his trainers. I can't see the rest of him from here but I imagine him massaging the tiny body with the towel, perhaps freeing the nose, the mouth of all that gunge.

I see his feet back away from the window. He has picked up the child, perhaps, clutching it to his shoulder, or draping the little body over his forearm. His steps are economical, efficient.

Determined. For all his love of staying in the background, I've always known my son to have a certain steeliness. It will stand him in good stead, because I fear things will end badly here, one way or another. That child is damaged goods. A dire consequence. That's why I put him down there. The miller knows what to do with a consequence.

Arthur comes to find me on the bridge behind the mill. I'm staring down at the spot where the lade and the river meet; two stories colliding. Glancing up, I see the tail lights of the ambulance disappearing up the track, blue light spiralling through the trees.

'Why didn't you phone for help?' He looks dishevelled. His hair is all over the place and there's a smear of blood on his face where he's rubbed at his eyes. 'She could have bled to death. And the baby . . . you cut the cord and tied it with string. What were you thinking?'

I shrug. I don't have any answers. 'The baby – he didn't cry, you know.'

'That didn't mean he wasn't breathing. Why did you take him away? Why?' Arthur is scraping his hair back, rocking on his heels as if his anguish has no place to go. 'You left him on his own, in the cold. Why?' It was a plea. *Why?*

I shake my head. Sirens are approaching. There is so much my son doesn't know. 'I suppose the baby got in the way. You deserve to be happy, but not with someone so unreliable.'

'So you were willing to let the baby die?'

'That baby is the product of a betrayal. It's tainted, corrupt.'

'People are allowed to make mistakes.'

A police car appears, pulls up at the bottom of the track. I squint into the blue flashing light.

'What are they doing here? They've flattened the winter pansies.'

Two police officers, one male, one female, are walking towards us. They seem to be in no hurry.

'Lucie managed to tell me about . . . about what you'd done, when they were putting her in the ambulance. The paramedics called the police. I'm praying she's wrong, but we need to know the truth.'

'I'm afraid I was never as forgiving as you, Arthur. I loved your father but I couldn't love unconditionally. I've done some things . . .' I produce Lucie's mobile. 'Please, give this back to Lucie. I do hope she makes a good recovery. I might not be able to visit for a while . . .'

The breath is leaving me. All I can feel now is the steady drumming of my heart. I'm aware of Arthur asking me question after question, while the young female officer approaches me to confirm my name, my address, my date of birth. I feel strangely calm as they read me my rights. It's like one of those cop shows – the handcuffs being snapped on, and the hand on the head bending me into the back of a police car. But they have obviously decided to take a softly-softly approach.

'Mrs Muir, we're going to have a chat down at the station. Perhaps you could help us by beginning at the beginning.'

'That makes perfect sense.' I nod agreeably. 'Let's start with the mill, shall we? It all starts and ends there.'

Lucie

The baby is wearing the sort of hospital gown they reserve for infants who have been abandoned in alleyways or whisked into care – or whose mothers have been unwilling to face the consequences of their actions. He doesn't seem too bothered by it. He is a very strange and interesting little person and I'm just beginning to realise he's all mine. The notion is exhilarating and terrifying in equal measure. I hug him a little closer, trying to ignore the cannula taped to my hand.

The Irish staff nurse was eager to tell me the nitty-gritty of his delivery, the bits where I was floating somewhere up in the rafters. I had a postpartum haemorrhage. Mac cut the cord with a Swiss army knife and tied it with old-fashioned jute string. *Sure, that's how it would have been done, long ago, but aren't we lucky now that we have antibiotics? The poor little chap. He's been dead lucky altogether.*

Lucky is a word that's cropped up a lot since we were admitted.

The boy yawns. His lips are crumpled and milky, like flower petals about to bloom. There's something about Reuben in the bow of his top lip – and I think, what a weird thing to notice. I suppose kids are the sum of their parents' parts. Anita, my very first visitor, brought us a little white brush and comb set, and I set about brushing his silky black hair for the umpteenth time. Anita tells me the first hair always falls out, but I hope that isn't true. She also brought a little white cap and some scratch mittens, but I can't bear to cover up any bit of him – not his lush hair or his miniature fingernails, so shiny and sharp. Everything about him is new and untried, and I like it. He is a fresh start.

Anita told me darkly that Mac has been remanded in custody

and Arthur is sorting things out at home. Everything is fine, and I'm not to worry. He'll be in when he can. I ask her to buy me the things the midwife tells me I'm going to need: nursing bras and big pants and sanitary products. I'm glad that they've stuck me in a side room and I don't have to be in the main ward and see the shiny balloons and the couples and the babies in their carefully chosen going-home outfits.

My favourite Irish nurse hurries in with a glass of water and some paracetamol. 'So did you call your folks yet?' She nods towards the locker where Anita placed my mobile. Arthur had given it to her to bring in, along with some hastily purchased toiletries.

'Not yet. I just need some time to work it all out in my head.'

The nurse chuckles and watches me down the painkillers with an eagle eye. 'Sure, babies bring love with them, don't worry about that!'

Not this baby, I think sadly. I kiss the top of his head, which still smells faintly of me. His soft mauve eyelids flicker and I wonder if he's having bad dreams about his start in life, being all alone in that cold, deserted basement. If Arthur hadn't arrived and cleared the mucous from his little face . . .

I can't wait to see Arthur again. There are so many things I want to say to him, but I don't know where to start. I suppose they'll all come out in time.

I doze off, and when I open my eyes some time later, Arthur is standing there holding two carrier bags of baby clothes and a bumper pack of nappies.

'I'm not sure if this is the right kind of stuff. I've never done this before.'

He looks a bit haggard and his shirt is crumpled like he's been wearing it for a long time. Behind his gold specs, his eyelids are puffy and vulnerable and it somehow reminds me of the baby. Strange that. I pat the bed, but he doesn't sit down. He paces to the cot and eases the blue blanket from under the little one's chin.

244

'Don't wake him up!' I hiss, and when he turns to look at me there are tears in his eyes. I pat the bed again. 'Tell me what's happening.'

He sighs and returns to me, the bed sagging beneath his weight. I hold his hand, move my thumb over the skin. I've become so wrapped up in the baby, his hands seem gigantic and tough in comparison.

'My mother's been taken into custody.' He raises his shoulders and drops them, as if he still cannot quite believe it. 'She confessed to everything. Told the whole story as if it was a –' He throws a hand up in the air. 'As if it were one of her fairy stories. She killed my father as well as Anna Madigan.'

I catch my breath. I hadn't known that bit, but it kind of makes sense. 'Did she turn on the water when he was working on the machinery?'

Arthur nods. His gaze is fixed on the wall, and I can see the tears glittering, unshed. 'She admitted it. She did it deliberately. He was in love with . . .'

'Anna Madigan. I guessed that bit.'

He nods. 'She got back in touch five years ago and my mother invited her in. She drugged her, then suffocated her with a pillow and left her body to rot in the tunnel beneath the wheel.'

His voice cracks and I open my arms to him. We hold each other for a long time, until my sore breasts remind me I've just had a baby. Gently, I break the contact. 'I was right about Floss. Floss spent her days looking for Anna.'

'Ma took her in and drove Anna's car to Tentsmuir, abandoned it so that they'd think she'd gone missing. It seemed to work. Maybe she would have got away with it.'

'No. Your past always catches up with you.' I look past him to the cradle and the sleeping child. 'Always.'

I did make that call. I spoke to my mother. There were tears and disbelief and vague plans to visit. Jane took over.

'I thought you'd put on weight,' she said. 'And you've been smoking and drinking...' She tutted. 'How could you not know?'

'It happens,' I said. 'And there wasn't that much smoking and drinking. The baby's had much more important things to worry about.'

'Do you have a name?'

'I'll have to think about it. He was . . . unexpected.'

There was a muffled sound at the other end, a sort of *hmm,* which I didn't think was appropriate for a new auntie, but I suppose the circumstances are far from ideal.

Jane visits the day before I'm due home. *Home.* Arthur wants me to stay on at the Miller's Cottage. There are a million reasons why I don't want to see that mill every morning, but it will have to do for now.

I hear my sister before I see her, the clopping of her heels along the vinyl corridor, and then she appears. She looks young and pretty and groomed, wearing a grey plaid dress and black tights. Every inch the popular aunt come to meet her new nephew. She's carrying a pack of Pampers and a gift bag with blue bunnies on it.

The baby is lying in my arms, sated with milk. His tummy is filling out like a little puppy's. I expect Jane to coo, or try to take him, or at least to kiss me on the cheek, but she doesn't. She sets the nappies on the floor and lays the gift on the end of the bed like an offering.

'A couple of Babygros,' she says awkwardly. 'I don't suppose you had time to get a layette together.'

I have no idea what a layette is, but I agree with her. 'It's all been quite dramatic.'

'Hmm.'

What the hell is wrong with her? A sinking feeling takes hold of my stomach. Sensing the change in me, the baby squirms and fusses in his sleep. 'Do you want to hold him?' I jiggle him a little on my arm, an invitation.

Jane steps forward, gazes down into the baby's face. And then she raises her eyes to meet mine.

'I know,' she whispers.

'What? Know what?'

The baby gurns and draws his knees up.

'Don't bother with the lies. I know what you've been up to behind my back. With Reuben.'

'I don't know what you're talking about.'

The baby begins to mew, and I realise how fiercely I'm holding him. The world shrinks to this – to me, my sister and the baby who will forever come between us.

'I've known for months.'

My breathing is coming in shallow gasps. Everything goes monochrome, as if I'm about to faint. It's happening at last. The waiting is over. My voice is reduced to a whisper, and the baby, starting to cry in earnest now, almost drowns me out. 'How?'

Jane's face is set like a mask. Her eyes are dry. 'That poem, Lucie. It was your handwriting. How could I not know? You're my sister. We wrote stories together, remember? I proofread your essays, for goodness' sake. You lied to me. Your family. And apparently you've been lying to yourself. I wanted you to come clean. We might have been able to salvage things, if only you'd shown some remorse. I gave you the chance when you came home, but you chose to keep up the deceit. And now this . . .' She waves a hand at my son. 'I can see Reuben in the curve of his lip, his eyes, his hair.' She gives a laugh which is far from pleasant. 'It's always the person you least expect. The person who's closest. How could you betray me? My own sister.'

My own sister, my own sister. How could you?

The baby's cry takes up her words, turns them into an eerie keening that soars up to the white ceiling, becomes, for a moment in time, the unstoppable music of the bone harp.

My own sister. How could you?

Epilogue

Lucie and Anita watch from the cottage as a white-suited figure ducks below the police tape and enters the mill.

'Who's that?' Lucie whispers. She whispers most of the time now, because the baby barely sleeps. He wakes up in the night, screaming, and won't be silenced.

'That's my tutor, Professor Stewart,' says Anita. 'The police call him the Bone Man.'

Next time Anita is on campus, she bumps into the Bone Man. He has a full white beard and a merry expression. When he's not in a forensic jumpsuit, he dresses from head to toe in black. He tells her that he's very excited by his findings at the mill. He puts a finger to his white moustache. 'It's an ongoing case, so not a word to anyone! The police have left no stone unturned, quite literally.' He chuckles at the witticism. 'The millstones have been dismantled and scoured for evidence. Our preliminary tests have been quite extraordinary.'

'Really?' Despite the horrible turn of events, Anita's interest is piqued.

'We found powdered bone commensurate with the age and sex of the alleged victim, but we also discovered something else, something much older. Mac was a colleague of mine, although we moved in different circles – science versus the imagination, eh!' He raises his snowy eyebrows at the quip, but when Anita fails to smile he clears his throat and moves on. 'So I am aware of her work in the field of local folklore and tradition. Indeed, the whole damn business is extremely –'

'Professor,' Anita cuts in. 'What did you find?'

The man rubs his beard. 'In the deep grooves on the grinding surface of one of the millstones, we found historic fragments of bone, together with filaments of human hair. Too early to say how old, but we're certainly talking in terms of centuries. Now, I do know the story of the two sisters associated with the mill – I was chatting to Mac about it not six months ago. And of course it would be wrong to jump to conclusions . . .'

'No, we mustn't jump to conclusions,' Anita agrees. In the deep grooves of her mind she can hear harp music, like the soft fluttering of birds. *Thrip thrip thrip*. 'After all, it's only a story. Isn't it?'